SOVEREIGN ASSASSIN

ROBERT NEW

First published in Australia in 2021
by Shooting Star Press

PO Box 6813, Charnwood ACT 2615

info@shootingstar.pub

www.shootingstar.pub

ABN 63 158 506 524

A catalogue record for this book is available from the National Library of Australia.

NEW, Robert.

Sovereign Assassin

ISBN: 978-1-925821-82-6 print

ISBN: 978-1-925821-83-3 ebook

Cover Design by Cathy Larsen, https://cathylarsendesign.com/

NOVELS

- Incite Insight
- The Conversationist

SHORT STORY COLLECTIONS

- Colours of Death: Sergeant Thomas' Casebook
- Mug Punter: Three Capers
- Movemind: Speculative Short Stories

FOR CHILDREN

- Eddy's Treasure (written with Michael New)

CHAPTER 1

Her Royal Highness, Princess Niobe Ancora of the tiny European country of Tantalia, was trapped beneath a large, muscular man, who seemed intent on killing her. Once he let go of her arms to put his hands around her throat, she knew there'd only be a short time until she passed out. The princess attacked the only viable spot, his groin, punching it with the middle knuckle of the index finger of her right hand. With a yelp her attacker leapt off her.

"You hesitated," her instructor, Gethan, complained to the princess. His voice echoed slightly in the basketball-court-sized hall.

"You made such a fuss last time I pulled that move—"

"A well-trained person wouldn't hesitate or worry about their attacker's comfort."

"Then train me better," the princess countered with her usual bravado.

Gethan pressed on his inner thigh as he hobbled a few metres away to check on himself. "That's going to leave a mark."

"Stop pretending you don't enjoy it when I hit you so hard. Only a masochist would sign up for this job."

Gethan turned back to his charge. "I wasn't complaining. You cannot be less than a hundred percent in a fight. Always strike as hard as you can. Let's go again."

"Why do we have to train so hard?"

"Your father is deteriorating. The cancer will soon win its battle. You need to be ready to execute your plan."

Niobe felt an anger rise within her. How could Alban Crab, a prominent Tantalian businessman, have knowingly allowed people, including her mother and father, King John and Queen Marigold, to be exposed to so much asbestos? And how could the courts of Tantalia allow him to get away with it? His lawyer had utilised a technicality, which had allowed Alban to escape with only a small fine. He'd gotten away with regicide. Her mother had passed from the same illness four years ago.

A few moments later, Gethan yelped again. "Good. And you managed to get the same spot. Let's maybe work on mindset for a bit, otherwise I won't be able to walk straight."

They sat cross-legged and facing each other on mats, which had been laid on the polished wood floor.

"Why should you make someone afraid of you?" Gethan asked.

"Because it weakens them and makes them easier to attack."

Gethan looked like he was debating whether she had the right answer. He always paused. Niobe was sure it was just to make her sweat. His expression would always be as though he was trying to impersonate an ancient philosopher, but his full head of grey-flecked brown hair and lack of beard meant he never quite pulled the impression off, despite some lines on his face.

"Okay, so *how* do you make someone afraid of you?"

"Tell them what you're going to do to them."

"Such as?"

"I'm going to stab you in the eye."

"Wrong. You're being too specific. If you want to threaten someone, make them go to their dark place."

"How?"

Gethan looked into Niobe's eyes and said, in a tone which was firm but contained a hint of the pleasure such an action would bring, "The things I could do to you with a coat hanger."

Niobe shuddered, then smiled.

"See. You put your own spin on that, which is darker than anything I could come up with," Gethan said.

Niobe wasn't so sure. Gethan may not be as lacking in empathy as she was, but he was highly skilled in the art of war, including interrogation.

"Next question." Gethan pulled a card from a pocket he'd sewn into the jacket of his *gi*. "What's this?"

The card contained a simple image:

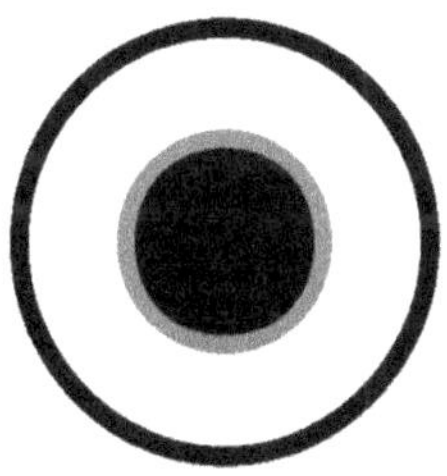

"An eye."

"Hmph."

"The window to the soul?"

"Better, but still wrong. When you can answer it, you'll be

ready. Hopefully, that will be soon. My only hint is that it's called the Riddle of the Eye for a reason."

Gethan placed the card on the floor in front of Niobe. "Meditate on the card for half an hour. Maybe its truth will reveal itself to you. Afterwards, come to your father's chambers. He wants to talk with you."

Niobe nodded, brushed her hair behind her ears and closed her eyes. Gethan would leave a timer to let her know when the meditation should end.

NIOBE TOLD herself to clear her mind, but the more she tried to dismiss her thoughts, the more replacements seemed to flood in.

A thought arose. Kill Alban for murdering your mother and father. She dismissed the thought, as per her training.

Was she afraid she'd enjoy killing him? What would killing a man mean to her? She dismissed these thoughts too.

Why couldn't she admit she was a sociopath and wanted to kill a man? Who was she? Why did she exist?

She began to repeat 'stop it' to herself, and tried to make the card her focus.

Deep inhale. Long exhale. Repeat. Control.

Several minutes later Niobe achieved her meditative state. For chunks of time, it was like she wasn't thinking anything at all. Often this was when an epiphany would occur for one of Gethan's puzzles. Today, she couldn't get past the idea of the image being an eye. When the timer went off, she audibly exhaled. Maybe she'd get it next time. At least now, she could go and see her father.

* * *

THE PALACE WAS A LARGE, seven-storey, circular sandstone building with a cone-shaped roof. The top third of the roof was made of glass, which allowed for a garden to be at the heart of the building below. Niobe liked to joke it was like they'd built the world's largest and fattest turret but had forgotten about the rest of the palace. Because the building was circular, and had evenly spaced windows, no matter which direction you approached from, it always looked symmetrical. The interior garden was meant to keep the nobility 'grounded'. King John's room was on the top floor on the eastern side. These days it resembled a hospital ward, with a hospital bed, crash cart and various machines. The king would get up for about an hour each day before he'd cough up blood and return to bed. He still made a monthly address to the Tantalian people. Niobe wondered if they realised how hard this address was for their king. It usually meant having fluid drained from around his lungs and peritoneal cavity first. At least this made him more mobile for a few days.

* * *

NIOBE ESCHEWED the lift and bounded up the staircase to the top floor. By the time she reached the seventh floor, her breathing rate had increased, but she didn't feel out of breath. Gethan stopped her as she approached the king's room.

"How did you go?"

Niobe knew he was asking about the symbol, but when she reflected on her thoughts, she realised there was a more pressing issue.

"I had trouble clearing my mind."

Gethan seemed to understand.

"Your father?"

"Yes, but more about what his death means in relation to the purpose of my life."

"You do seem to want to search for the meaning of life through death."

Niobe nodded. He was right. Ever since she was a child death had fascinated her. Her parents had become concerned, after catching Niobe putting a kitten into a tumble dryer at the age of five. Catching her again, a month later, drowning the same kitten had led them to hire Gethan to do what he could to mould her into a 'proper' royal, before the behaviour compounded.

"And yet, you still don't realise it's a terribly unimportant question."

"Huh?"

Gethan leaned in as he spoke. "'What is the meaning of life?' is an unimportant and boring question. The important question is what is the meaning of *your* life?"

Niobe felt like a bubble had popped in her mind.

"Answer that and you'll also answer the first," Gethan added.

"You know I hate that you have a point, right?"

"Of course. I've been responsible for much of your development since you were a child. I know you better than you know yourself."

"So, what has your almost twenty-year observation revealed?"

"Someone who can't tell me the meaning of a little drawing."

Niobe laughed. "If you'd deflected my strike that well this morning, you wouldn't have a new bruise. Besides, I think I solved it on the way over. It's the diagram of—"

The door to the king's room opened, and the king's personal secretary-cum-nurse, Patterson, beckoned them in.

"Stop nattering the two of you. The king needs to see you

urgently." Patterson wagged a long, thin finger at them, but his blue eyes shone with amusement.

Niobe and Gethan nodded with mock sheepishness and entered the room. King John was propped up on his bed. For someone so close to death, he looked surprisingly healthy, mostly due to the light in his hazel eyes. The only external clue to his illness was the oxygen tube around his face. His silver beard, and hair, both thinned from chemotherapy, were brushed, and he presented well.

The king turned to his servant. "Thank you, Patterson, I'll be fine alone with them for a while."

Patterson dutifully shuffled out of the room, his old-man gait betraying his age. Niobe knew he'd station himself outside until they left.

King John nodded for them to sit at the foot of his bed. "How's the training going?"

Niobe glanced at Gethan. He paused for just long enough to make it clear he was seeing if Niobe would jump in with a response. "Your Majesty, I can't fault her martial arts. Other than she's too careful about hurting me. She's lagging a bit in the other side of her training."

"Have you given her the Riddle of the Eye, like I asked?"

"This morning," Gethan replied.

"And?"

"Not even close."

The king sighed, which triggered a spate of coughing. He dabbed a handkerchief to his mouth. It came away with pink on it—blood and saliva. Niobe winced at the sight and took a moment to daydream about what she'd like to do to Alban. Maybe if she could get in a hard enough kick, she could break his pelvic bone and rupture his bladder. Niobe saw her father react to her scrunched face.

"Now, now, my dear. I'm not gone yet. I would like to see you solve that puzzle though; I know when Gethan's predecessor gave it to me it elevated my development considerably."

"But I came up with a solution," Niobe protested.

"It's wrong," Gethan said.

"How can you be so sure?" Niobe pouted. She hated being wrong.

"Too soon. I say this in front of your father, my king; you know I love you like a daughter, but you're not there yet. Your movement and attitude would change."

King John nodded in agreement.

"Humour us though. What did you think it was?" King John asked.

"It's a diagram of the observable universe. We're the dot in the middle. The lighter outer ring in the middle is the boundary of space from which light will eventually be able to reach earth. The light from stars outside that area will never reach us due to the universe's expansion, and hence never be seen by humans. It's why the sky at night only has points of light and isn't all white. The white space is the unobservable universe, and the outer ring its boundary."

"Not bad. But wrong. It's at least an improvement to your earlier response," Gethan said.

"I have something I need you both to hear," King John said with sudden authority.

Niobe and Gethan gave him their full attention.

"The plan you two have, I want you to stop it."

"Your Majesty?" Gethan queried.

"I know I supported it a few years ago, but not now. Being the monarch is not a licence to kill, even though it affords immunity from arrest for any crime. Once you cross one line, and the one I've asked you to consider crossing is the most serious, then all the other lines disappear. I don't want my people to be ruled by someone like that. More importantly, I don't want my daughter"—he reached for Niobe's chin—"to be someone like that."

"But all our training," Niobe said.

"Is not for nought," King John replied.

"The plan gave me purpose. You can't take it from me." It was the first time in years Niobe remembered feeling angry with her father. His, and her mother's, approval of her desire had meant the world to her.

The king's eyes looked sad.

"Just tell me, why?" Niobe implored.

"Watching your mother go through what I am now was the most horrifying part of my life. How the disease stole her dignity and health. The suffering she went through … I succumbed to my base nature and wanted revenge. I thought it coming through you would be … the most prudent choice and give you some closure, especially once we're both gone. It'd be a means of moving on. But pretty much all I do these days is reflect upon my life and legacy, and how I can help you achieve your own. My search for meaning has ended. To put it simply, there will come a point after you die when someone thinks about you for the last time. The memory of your life on earth will end, a truly permanent death. We're dust, nothing more… Revenge is so petty."

"But, Dad, I—"

"But nothing." King John launched into a series of bloody coughs.

"I know you're trying to figure out your purpose, and training to kill the man who took your mother and, soon enough, me, has given you that sense of direction. I don't want you to feel the obligation for revenge, nor bear the cost of taking someone's life."

"You know while you may have supplied training and preparation, you didn't give me the desire. I want to do this. Geez, I'm nearly closer to thirty than twenty. Do you really think you could make me do something I didn't want to do? Do you think you can stop me doing something I want to do?"

"No, you've always followed your own path. On this though, I want you to find another way to move past our deaths, and your subsequent ascension to the throne. I want our people to be proud of you." He turned to Gethan. "Gethan, you must see this happen."

Niobe scowled. It wasn't fair her father was doing this to her, but then he was just expressing his desire, and so didn't deserve the dark look she was giving him. But roping Gethan into it was a bridge too far.

"Niobe, I want you to feel freedom from constraints of the past. Think about what religions teach about a benevolent deity forgiving sins, what Nietzsche says about rising above the constraints of social laws and being above the triviality of man. Think about what Shakespeare says about man being a quintessence of dust. All these things lead to the state of being in the now. If I let you go ahead with your plan, I'm afraid people will come for you, and you'll never achieve that state, and never be the best you, you can be. Worse still, you'll never be truly happy."

"But avenging the death of you and Mum will make me happy."

"If you do it, you'll always carry it with you. That will stop you from achieving your *self*." He turned to Gethan. "You've taught her Maslow's hierarchy?"

"Of course, Your Majesty." Niobe admired how Gethan remained respectful. These days, her father often asked questions he knew the answer to. It was as though a side-effect of his medication was a poor memory.

King John turned back to Niobe. "All those stages on the hierarchy from having your food, safety and basic needs met, to the esteem of your peers and self, lead to a great state of being."

King John paused. Niobe took the bait. "What state is that?"

"The freedom from worry. That is what I want for you, and what Gethan, your mother and I have tried to teach you. Moving up the hierarchy means you become free from those concerns below your level. When you are free from worry, you can explore and become your own true self, or as Maslow called it, achieve self-actualisation."

That was wrong. She could only be her real self through killing Alban. The man deserved to die, and Niobe was determined to make it happen. But the mood of the room was against her, so she played along.

"How can I get past those concerns though? I mean—"

A loud knock echoed around the room. "Enter," King John commanded as loudly as he could manage. The door opened, and Patterson strode into the room with unusual haste.

"Your Majesty, I have some urgent and wonderful news from the PM."

The king nodded.

"Tantalia's ratification of the treaty for membership of the EU is complete. We're now an acceding country."

Niobe worked to memorise the smile on her father's face. That's how he should be remembered. That was the image she'd use to remind her what Alban had taken from her. It would join the one of her mother's mirthful grin when teasing Niobe about her first crush. King John opened his arms and she accepted the hug.

Gethan cleared his throat. "What is the date for the ascension?"

"New Year's Day," Patterson replied.

"Two months. I hope I live to see it," King John said.

"So do I," Niobe and Gethan said in unison.

"It's your life's work, Dad. You did it."

"I wish your mother could have seen it too."

Niobe hugged her father again. Her rage at Alban, compounded with her frustration at her father's unexpected obstruction of her path, overwhelmed any sense of sadness, but she knew tears were an appropriate response, so she took a tissue and dabbed her eyes.

CHAPTER 2

A blast of wintery air accompanied Niobe's entrance to the training hall. It'd been a white Christmas, celebrated by the palace in grand style. Now it was New Year's Eve. Tomorrow, Tantalia would join the EU.

After a vigorous workout, Niobe and Gethan assumed a cross-legged position opposite each other. It was time for the more esoteric side of their martial art training.

"If you're not going to kill your enemy then always leave them with two things left to lose," Gethan said. He shifted so he was kneeling. Niobe knew this meant he would keep asking questions and talking, but at some point, lash out and strike at her. Her goal was to answer the questions and block the strike. Awareness and a-wary-ness was how Gethan described it.

"Why two?"

"When there's nothing left to lose, your enemy will come for you with everything they can, but, more importantly, they will take risks others won't. Unpredictable, self-sacrificing risks. If they only have one thing left that puts them in a position of power, perhaps even more than if you leave them with nothing left to lose. If they use it correctly, you'll have to protect the one thing they have left, to prevent them coming for you with all they can. That weakens your position and disrupts efficient use of your time."

Niobe nodded. If someone wasn't interested in self-preservation, they could achieve things others couldn't.

"How do you prepare for firing a rifle or gun?"

"Clean the weapon, check it's loaded and the safety is on."

"And?"

Niobe scratched her head. "Soak your fingers in a tin of pineapple pieces for half an hour."

"Why?"

"Doing so alters your fingerprints for a few hours."

"Good."

"What's this?" Gethan flicked the Riddle of the Eye card into the space between them. Niobe was sure he would choose this moment to strike as she had made no progress in solving the riddle over the last eight weeks, despite an attempt each week to do so. She was sure Gethan knew how frustrated she was it hadn't been solved, and that the subsequent feelings the card produced in her would make for a golden opportunity to catch her off guard. He didn't move though. Was he waiting for her to respond?

She thought through all her previous responses: eye, window, model of the universe, sun and planets, model galaxy, breast, the palace, a sports stadium. At least the last two had elicited a 'Why?' rather than the usual grunt of disapproval.

"It's an auditorium," Niobe said.

"You said that last time."

"No, last time I said it was a sports stadium. This time I'm saying auditorium. A place to be heard."

"Continue."

"It's like when they do a concert in the round, like the Royal Opera did last year."

"You were a guest on opening night, no?"

Niobe nodded. "And as my de-facto bodyguard, you were with me, so you know the answer."

Gethan smiled. "And where did we sit?"

"In the Royal Box."

"Which would be where in your interpretation of the image?"

"Here." Niobe pointed to the outer circle.

"Continue."

"That's it. That's what I think it is."

"An improvement, but still wrong."

Niobe cursed under her breath.

"Now, now. You know there's nothing wrong with my hearing."

"Next time I'll say it loudly then."

Gethan laughed. "Always so bold. Don't lose that; it gets you closer to the answer you seek. Did you know, it's been nearly two months and we still haven't discussed what your father said."

Niobe had been waiting for Gethan to bring up the topic since that day. He wouldn't let her start it either. He'd made that clear the three times she'd tried. She couldn't figure out why he wouldn't allow her to discuss it.

"I know. I'd hoped that for Christmas he might undo his decree. I guess I'll have to hope it's more of a new year's thing?"

It was at this moment Gethan made his strike—a spear hand, *nukite,* to her throat. Niobe only just caught the movement in time. In her cross-legged state she didn't have the same freedom as when standing, but she was able to drop her chin to her chest and twist her upper body to her left so that her cheek and shoulder acted to parry the blow. As she moved she kicked her right foot out, making satisfying contact with the base of her big toe to Gethan's temple. He crumpled to the floor. Moments later he stood and took a few deep breaths.

"Very well done. But if you're going to continue to be that accurate with your kicks, we'd better do some more *kappo* training. I think you're ready for the next form."

Niobe was fascinated by this ancient resuscitation and healing art. Some of the techniques accelerated healing and others restored breathing or consciousness. The 'forms' she'd learnt were movements which blended the various techniques into a flowing, energising sequence. Along with her *kata* for martial arts and gymnastics, they were better than dancing for making her feel a joy of movement.

"I don't think you've ever praised a kick of mine so highly."

"Probably not. It'd just go to your head, and you're already a… a…" Gethan looked to the door.

"I hear them too. Someone's coming," Niobe said.

"Who is it?" Gethan asked.

"Patterson. Only he shuffles like that, but he's rushing."

Gethan nodded and waited for a beat. "Excellent. If you only knew how close you are to breaking through. All you need now is to—"

The door opened right at that moment. Niobe unsuccessfully tried suppressing a smile at Gethan's timing. Patterson glanced around the room and, as soon as he spied them in their shadowed corner, spoke with a previously unheard urgency. "You need to come now. The king is dead." As he came closer to them, it was clear his eyes were red from crying. Neither Niobe nor Gethan bothered to put on their shoes as they ran to the palace.

CHAPTER 3

Niobe had known this moment was imminent for weeks, yet hearing the words aloud still put her in a state of shock. King John was meant to live for another day, so he could see Tantalia, the country he loved, become a fully-fledged member of the European Union. Once at the palace, for a change, Niobe caught the lift with Patterson and Gethan, since it would get her to the top more quickly. When the doors opened, she pushed past Patterson and Gethan and ran to her father's side.

She climbed on top of his bed and hugged him, instantly knowing Patterson's words were true. There was no life left in the body. Even lying down, her father was a 'dead weight'.

"Out," Niobe commanded as the other two followed into the room. They dutifully spun on their heels and waited outside.

"You should have died hereafter," Niobe said, paraphrasing Macbeth, having gained a rare insight into someone else's emotions. Speaking aloud made her thoughts seem more real. She wiped her tears off her cheek with her sleeve.

Niobe was unsure if they stemmed from frustration or sadness.

"Why have you and Mum left me? I'm not ready to be an orphan, or face this world without you." Niobe knew this was true; her parents had understood her better than anyone else and accepted her unconditionally. Still, as long as she had Gethan, she wasn't truly alone. At least he could comfort her.

"Why did you tell me I couldn't kill Alban for you as we planned? Why wouldn't you want me to have that peace? I don't understand."

Niobe implored the body to give her a response. To give the answers she so desperately wanted. She held the body for what felt like an age. When she finally released him and drifted to the door she knew one thing for certain: despite her father's wish, it wouldn't be long before Alban Crab would die.

THAT EVENING, Niobe sat gazing into the fountain in the internal garden of the palace. Niobe loved its ornate marble sculpture. It depicted a scene of Echo falling in love with Narcissus and was based on a painting by Poussin, which, unlike other such paintings, had Eros—better known by his roman name Cupid—playing a role in the tragic story. In the myth, Echo fell in love with Narcissus who had already fallen in love with his own mirror image. Narcissus spent his days gazing at his reflection in the water of a pond while Echo slowly faded away, leaving only her voice behind. Niobe often pondered each character's perspective in the painting and fountain. She liked the idea that the tragic story was caused by a mischievous Eros. Today, all she could think was that she was Echo, in love with something she could never have, although in her case, it was her father's support for killing Alban, being denied.

The noise of a door opening made her look up. Niobe watched Gethan approach. It was clear he'd come to find her. His hazel eyes were red with grief.

"How'd you find me?" Niobe asked, hoarsely, an effect achieved by screaming in frustration under the water of the fountain several times over the last hour.

"I knew I'd find you here. It's where you come when you're upset," Gethan said.

"Usually, that's with you."

"I always have your best interests at heart."

"Yet, you won't address the elephant in the room."

"We'll get to that. How are you feeling?"

"Like my heart's been ripped out. Except that I can still feel it convulsing in my chest."

Gethan nodded. "Me too. He was a great king and an even better man."

"I mean because I can't plunge a spear hand into Alban's side and rip out his intestines. It aches"—Niobe tapped her heart—"I know you loved Dad."

Gethan took a deliberate breath.

"If you're my surrogate daughter, he was like my older brother."

"If he chose you to educate me, he must've felt similarly about you," Niobe said.

"I'm pleased you understand."

Niobe took a last look at the water spouting from Eros' arrow onto Echo, which then bounced from Narcissus into the pool. Niobe decided she wouldn't be left as a hollow voice. She wanted to be Eros—the one manipulating events. The one in charge. She turned to look Gethan in the eye. "There's no way I'm going to abandon my revenge for this. Alban stole my father's life the day before he achieved his life's goal." Niobe knew her anger was writ large upon her face.

"You're upset, understandably, but this is a time for mourning, not revenge."

"I want you to help me kill Alban."

"Let me answer with a question. Do you know why I wouldn't discuss your father asking you to cease your quest with you?"

Niobe shook her head.

"It was because I wanted you to think about all the things he said and work out what they meant to you. If I started offering opinions, or acting as a sounding board, it would prevent you from reaching an authentic decision. I will support you on your quest, at least up to a point."

Niobe looked at Gethan's face, desperate to know what he was going to say.

"I will train you to the very best of my ability as per my charge from the king. But once you embark upon your quest, I will try and stop you, since the king commanded it. My loyalty was sworn to him, not you."

When her parents had hired Gethan, it was because they weren't comfortable with what they'd called her insufficient concern for life. Gethan had trained Niobe to give her a sense of knowing she would have the skills to kill a human if she wanted to. Gethan had said her parents hoped this knowledge would be sufficient to make her feel the act itself was unnecessary. This was based on the logic of her parents' own experience in martial arts training, which had led to them being capable of defending themselves, and hold the knowledge they'd be okay in a fight. This led to a loss of intimidation when dealing with people and, due to the subsequent reduction in fear, an increase in empathy. After Queen Marigold was diagnosed and effectively given a death sentence, King John had wanted revenge and realised Niobe was the perfect instrument for the job. The years of training hadn't diminished her desire. With Niobe's enthusiastic approval, her training switched focus to let more of her true nature emerge. Niobe was still angry that King John had changed his mind while on his death bed.

"But when I'm queen—"

"You're already queen, Your Majesty. You may not be sworn in, but you are now the queen, and I have not sworn an oath to you and"—Gethan lowered his eyes—"nor will I."

Niobe was dumbfounded.

"You're abandoning me on the day my father died. On the day I need you the most?"

She felt her generalised frustration turn to focused rage.

"One day the scale will fall from your eyes, and you will know my actions are a declaration of affection for you. I can't serve you when you're the queen."

"Affection. Is that all?" Niobe said angrily.

"Your Majesty, I was simply implying purity, instead of … sexuality. You know I love you like a daughter."

Niobe filled her lungs with air, exhaled and repeated the motion. "Exactly. I was always so blessed to have two fathers. My real dad and you. Having the two of you was crucial when Mum passed. And you're telling me I've lost both of you at the same time." She hadn't felt so impotent since the moment she'd learnt of her mother's diagnosis. Her horror at the feeling within, and her anger at the fact tears started falling made her want to scream.

"I'm not abandoning you, but I can't support you."

"Then declare loyalty to me." She hated the desperation in her voice, hated that she was pleading. "Help me."

At least Niobe could see Gethan was emotionally torn with his decision. He took a few breaths before responding.

"I can't believe how skilled you are at manipulating me, but I'm not going to let you get away with it this time. Your marksmanship is approaching sniper level, and your martial arts are surpassing mine. All you have left to learn is to truly conquer yourself, but you can't do that until you get out of your own way."

Niobe tried not to let the fresh tears she felt welling fall down her cheeks. "How can I, when you've just said you won't help me?"

As he turned to walk away, Gethan handed her the Riddle of the Eye. "Solve this. When you're ready, let's talk."

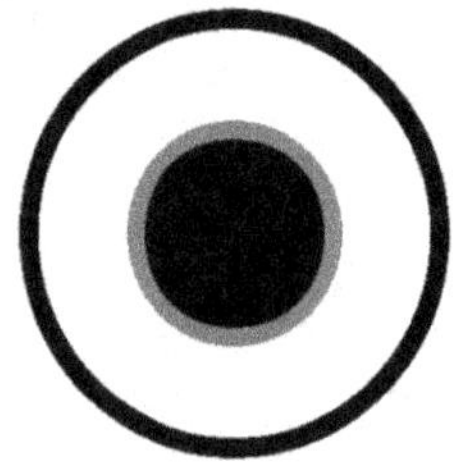

CHAPTER 4

Despite the king's death, there were still New Year's Eve celebrations throughout the country. Most were made smaller than planned. Even the fireworks, which normally would have been spectacular, seemed to have muted colours. When Niobe managed a brief moment of sleep, in between thoughts of her father, her new role as queen and Gethan, she dreamt of being on a beach on a warm, sunny day, lying next to the ripped-apart body of Alban. A cold wind rose up and made the waves larger. They pounded the sand and started forming a trench. The water darkened, as did the sky. The trench ran as far as she could see, morphing into the slow realisation the trench would keep going for as long as she travelled along it. This transformed into water from the trench flowing into the palace's fountain. That image was still in her mind when she realised she was in her bed.

Patterson knocked on her anteroom door a few minutes after Niobe had showered and dressed. She wore her usual training outfit; a light white t-shirt, black jacket and grey sweatpants, in preparation for her 6.00 am training session

"

with Gethan. Despite their conversation the previous day, Niobe hoped he'd be in the hall when she got there, as she wasn't sure what she'd do if he wasn't. He had suggested there was a negligible amount left to teach her, but that wasn't the point. Their workouts burnt through her dark energy, and no one but Gethan knew how hard to push her. Besides, she loved the feeling of mastery of her environment and opponent their sessions gave her.

Patterson seemed nervous as he approached. "Your ceremony is planned for this afternoon at 2.00 pm, Your Majesty."

She nodded as Patterson looked her up and down.

"Do you need a hand getting ready?"

Niobe looked at her clothes. "This is just for the morning. If you arrange for a suitable outfit to be ready on my bed, I'll change into it after lunch."

"What about the rehearsal?"

Niobe tilted her head and gave him a quizzical look.

"The rehearsal for the funeral is at noon. A run through of where you need to be and where you need to move from, to and when. They'll follow with the blocking for the inauguration. The funeral will be at one."

"I'll be here at quarter to twelve. I'll change into the formal clothes after the rehearsal."

Patterson still seemed ill at ease.

"Is there something wrong?"

"It's just … I'm used to serving the king and helping him get ready for things. I've done it for over thirty years. I'm not sure what's appropriate for me to do with you. Perhaps you'd be better served by a female aide? One closer to your age … like the one your mother used to have."

"You afraid of seeing me naked, Patterson? Aww." Patterson blushed. Niobe had to stop herself peeling off her clothes then and there to break the ice … and amuse herself at how much he'd squirm. Should she just lift her shirt?

"What if I ask you to get me tampons?"

Patterson's face went from pink to salmon.

"Really? You used to put diapers on my father when he was too sick to get out of bed, but me having a period is too much?"

Patterson looked ashamed.

Niobe shook her head in mock disbelief. "I could use your counsel. Please maintain your role for me. If, or when, you see me naked you are to keep what you see to yourself, understood."

Patterson nodded. Niobe wondered what he'd make of the thick scar on her side from a training mishap, and her kanji tattoo, both of which she'd kept from her parents on Gethan's advice.

"I'll see you here to get changed at 12.30 pm for the funeral and 1.30 pm before my inauguration starts."

"Will that be enough time? What about make up?"

"A quick application of lipstick, mascara and moisturiser will only take a couple of minutes. I'm not like other girls, Patterson, but I think you know that. I only need a moment to get dressed."

* * *

NIOBE ENJOYED the crispness of the winter's morning air as she walked to the training hall. The chill suited her mood. She was still replaying her father's final wishes and her conversation with Gethan. She approached the hall with some trepidation. Would Gethan be there? How would she be received? Would he be able to look her in the eye after he'd said he would campaign against her if she tried to enact what had been

25

their plan and goal for nearly six years? Niobe hesitated at the door. She listened to hear if there were the sounds of anyone inside. Her heart pounded as she turned the handle. Pushing the door open, she saw a hall which, to her relief, wasn't empty, as Gethan was sitting in the centre of the room surrounded by twenty sheets of paper with the circle symbol printed on them. The papers formed a figure eight on the ground. Gethan was in one of the eight's circles. He beckoned Niobe to sit in the other. She took off her shoes and walked, cat-like, on the balls of her feet, barely making a sound. Gethan had done this once before, and an arrow had shot at her from an automated bow. Due to her dropped guard, she hadn't seen it coming. She'd learnt a valuable lesson, but at the cost of a scar. Niobe had refused Gethan's request to let her get proper medical atten-tion as she'd wanted the scar as a memento. It would also be a useful way of triggering his guilt as he had set the bow with too much tension. This time though, nothing attacked her as she made her way over and sat in her side of the figure eight.

"Thank you for coming, Your Majesty. I wasn't sure you would."

Gethan was breathing shallowly, and his gaze occasion-ally darted around. These were cues Niobe recognised.

"I've never seen you look worried before."

"Many ways this scenario could play out have run through my mind," he said. "In one you're here to say goodbye to me, and I'm executed as I leave the hall. In another, you convince me to change my mind. In another still, we find a way to make this work with neither of us having to compromise. I'm hoping for the latter."

"Oh, Gethan, I'd never let anyone *else* kill you. Besides, if I were to do it, I'd do it in a way where you'd know what was happening but couldn't avoid the consequence. I'd watch from right beside you."

Gethan shivered.

"You're right; people do take such things to their dark place. I don't want you dead, nor out of my life. So, how do we make this work?"

"You need to solve the Riddle of the Eye. I can't solve it for you. There are rules, you see. But, I can nudge you in the right direction."

Gethan's breath still betrayed his state of mind, but at least his gaze was now on her.

"Do you remember Isaac Newton's translation of the Emerald Tablet?" Gethan asked.

"You made me memorise it word for word."

And with that, Niobe felt them revert to their usual student and teacher roles. Gethan even started breathing normally.

"Well go on then. Latin first. Start from *separabis*."

Niobe began to intone: *"separabis terram ab igne subtile ab spisso suauiter magno cum ingenio ascendit a terra in coelum iterumque descendit in terram et recipit uim superiorum et inferiorum sic habebis gloriam totius mundi ideo fugiet a te omnis obscuritas haec est totius fortitudinis fortitudo fortis quia uincet omnem rem subtilem omnemque solidam penetrabit—"*

"Meaning?"

"Separate thou the earth from the fire, the subtle from the gross sweetly with great industry. It ascends from the earth to the heaven and again it descends to the earth and receives the force of things superior and inferior. By this means you shall have the glory of the whole world and thereby all obscurity shall fly from you. Its force is above all force. For it vanquishes every subtle thing and penetrates every solid thing."

"And that, my dear, is how I want you to be."

Gethan stood, gave a slight bow and said, "Meditate upon it for an hour. I'll be in my room in the palace after the funeral and your ceremony."

"You're not coming?" Niobe felt a surge of panic. Gethan tilted his head slightly and spoke as though he was about to be overcome with emotion. "Of course, I am. I'll be right by your side, if you'll let me?"

Niobe nodded.

"Thank you, Your Majesty."

* * *

WHEN THE ALARM went off an hour later, Niobe took a stroll through the Greater Gardens, which were off to one side of the palace. She stopped by the pond she'd asked to be constructed a few years previously. Once it had been built, she'd seeded it with a very particular strain of cyanobacteria from a German freshwater lake she visited for the purpose of obtaining a sample. Today, she was pleased the pond wasn't frozen over from the chill in the air. She was even more pleased to see the run-off nitrogen and phosphorus of the garden's fertiliser had allowed a bloom of the cyanobacteria to form.

* * *

NIOBE KNEW the funeral for the king would be nationally televised. A life lived in the public eye had made her used to speaking in public, but this was her father's funeral, and she was about to be anointed queen. It wasn't just the speech of a grieving daughter, like she had given when her mother passed, it was also a statement about how she would act as figurehead of the country. Niobe just wanted to mourn her father her way, through reflecting on what his loss would mean for her. It made her unsure how her speech would go. Would she give away that she had abnormal emotions? That could lead to undesirable complications.

The Prime Minister, Zacharias Brenk, was the first to speak. He was in his sixties and had been PM for nearly two decades. Tantalia's electoral system didn't allow party politics. Candidates were elected to represent their district, and the PM was voted for by the parliamentarians. Zack had maintained his role through masterful charisma and political acumen. Zack's voice trembled as he spoke.

"It is with great sadness we mourn the passing of King John Andreas Wim Ancora. King John made it his life's work to improve the status of this country. He worked tirelessly with the government to build relationships with foreign nations and lift the living standards of Tantalia through improved trade. As Prime Minister, I occasionally had to tell him he was too ambitious. One such occasion was when he said he wanted to invite Autarchos' President, Jork Dressov, to dinner at the palace to discuss Autarchos and Tantalia's relationship. He wanted to help them join the EU alongside Tantalia. This was a decade ago, long before Tantalia achieved that objective. I pointed out that just because we shared a border with them, it wouldn't mean Jork would work with us. In fact, when the offer was made, it only served to increase Autarchos' resistance to foreign relations. Something King John tried to change for the last decade.

"King John campaigned throughout his life to raise standards of living. He personally funded scholarships and improved the brain gain of the country through his directive to parliament to attract the best and brightest immigrants to our country. Joining the EU was his most ambitious goal, and I'm pleased he lived to know it was achieved, even if he didn't survive until it came into effect this morning. King John was a good man. He loved his wife and daughter. In our private talks he would often mention them, particularly Niobe, who he felt blessed to have as his daughter. He admired her so much."

The words hit Niobe right in the little conscience she had, for she was about to disobey his dying wish. She felt her throat become rigid and forced herself to remember the times she'd felt out of control to amplify the emotion she needed to sell.

"Let's hear from our queen."

Zacharias stepped down from the lectern and gestured to Niobe. Niobe took a breath, which bordered on being painful, and stepped up to the stage, as a tear rolled down her cheek. The thoughts had worked.

"My fellow Tantalians. I come before you today with two hats on. The first is as a grieving daughter. Sadly, this isn't the first time I've presented to you as such. Secondly, I'm also your new queen. I'll speak more on the latter later, when I'm sworn in. For now, I need to talk to you about King John. To me he wasn't a king or statesman or leader, he was just Dad. My dad. My father. I don't know how to sum up his influence on me. I'm an only child, so perhaps that's why it seemed like he gave me so much attention? Mostly, he'd make time for me if I said I needed it. Sometimes there were matters of state… My father was wise, one of the three wisest people I know. Knew."

Niobe glanced at Gethan. Would her tears convince him to hang around?

"He knew, one day, I'd be given the responsibility for leading this country, so he made sure I would be ready. From age five, he made me study philosophy and martial arts, alongside a regular curriculum. It's only since my mother died that I really grasped why he saw these things as being important." Niobe again glanced at Gethan. Had she let slip a few too many of her intentions? She'd have to make it seem like she meant something else. "My favourite times as a kid were when he and Mum trained with me. Dad loved martial arts, and I think he would have instructed me himself, if his schedule had allowed it. When Mum got sick, he stopped training in order to be with her. When his diagnosis came through before she died, he refused to tell her. He knew how much pain it'd cause her to know he'd soon suffer the same fate. Both my parents were fighters, and they certainly beat the odds for life expectancy from their illness."

Niobe paused, allowing the words to catch in her throat. She was pleased her tears were making it hard to read her notes. The effect was immediate. There was a collective 'ahwww', which made it hard for Niobe to repress a smile and regain control of her display. Her sobbing increased as she channelled her righteous anger at the person who'd made her parents sick, into her presentation of sadness.

"Dad knows I blame Alban Crab for my parents' deaths. It was his dying wish I make peace with Alban, so I've invited him to my reception this evening. Mum loved me and I loved her. Dad loved me, and I loved him. To say I'll miss them doesn't do it justice. I felt so lucky to have them as my parents, and King John as my dad. He inspired me. Every single day, he inspired me. He helped me become a better person, so I'll honour his wish."

Niobe had more written, but was too angry with Alban to continue. She glanced at Gethan to see if her act of being overcome with emotion had fooled him. Would Gethan buy the act that she'd forgive Alban? He'd always been the best at spotting her lies. Regardless he'd at least be at the reception to keep an eye on her. Surely he wouldn't really try to stop her out of some misguided loyalty to a now dead king?

* * *

THE CORONATION for Niobe to become queen began punctually at 2.00 pm. It began with another retrospective on King John. The main narrative was the history-making role of the king's fight to transform the country from an emerging to a developed market economy, worthy of joining the EU. Alban Crab's role in both the king's and queen's cancer was covered, but the video ended with the king saying a piece to camera in which he forgave Alban for his actions. Niobe forced her expression to remain neutral. Her father's message to Alban was clearly meant for her, since it had been recorded in the last month of the king's life. The message had the opposite effect. Niobe was more determined than ever to kill Alban. The only difference was now she had a time frame. He would die tonight. Any other time frame would give Gethan too much opportunity to put up a counter-offensive.

FIRST ASSASSINATION

"Princess Niobe Allison Andrea Ancora, do you accept the role of queen as stated?" Zacharias intoned. His rich voice filled the majestic chapel, even before it was amplified by speakers.

Niobe kept her hand on the ceremonial bible and looked the prime minister in the eye. "I do," she said.

"And will you execute the role with the best interests of Tantalia at heart?"

Niobe suppressed a smile. *Execute.*

"I will."

"Per article seven of our constitution, I declare Niobe Allison Andrea Ancora, Her Royal Highness, Queen of Tantalia. Congratulations, Your Majesty."

The massive crowd's thunderous applause created a strange feeling within Niobe. For her whole life she'd been trained to think about what her actions might mean to others and what it meant to be a leader and a royal. Here was that writ large. She owed these people for giving her the life she'd had until this point. They were the ones who'd afforded her the luxury of her training. Who'd allowed her to feel in

"

control. The focus on her mission had made her neglect the repercussions of her ascension to the throne. Tantalians seemed to adore her. Niobe felt an unexpected sensation of ownership. These were *her* people. She would protect them. They would want her to lead them through the adjustment period, not only as their new monarch, but also as the leader of the country as a new member state of the EU. Trade, people movement and the wider political landscape would change. Her powers as queen were not dissimilar to other EU monarchs, however, unlike the Queen of England, who had similar prerogatives but acted as barely more than a figure-head, Niobe was expected to be active in shaping the country. Her role in the political landscape of Tantalia was more presidential than regal.

Niobe's full-length, fur-lined, purple cloak shimmered in the sunlight breaking through the clouded sky. She smiled and waved. Cameras flashed by the tens of thousands, and another loud cheer filled the air.

Nominally, she had twenty minutes to change clothes between the coronation and a reception at the palace, but she had grander plans, which would require moving efficiently.

Niobe mentally rehearsed her plan as she accepted a kiss on the cheek from the prime minister. A procession line of dignitaries waited patiently for a similar ritual. This was the worst part of the afternoon. They'd never kiss the king like this, just shake his hand. It felt too personal. If only she'd anticipated it, she could have made a decree.

Niobe was pleased when she saw Patterson a few people away. When she got to him she held him in close as he went to kiss her cheek and whispered, "I need a mortar and pestle, some masking tape and a new bottle of children's pain relief, the one that comes with the syringe. And, Patterson, be discreet."

Patterson nodded and spun on his heels to obey the request. Niobe's smile widened. Her plan was taking shape.

* * *

AFTER ENDURING another half hour of platitudes and coronation bureaucracy, Niobe was, at last, able to return to her room in the palace. She knew she'd be expected downstairs at the reception within a quarter of an hour. Time was of the essence.

Niobe found her jacket where she'd left it under her bed and removed the sample she'd taken that morning from the pond. She scraped the bacteria from its plastic bag, into the mortar and pestle. She knew the substance would degrade if exposed to light or water, so she placed a red shirt over her lampshade. Grinding the bacteria, which was often wrongly called blue-green algae (it wasn't algae), was harder than she'd anticipated due to its slippery nature. Niobe muttered to herself as she worked. "It's a good thing I'm not trying to get a pure sample. That would require specialised equipment. But you, my pretty, will do the job."

After a few minutes, a small pool of green viscous liquid sat in the bottom of the mortar. Niobe extracted the 5ml syringe from the children's pain relief medication and used it to remove 3 ml of the fluid. She then used the masking tape Patterson had obtained for her to cover the syringe so light wouldn't affect the extract. She would have preferred a proper, medical syringe, but that would have raised too many questions. Besides, it wasn't her intention to inject the solution into Alban.

The extract contained anatoxin-a, a substance which had originally been given the prosaic name, Very Fast Death Factor (VFDF). A pure sample was known to be able to kill various animals within a few seconds of ingestion. It would only take about 5mg to kill a human, but this was just an educated estimate. How much in the solution was anybody's guess, but it should be much more than required for the job. The poison wouldn't act with its usual speed due to the impurity of the sample. With luck, it would take hours and Alban would suffer before dying.

Niobe taped the syringe to her arm using more of the masking tape, and put on her long-sleeved top. Niobe checked her reflection and smiled. The syringe wasn't visible. Her cleavage was also shown by a deep 'V' cut in the front of her top. With a strapless push-up bra on, her C-cup breasts looked impressive, even to her. Niobe knew no one would be looking at her sleeve.

* * *

Niobe's entrance to the reception brought an immediate hush to the room. This was followed by a loud applause as Niobe was led, by Patterson, to a waiting lectern. She found it hard to match his shuffling gait, and once she was free of his arm, she strode to the microphone.

"Thank you for your warm reception this afternoon. To be honest, I've been grieving my father so much, I didn't think about how you might receive me as your queen. According to my father, and my royal counsel, Gethan, I am not a philosopher king, or queen, as I am too young and"— Niobe turned to look Gethan in the eye—"haven't studied enough to earn that title. I hope you, my people, will allow me to grow into the role bestowed upon me. I will perform my function to the best of my ability and without fear or favour. My father wanted the best for this country and worked tirelessly to raise its status, prosperity and, most importantly, its level of happiness. I aim to continue this legacy and do what I can to ensure Tantalia continues to elevate itself amongst established economies. Thank you for entrusting me with this role. I'll finish with a quote from my favourite poet. It sums up my determination to fight for Tantalia's place in the world. 'And with each shot fired she affirms her movement, saying enough, enough, no. I will see my own blood flow, before I let you take my land or my liberty.' With each of my actions, you'll know my love for this country."

Niobe had heard a lot of applause at the innumerable royal events she'd attended over the years and had learnt the difference between polite and rapturous clapping. The noise was surprising—they seemed to really like her. She wondered if they'd still love her if they knew how much she wanted to kill?

Niobe would engage what Jung would call her *animus*. The male part of the female psyche would help her find a way to get to her enemy. While Niobe didn't believe in such gender division, she acknowledged the power of a mental framework for activating a mindset. This was her way of finding the hunter-killer within.

Alban was a predator too, and would be wary of Niobe, given her vocal opposition to him in the past. He would be susceptible to flattery though. She'd have to find a way to use that against him. A plan revealed itself, but it would rely upon how well she could read him and control his thinking. Fate would play a role in the outcome. It was not how Niobe wanted him to die, but it would suffice.

* * *

AFTER QUEEN MARIGOLD was diagnosed with mesothelioma, Niobe was angry at the loss the cancer would bring. What would the absence of her mother, who was always good at calming her down, mean? Growing up, the queen had always impressed upon Niobe how much she wanted to have grand-children, and her hope she and the king could abdicate a year or two after Niobe started a family, so they could look after the kid or kids while Niobe was queen. The king had first coughed up blood a month before the queen died. This was when the plan had kicked up an extra gear and Niobe trained harder to extract a discreet but permanent revenge on Alban. At one of their earliest training sessions after her mother died, Gethan had asked Niobe how she wanted to do it. They had been in what had become their usual post-workout meditation spot. Gethan helped her into a meditative state and asked her to visualise what she'd do.

"I want it to be by my own hand. I want to stare into his eyes as he dies, so he knows it's me ending his life. I'd like to hurt him first though, lots of body punches, maybe crack a rib or break his jaw with a kick. I'd really like to break the index finger and maybe the middle finger of his dominant hand. Is that the right or left? He'd never again be able to grip a hose like the one he'd used to spray asbestos dust on chil-dren or my parents in order to demonstrate how 'safe' it was. I wouldn't go for the actual kill until he was in extreme pain and knew with certainty he was about to die. I want him to be afraid as he dies—to not be at peace. Only then will I produce the knife and stick it into his lungs, so he drowns in his own blood, like he made Mum. That's what I want. Then I will move on happily knowing he suffered."

Gethan had nodded in reply and placed a paternal hand on her shoulder. "As the king commands, we'll make that happen."

He'd fine-tuned their training for lethality, rather than self-defence, ever since.

TANTALIA HAD ONLY one recognised distillery, which was given royal assent in the nineteenth century. It used water from a large tributary to the main waterway through the country, the Paine River. The Tantalian river was named after the scout master who'd led the development of a hiking trail and campsites along the banks of the river, and was unrelated to the Chilean river which shared its name. It was a popular two-week hike, which ran the length of the country. The distillery had produced a thousand commemorative bottles of whisky in preparation for the changeover of the monarch. In the last twenty-four hours they'd worked to hand-label each bottle with the date. A few miniatures had also been produced. These were meant for royal staff. On the way into the reception hall, Niobe asked the waiting Patterson to bring her his miniature. She promised to replace it with a full-sized bottle, as it was more fitting for his status in her life. Niobe was sure he looked pleased with the request. She wondered if it was due to the bottles already listing online for thousands of euros.

Patterson reappeared just as Niobe spied Alban for the first time. She was about to scowl but managed to convert the expression to what hopefully appeared a non-evil smile. Alban's short, silver hair and natty pinstriped suit stood out in the crowd, but this seemed an intentional choice. He looked happy to be mingling with the country's elite. Niobe quickly and quietly slipped to the bathroom. Once safely in a stall, she partially uncapped the black glass miniature, being careful to lift back the cap leaving a couple of the attachments intact. Raising the cap meant she could squirt the syringe into the bottle. A small amount spilt down the side, but no matter, enough got in. She put the cap back on and gave the bottle a little shake. The extract would blend in well. She hoped the cask-strength alcohol would slow the degradation enough for her plan to work.

Niobe wiped the bottle, then decided to obey the first rule of public life—never pass up the opportunity to sit down or pee. After finishing her business, Niobe returned to the party being held in her honour. It wasn't long before Alban Crab was being walked towards her by Patterson. Niobe noticed Gethan some ten metres away watching her out of the corner of his eye. When he saw who Niobe was about to talk to, he made sure she had his full attention and stood square on to her. He even forced eye contact. The message was clear— don't try anything. A curt nod was her reply. For extra emphasis, she mouthed, "I won't".

Niobe wondered if Gethan had divined her plan. She'd made it knowing it was far removed from what she'd told him she wanted to do, but as he sometimes said, he knew her better than she knew herself.

"Your Majesty, this is Alban Crab," Patterson said with one arm on Alban's back and the other out in front from guiding Alban through the crowd. Niobe noticed the contrast in the similarly aged men's faces. Where Patterson's was the warm face of a kindly grandfather, Alban's was the face of a predator, assured and ruthless.

"We've met," Niobe said, only just keeping an icy tone out of her voice. Coming face-to-face with the man she most wanted to kill produced strong emotions, yet they needed to be hidden for her plan to work. She forced a half-smile, but was aware her eyes didn't join in. She struggled to contain her desire to start maiming Alban and hoped her twitchiness would be interpreted as nervousness.

"Your Majesty, congratulations on your ascension to the throne," Alban said. It was clear he was trying to sound charming. Niobe wondered if he realised the crassness of his words. After all, he was the reason her parents had died and made her queen.

"It was my father's dying wish that we make peace with

each other." Niobe was pleased this statement would provide an excuse for her body language.

"I never understood why you blamed *me* for their illness."

Inwardly she raged: It wasn't an 'illness,' it was cancer. A cancer which took years to kill them. They felt their life ebbing away and the loss of their senses, freedom, hair, and mental faculties from the chemo and radiation therapy. They felt like they were suffocating, numerous times, from the fluid around their lungs, and here he was brushing it off as an 'illness'. Fuck him.

She smiled. "To show acceptance of my father's desire, I have a miniature of the commemorative bottle of whisky produced to celebrate my ascension to the throne. No other guest is receiving one. Please savour it. Drink it slowly, on a special occasion."

Alban nodded, and received the whisky with the hint of a smile. Niobe was pleased to notice it. He could take bait. He was probably already planning to *skol* the drink.

They made some small talk about the economy and the impact of joining the EU. Alban seemed interested in what was being planned for the upcoming negotiations with Australia over a free trade agreement. Niobe said it might depend on who the Australian prime minister was by the time of the talks, after all, they'd recently had five changes of leader in six years. Since the talks had been provisionally started before Tantalia's ascension to the EU, the EU members had given them dispensation to continue them. Though any agreement would have to be approved by the EU and added to their free trade agreement with Australia.

* * *

Niobe moved on to the next guest, all the while keeping Alban in her sights. She waited until he headed towards the bathroom, then slipped away from the person she was speaking to, taking advantage of a moment when Gethan took his eyes off her. Niobe followed Alban down a narrow corridor and right into the bathroom.

Seeing Niobe visibly startled Alban. Niobe held up her own miniature whisky.

"I thought we could bury the hatchet properly, with a drink." Niobe stopped herself adding she'd rather bury a hatchet in his head.

"I thought I was meant to save it for a special occasion." Alban's smugness irritated Niobe, but she held her smile. "Isn't this one? Your queen would like to share a drink with you."

"Okay." Alban sounded reluctant, but dutifully uncapped and raised his bottle for a toast. Niobe was pleased his cap still 'cracked' when Alban twisted it open. It was a little touch which would help her plan work.

"*Slàinte*," Niobe said. They clinked their miniatures together.

Alban grunted and downed his bottle in one gulp. It was a clear 'stuff you' after he'd been told to savour it.

Alban coughed as the alcohol hit. "Hmm. An oddly bitter whisky. I like it."

"I like it too, especially its effect."

"Yes, it's rather warming."

Niobe smiled, not at how her reverse psychology had made him drink, but that her mission was complete and Gethan hadn't witnessed it. The poison would kill Alban in anywhere from minutes to hours. Hours would have the added benefit of him suffering more, but also the advantage of him having left the palace. Niobe's heart raced with excitement. Alban was as good as dead. It was such a rush.

Niobe watched Alban closely, looking for signs of the poison taking effect. Alban, for his part, started looking increasingly uncomfortable. Although, Niobe reasoned, that could simply be due to being in the men's room with a woman, and the awkwardness of being around someone whose parents' deaths he was responsible for.

"So, what will you do as queen?" Alban asked.

"Defend my people, in the best way I know how." Niobe noted the veracity of her reply. It was her real intention. She realised Alban's imminent death meant she could be totally honest with him. Was that why villains confessed all in the movies? It was cleansing.

"It must be hard for you, having your parents pass while you're so young."

Niobe began to wonder how much longer she could remain away from the party. Surely someone else would come into the bathroom soon? But she was compelled to stay. She had to see the process begin. She had to see the look in his eyes as he realised something was wrong.

"Yes, it has been very hard. I'm concerned my royal counsel, Gethan, will leave me too. He would have done anything for my father, but I'm not sure he'll do the same for me."

At last the first bead of sweat appeared on Alban's brow, but was it caused by nerves or the poison?

"Are you feeling okay? You look a little unwell. Maybe you shouldn't have drunk your drink all at once?"

"I'm fine," Alban declared stiffly, in defiance of more sweat beading around his thin hairline.

Niobe opened a stall door and directed Alban to the toilet. She watched him hesitate as though he wasn't sure whether he needed to sit or kneel, before he settled on kneeling. Niobe drew the door closed and smiled as she left the bathroom. The Very Fast Death Factor had taken hold.

As Niobe left the bathroom, she ran into Patterson who seemed to be entering.

"Your Majesty?" he questioned. "This is the male bathroom."

"I know, I heard someone being unwell. Maybe you could arrange some help and transport for them?"

"Certainly, Your Majesty." Patterson seemed happy for the task.

"By the way, Gethan is looking for you. I suggest you enter via the reception hall's west entrance to catch him."

"Thank you, Patterson. You're a great help."

She made her way back to the party, making sure to enter via the east entrance. A few moments later she waved to Gethan across the room. He seemed relieved to see her.

* * *

NIOBE AND GETHAN had completed their morning workout and were sitting in their usual position facing each other for the other half of their training. With her sweat still evaporating and her heart still beating at an accelerated rate, Niobe was caught off guard when Gethan said, "I'm not sure whether to be pleased or upset with you."

She met his gaze squarely. "What do you mean?"

"You moved differently today. That kind of change doesn't just happen. You've either killed Alban or solved the Riddle of the Eye. Either way, I don't know how you managed it. I can't see you getting the riddle just yet, although you're close, so I'm guessing you somehow completed your assassination?"

Gethan's voice had an edge, but Niobe couldn't determine if it was stern, or formal, like the tone you used when speaking to someone you admired. Niobe felt the edges of her mouth curl upwards.

"How do you feel?" Gethan asked.

"I thought it would be different," Niobe replied. "My rage

has gone, and I feel a sense of serenity, unlike anything I've felt before. But I must admit some concern over your response. But for what it's worth, I don't know I've killed anyone."

"Don't play semantics. What do you mean, you don't know?"

"I gave Alban a bottle of poisoned whisky. I knew you'd try to stop me if you saw me starting a physical attack, so I found another way."

"But he might not have drunk it yet?"

"No, I watched him drink it."

Gethan leapt up with a speed other near-fifty-year-olds would kill for and ran towards the door. "Meditate on what you've done," he called out before he left the hall.

Niobe hoped he'd be too late to save Alban, after all, the impure sample may not have had enough toxin to kill him. She thought back to the night before. The rush when he'd drunk the poison was like a reward for the years of desiring to see him die. She knew wanting to commit murder wasn't 'normal'. Her parents had made that perfectly clear to her when she was a child. But individuals were separate entities from society, so surely any individual's perspective of right and wrong would take precedence over society's view. Her assassination of Alban wasn't wrong from her point of view. She was more than comfortable with her actions. Was her perspective above that of her country? Should individuals be allowed to disobey rules inconsistent with their own principles?

* * *

THE NEXT DAY, the newspapers reported that Alban Crab had died from a cocaine overdose. Niobe remembered that Very Fast Death Factor could be synthesised from cocaine. The chemical test the medical examiner ran must have responded to the similarity of the molecules. She smiled. She'd gotten away with it. Except Gethan knew. In fact, he'd prompted the discovery of the body when he'd phoned Alban and spoken to his personal assistant, nominally on an administrative manner. The assistant had gone to his home to check on Alban and found him slumped on his desk.

But what Gethan would do next, Niobe wasn't sure, especially after she'd defied him. She'd already received a note to say he was cancelling training that day.

* * *

THAT NIGHT whilst trying to fall asleep, Niobe thought about how much better it felt to be a Tantalian now Alban had been removed from the social discourse. Haiti, Cuba, the Zapatistas in Mexico. How many revolutions had begun on New Year's Day? Tantalia's revolution was just beginning, and not only because they were now a member state of the EU. Tantalia might not know it, but they now had an assassin as their queen. Niobe would kill again to make her country a better place. The revolution would be quiet and less violent than those other revolutions, but no less significant. When she fell asleep, Niobe dreamt of black dominoes falling on a white table. At one point the dominoes split into two parallel paths that were meant to join together further along the set, but one path was blocked by a pile of three dominoes just before the point of convergence. In the morning, when she awoke, her thoughts kept circling back to her inauguration; something about the crowd kept bugging her. Once she realised what it was, she knew she'd solved the Riddle of the Eye.

CHAPTER 6

After a light breakfast, Niobe practically skipped to the training hall. The relative warmth of the last few weeks had given way to a cold snap, and the air didn't just have a chill, it felt like it contained slivers of ice. Mastery of Wim Hoff breathing practices meant the cold rarely affected Niobe. However, the winter meant she missed the scent of the garden when it was in bloom.

Resisting the urge to fling open the door, Niobe slipped quietly into the hall. She felt herself smile, and exhale, when Gethan came into view. He beckoned to a spot in front of him. Niobe crossed the hall and mimicked Gethan's posture as she sat on the floor.

"I'm upset with you for disobeying your father and me. You broke the rules. I'm still deciding what to do about it."

"You've always taught me rules are not absolute dictates which must be obeyed without question."

Gethan inhaled. Was he gritting his teeth? Her response must have struck a nerve.

"Rules are valid if they are grounded in justice, and a commitment to justice carries with it an obligation to disobey unjust rule, that's true. But, you didn't break an unjust rule, you killed someone and broke the social contract."

"That we give up the freedom to behave as we please, or immorally, so we can be part of society."

"Exactly. You don't have the right to kill on a whim, or worse, for some petty revenge."

Her new interpretation of the Riddle of the Eye gave Niobe a confidence she'd never known. It wasn't unusual for her to answer Gethan back, but now she found herself outright challenging him.

"Interesting, so what about all those years spent training me specifically to kill Alban?"

"I hoped you'd surpass the desire. I went along with your father's plan out of loyalty to him, but I hoped our training would help you realise killing him wouldn't change the situation you're in. So yes, I was pleased when he changed his mind, and I was, *am*, determined to uphold his wishes. You outsmarted me. I didn't believe you'd do anything at the reception; it was too public, and you always said you wanted his death be a physical punishment by your own hands."

"You taught me that if your enemy believes something to be true, which you can change to be untrue, then you should use it to wrong-foot them."

"So I did." Gethan shook his head. "So, does that mean I'm your enemy?"

"My thoughts about Alban weren't conditional upon anything; they were an absolute. Alban didn't just deserve to die, he needed to die for the betterment of the country."

"So, legal rights are unnecessary? Your opinion is sufficient justification?"

"Social contracts aren't essential for moral action. I guess, I feel like I'm above that constraint. I realised at my inauguration that I wasn't merely killing him for myself. He wasn't the means to an end—for me to consolidate my grief and anger into a solvable puzzle. Killing him was an end, in and of itself."

"So, you're saying a corollary would be that rules which don't promote general welfare should be changed to meet the greatest good for the greatest number of people?

"Yes."

"But that may mean you need to compromise."

"That's what democracy is about."

Gethan had a look on his face Niobe had only seen a few times before. He was beaming with pride. As he threw the Riddle of the Eye card into the space between them it was as though he knew she'd solved it. "What's this?"

"A prison." There was a slight upward twitch at the corner of his mouth. She was right.

"Continue."

"It's the panopticon, a prison, like the *Presidio Modelo,* where the cells are located in an outer ring, like the larger circle of your drawing. The white space between the ring and the centre is a courtyard. The two tones of the central circles are to indicate a tower rising up. The prisoners are thought to be able to be controlled through knowing they're always being observed. Their cells have windows to the inner court-yard and to the outside of the prison. The occupants are always illuminated or backlit. By being constantly observed and having any wrong behaviour instantly noticed or responded to, the prisoners learn to control their behaviour, particularly any behaviour breaking the social contract, due to the power of the 'gaze' upon them. The key thing in the design is a reflective coating on the tower so the prisoners can't see the guards."

"Why is that important?"

"So, after a time, the guards don't actually have to be there. The prisoners don't know when they're being observed or not, so they'll continue to behave as though they are. What will actually control their behaviour at that point won't be the gaze itself, but their perception of it. It won't matter that the perception is of something which isn't there."

"And what does this mean for you?"

"I realised last night that I've been living in my own prison due to fear of the gaze. I've been so caught up in how everyone thinks of me—you, Mum, Dad, the public. I've always been told I have to behave like the perfect little princess. My behaviour has been dictated by expectation, wanting to fit in, to be *seen* to be doing the right thing, to be taking action over my parents' deaths, to be queen. I haven't actually worked out who I am in the absence of the gaze, the absence of other people. Killing Alban has freed me. It's not a burden like my dad thought it would be, it's the opposite. I'm the one who's been in my own way, who's created my own *estoppel*. That block has been removed. I'm now truly, and for the first time, myself."

Gethan smiled. He seemed proud. Niobe enjoyed being able to share her new understanding with someone who grasped the significance of it.

"You've reached identity achievement as Marcia called it; mostly by getting out of your own way, but also through exploring and committing to who you are. The social-self and the personal-self become one. Your person and persona are the same. That is a phenomenal achievement, but could put you at risk if the public don't like it. I knew you were close with your description of the auditorium and the change in the way you moved at training the other day. You abandoned set forms. Do you understand why I couldn't just tell you the solution to the Riddle of the Eye?"

"If you had, it wouldn't have the same meaning for me. I

needed to reach the understanding myself to see how important it was, and how it applied to me. I was the creator of my own prison and I was my own jailer, because I submitted to the gaze, just like other people do when they consume social media and advertising."

"I've been responsible for your physical and mental development for a very long time now. Today I have completed that role. Thank you also for letting me see what I need to do now, especially after the last few days."

"What are you saying?"

"You don't need me anymore. You think I'm your enemy, even if you didn't say it. I don't want to be your next victim. I'm leaving the palace. *Today.*"

Niobe was too stunned to speak as Gethan stood and walked slowly from the hall.

SECOND ASSASSINATION

Gethan left a letter acknowledging Niobe's achievement of self-actualisation, and of her personal strength and expert level of martial arts. The letter reaffirmed his opposition to her actions vis-à-vis Alban, and her disobedience of King John's orders. He also nominated a replacement martial arts trainer for her.

Niobe checked and was advised that after obtaining his last pay, Gethan had disappeared. She wondered where he'd gone, and why he'd left the palace rather than take on a new charge. He could easily have stuck around to keep an eye on Niobe, even if he was no longer training her. After all, Niobe's cousin, Ebony, was a teenager and was displaying rebellious behaviours, which indicated she'd benefit from a guide through the years ahead. Niobe had wanted to nominate Gethan for the role. He was her surrogate father and had guided her when her own father couldn't, particularly over the last four years. He was her confidant, her safe place, but now he was gone. This should have made Niobe feel lost, but she felt strangely unconcerned about not having a mentor. This upgraded version of herself seemed to be able to accept his choice.

What did worry her was what he may have meant by mentioning her father. Did the mention mean he'd continue to work against her? What if she wanted to kill again? Would he really try to stop her?

Two weeks after Gethan had left, Niobe had her first meeting with the Australian Prime Minister. They spoke about the trade deal Tantalia's Prime and Foreign Affairs ministers were negotiating. Ultimately, Niobe would have the final say in whether the deal received her royal assent to become law, so she was grateful for the opportunity to understand it better. Australia was a relatively small country in population terms, but still six times larger than Tantalia, and the trade deal had relatively few items. Any agreement would have to go through the EU, but she was confident a deal could be done which would benefit both parties. After all, Tantalia had specialist medical equipment and tourists the Australians wanted, and they had the aluminium and iron Tantalia needed. The meeting was long, and quite boring. More than once, Niobe found herself daydreaming about different ways of killing the PM for no reason other than how easy it would be to do if she wanted to. The worst moment of the meeting was when she let her secret thoughts slip when she accidentally said murder rather than merger. Thankfully, no one reacted.

* * *

THREE WEEKS after Gethan had left, Niobe was beginning to find her feet in her new role as queen. She kept up her daily martial arts and meditation, but without Gethan training her, some of the lustre came off the process. Her regular thoughts about Alban produced mixed emotions. Happiness at the outcome, but regret he hadn't died by 'her hand'. Niobe began to dwell on what ending someone's life in a more intimate manner would feel like. She felt like she'd missed out by not watching Alban suffer, or take his last breath. For the previous five years, she'd daydreamed about what it would be like to plunge a knife into his chest, how the blood would pool after an initial spray, how he'd gurgle as his lungs filled with blood, and how his eyes would glaze over as he died. This had been denied to her thanks to Gethan's interference. She wouldn't forgive him for that.

Her new instructor, Nathan, struggled with the strength and intent of some of her attacks and defences, which fed into her desire for a challenge. She needed to feel alive again, like that night with Alban. She had no choice. She needed a new target.

Reading newspapers over breakfast seemed like a good place to start looking.

It wasn't front page news, even on a Monday, but on page three of the *Tantalia Sun* an article caught Niobe's eye. It was about the start of the trial of Donald 'Don' Azzure. He was being tried for the murder of a rival businessman, Ashton Weri. The trial was due to hear from its star witness at the end of the week, a woman who'd hidden behind some curtains when Don had entered Ashton's living room.

Niobe knew of Don and his reputation as an alleged crime-based businessman. She took out her phone. A search revealed a number of pictures from social events which had made the news. A few articles in the lead-up to the trial outlined the murkiness of his business practices. There was one quite favourable article about Don Azzure's business dealings in the *Tantalia Sun* though, written by a journalist called Drysen Silic. It was complimentary towards Don and the various members of his family who ran businesses in Tantalia. One thing which stood out to Niobe was Drysen's praise for Don's links to the country of Autarchos and its despotic ruler, Jork Dressov. In the article's words, 'at least someone is improving relations between our countries'.

Niobe scowled. Jork was probably conspiring with Don Azzure to enable the supply of drugs to flow between the countries.

Niobe began to smile when she realised Don would make a good victim. However, she wouldn't target him while the trial was still ongoing. Justice had to be allowed to run its course.

Niobe sighed and went back to her newspapers. It didn't matter what she read, her mind kept drifting back to Don Azzure. He was a stain on Tantalian society, and she couldn't think of anyone more perfect to be her next target.

The next morning Niobe scoured the newspapers for reports of the trial. The *Tantalia Sun* had barely a paragraph on it, reporting little more than that the trial had started. The *Tantalian Times* had a longer report, which indicated the trial's blockbuster day would be Friday, when the witness testified.

Wednesday's papers weren't any better, which made Niobe highly distracted throughout the day. She wanted to hear word of how the trial was going, but such information wasn't usually reported, so not knowing whether the courts would convict or release Don was frustrating.

By Thursday, Niobe was a bundle of nervous energy. She kept a muted news channel on the television in the conference room where she was having an afternoon meeting with the Tantalian Prime Minister. Niobe kept glancing at the TV. Surely, they'd mention the trial in the daily wrap-up? The witness was due the next day.

"Something on your mind, Your Majesty?" Zacharias asked.

"Sorry, Zack. I can't seem to focus at the moment. These

negotiations with Australia, coming to grips with my new role, even the trial for Don Azzure has caught my attention. It's all so much. I just don't know how to deal with everything at once."

"It must be tough for someone of your ... err ... age to take on so much so quickly. Even with all your training, it's such a large responsibility."

For a moment Niobe thought he knew about Alban, or her desire to kill Don Azzure.

"It is. Thank you for your empathy. I must admit—"

Niobe leapt up and raced past Zack to the remote for the TV. A headline had appeared on the screen. *Key witness in Azzure trial found slain.* A warning flashed up to say some viewers might find the report distressing.

Niobe unmuted the sound and turned up the volume. "... stabbed three times in the chest. Her son's throat was slit," the reporter said.

"Turn it off. That's too terrible to watch," Zack said.

Niobe quickly turned her wide smile into a forced frown and turned to the prime minister. "A few moments more. I want to know what this'll do for the trial."

The reporter continued, "...-come of the trial."

The reporter crossed to Morgan Henry, who was covering the courthouse. Morgan gestured towards the lectern behind her. "Thanks, Tom. Don Azzure's lawyer is about to make a speech."

Cameras clicked like crazy as the lawyer began to speak.

"Without the witness, Don may get off," Zack said.

"Shhh," Niobe said sternly.

"...tragic robbery gone wrong. Our condolences go out to the family. Of course, we had wanted Maria to testify. I'm sure she would clear my client, but alas that won't happen now."

"That's not true," Zack said. "He fought her right to testify tooth and nail. Surely people won't fall for that?"

"The gaslighting you mean?"

"Yes," Zack said.

"People are stupid. At the very least it will make them question what's real, and then they'll believe whatever story fits with their worldview."

"I guess so, I mean you muddy the waters with many versions of events, even with obvious lies and people will just ask themselves which version they want to be true."

On the TV, the lawyer continued, "…file for a dismissal. My client deserves to be acquitted of these charges."

Morgan turned back to the camera. "No word on whether the judge will grant it. We'll have to check back tomorrow."

"I'm sorry, Zack, I don't think I'll be able to concentrate on the rest of our meeting. Would you mind if we cut it short?"

"Of course, Your Majesty. I'd better get back to my office. It's likely that this trial will come up in parliament. I'm sure one of the members will want to make a name for themselves by using parliamentary privilege to accuse Don of being involved."

Niobe smiled at the thought of someone else using their positional rights to take otherwise unavailable action.

"Thanks."

* * *

THE NEXT MORNING Niobe read every newspaper article on Don's trial. Drysen Silic had written an article for the *Tantalia Sun*, which was sympathetic to Don Azzure's version of events. Most other papers, including the *Tantalian Times*, reported the story of the murders as being detrimental to the

Crown's case, leaving it likely that Don would get away with murder.

At 9.30 am, the judge in the case dismissed the case and demanded Don be released.

Don didn't yet know it, but he had stepped out of the frying pan and into the fire. Niobe couldn't stop smiling at the thought Don had limited time left on this earth.

A report on that evening's news indicated Don was likely to be celebrating his court 'victory' by staying at a hotel run by his cousin near the Tantalian and Autarchos border. Niobe guessed he'd probably have a bodyguard with him. Debating whether to kill the bodyguard or not led her to realise she didn't know the extent of their actions in Don Azzure's empire. Gethan had been her bodyguard for two decades, but was also quite involved in palace affairs as head of security, and had covered up a few potential scandals in his time. How involved was the bodyguard in the thuggery, drug distribution and racketeering? Since Niobe couldn't answer, the bodyguard did not meet her categorical criteria for assassination. She'd developed the criteria over the last few weeks after reflecting upon why she'd wanted Alban to die so badly. Per her two decades of mental training, she'd taken the personal, subjective notions out. For Alban it had meant overlooking his role in her parents' deaths. The five criteria Niobe had created were straightforward:

The victim needed to be an arsehole (objectively).

The victim needed to have incited or committed murder.

They needed to have shown no remorse.

They needed to have been tried for their crime but escaped natural justice on a technicality or their own interference with the trial.

Finally, their actions needed to have harmed Tantalia.

For Niobe you were either worthy or not. The final criteria was the one Niobe felt the most satisfaction about.

She would kill to protect what was hers—the people of Tantalia. She'd watch over them and be their secret assassin, taking out those who would cause the country harm. Niobe felt this was probably the most royal thing she could do. After all, hadn't past kings and queens had numerous enemies of the state executed, sometimes even solely to induce fear? The only difference was Niobe had the courage to do it herself and out of the public eye.

The criteria list had one weakness: she couldn't kill those who didn't meet the conditions it imposed. This was a problem for her next assassination and would influence what weapons she'd carry. Electric-shock weapons, such as a Taser, were something she hated using. The handheld ones had no range, and you ran the risk of shocking yourself if there was a struggle. The Tasers that shot cords gave you one shot to get your opponent. Niobe decided she'd use a suppressed shotgun from the hidden gun locker in her training hall. She'd have it fire 'bean bag' rounds. These would incapacitate the bodyguard long enough for Niobe to either strangle or choke them into unconsciousness, if they weren't rendered so by the shot. Then she could bind them so they couldn't move. The suppressor wouldn't make the shotgun silent, but it would make it sound like a loud clap rather than a gun being fired. In a hotel, it was unlikely anyone would notice due to the insulation between the walls and floors. Besides all these considerations, carrying a shotgun would make her feel more badass as she travelled to the hotel.

Niobe waited for the sky to turn black and the night to be late enough for few people to be out and about in the city. At such an hour, the palace staff would be at its minimum too. She snuck out of the palace the way she'd done as a teenager. She went into her bathroom, and, standing on the edge of the sink, reached up and carefully pulled the cover off the square-shaped fan in the ceiling. Some deft manipulation later, and the fan was now in the recess of the ceiling, leaving a hole she could climb through. Niobe raised her arms like she was about to dive off the counter. Instead, she jumped up. As her arms went through the hole, she spread them wide, so her body formed a cross. Her arms landed with a thud on the nearest beams. Wriggling side-to-side meant Niobe could shuffle enough to get a hand and elbow on each beam. From there, it was a simple case of doing a pull-up using her back muscles, more than her biceps, to push rather than lift her body up. Years of training made it easy. Niobe then pressed up with her hands, like she was doing a triceps push-down, and swung her legs into the ceiling. She looked at the hole she'd come through. Good, no nicking of the plaster on the way through. She'd be able to replace every-thing without a trace when she returned.

Within the ceiling, Niobe made her way along the rafters to the edge of the circular roof where there was a section of tiles she could easily remove and replace. Once on the roof, she went to the nearby drainpipe. One which had been ordered to be reinforced so long ago no one would even remember.

A quick scale down the pipe and hugging of the shadows enabled her to reach the training hall. She snuck inside and went to the back of the change room. Inside a locker, she pulled a hidden lever and typed a code into a panel. A red light turned green. She pushed the lockers sideways and opened a small passageway. Inside was a walk-in gun locker for her weapons training with Gethan. Niobe changed into a black hoodie, thermals and leggings, which she'd placed there over the last few days, and stuffed one of her pockets with a wad of cash she'd added for her mission. She placed a shotgun in a holster and slung it over her back, then put a long black coat over the top. She decided she didn't need any special weapon for Don Azzure. She would be the weapon. She also took the only other tool she'd need.

A light run through the shadows of the Greater Garden later, and she was soon at the fence line of the palace. Niobe couldn't climb the fence. It had motion and pressure detectors, but she had made a tunnel as a teenager and later maintained it in preparation for her 'Alban mission'. The tunnel was hidden by a shrub, but this was easily moved aside and back over the hole. To her surprise, there was a note from Gethan waiting for her. It simply read: 'Don't do it. Respect your father. -G.' He'd thought this tunnel was how she'd get to Alban.

Niobe wondered what Gethan was up to now. His note reaffirmed his loyalty to her father over her. Would he keep fighting her if he knew she was about to kill again? Niobe scrunched up the note and stuffed it in a pocket.

The tunnel was about twenty metres long. Niobe hadn't entered it in two years, but it was still functional. The smell of dirt made Niobe recall the first time she'd used it—at age fifteen—to sneak out to meet a boy she'd had a crush on. That night hadn't gone well for him. He'd tried to be in control and force her to do more than kiss. Niobe tried to explain she needed to be the one in control, but he wouldn't listen. A knee to the groin, a strike to his carotid sinus, and another to just below his sternum had left him gasping for air, and with a changed mind.

Several roots had grown into the tunnel, but they didn't prevent Niobe from making her way along its length. Soon she was free.

* * *

MAKING her way to the hotel was straightforward. Niobe caught a taxi and paid in cash. The hotel was eleven storeys high and had an all-glass exterior, which complemented the modern interior. From her use of an online mapping program, Niobe knew its base was a forty-metre wide square. Once inside the lobby, she went straight to the elevators as though she were a guest. The elevator let her in, but required a key card to get to the floor she needed access to. Niobe smiled and pressed the buttons the way emergency services were taught so they could get to a floor in an emergency, when every second counted. She went straight to the eleventh floor. Sometimes stereotypes existed for a reason, and she was confident the *Mafioso* would have booked out the entire top level. The elevator barely seemed to move as it went skyward. When the doors opened, Niobe steeled herself for any signs or sounds of people. At nearly midnight on a cold winter's night, there were unlikely to be many, if any, people around.

Niobe removed the Range-R device from her pocket—the only other thing she'd taken from the training hall. The handheld device was capable of detecting movement through walls. It was even sensitive enough to detect someone who was asleep, just by their breathing.

As she moved along the corridor, switching from side to side, it was clear she'd made a mistake. All the rooms seemed to be occupied. It pissed her off that she might not be able to complete her mission. Where was he? Thankfully, as she reached the south-east corner of the building, there were two empty rooms in a row on both sides of the corridor. The corner room was occupied by, it seemed, three people, two in a bed, and one near the door. The rooms either side were vacant. It was enough to create a zoned space for Don. This *had* to be his room. But why three people? Perhaps he had some company for the evening. She hadn't planned for that. Still, the shotgun had one round in the chamber and four in its magazine. Five rounds would be enough for two people.

Niobe knocked on the door. "Concierge," she called loudly. She readied the shotgun, enjoying the sensation of her heart thumping with excitement. She couldn't hear any movement, but when she saw the door handle turn, she took it as a good sign about the level of noise which would be heard by the other guests. The door swung open to reveal a man dressed in a suit. In another place, he could have been a stand-in for an action movie hero. He must have been two metres tall.

"Whadd'ya wan—" The loud clapping noise from the gun not only masked the words, it stopped them dead due to a bean bag round hitting the bodyguard in the head. From the way he crumpled, it was clear he was unconscious before he hit the ground. Thankfully, he'd fallen backwards, so Niobe was able to close the door as she entered the room. She pumped the shotgun to load a new shell and stepped over his body.

"Hey, what's going on?" a deep male voice asked.

Niobe walked down a short corridor past a bathroom and entered a bedroom, where she saw a naked man and woman on a king-sized bed. The man had a large blue tattoo on his chest and was unmistakeably Don Azzure. Their lovemaking had clearly been interrupted. She wondered how the bodyguard occupied his time while they were busy in here.

Niobe pointed her shotgun at the woman. "Go," she commanded.

The woman nodded and quickly pulled her clothes on.

"And if I let you go can I trust you not to say anything to anyone?"

"Y-Yes, t-tell no one," the woman stammered.

Niobe didn't believe her. She waited until the woman was halfway down the short corridor before she shot her in the back of the head, then she pumped the shotgun to load a new shell. The girl managed a half step before she fell next to the bodyguard. Niobe turned back to Don Azzure. "Stay."

He nodded.

Niobe put a zip tie around the bodyguard's wrists, all the while listening for movement from the bed. She returned to her soon-to-be victim.

Don Azzure had his arms behind his head, which left his well-built, naked torso exposed. He has a gun, Niobe thought, otherwise he'd cover himself. She could see more of the tendon in his right wrist, so she guessed that hand was holding it.

"I'm not sure what's the bigger crime: you getting away with murder, or me asking if that's a gun under there or if you're just pleased to see me?"

"Very funny, little girl. But what fool brings a bean bag to a gun fight?"

Niobe twigged he'd seen the blue tape on the base of the magazine which fed the shotgun. She wondered if he could also tell how many shots she had left.

"I'm not a fool," Niobe said and hummed a few bars from a showtune before saying "I can't say no"—her voice turned cold—"to killing you. Let go of the weapon."

Don tried to get his gun out to shoot Niobe, but instead howled in pain as she shot his arm just above the elbow. There was a chance she'd broken his humerus. Purple bruising instantly bloomed. The gun was flung to the floor away from the bed.

"I'm sorry about that. I wanted you to be unhurt when I kill you. Wait, that doesn't make sense. You know what I mean. I wanted it to be a fair fight. Get up. I'll give you a chance. I'll even let you put on underwear to cover yourself. It looks super cold."

"You little bitch. You'll pay for this."

"Oh, dude, you really don't get it, do you? Let me spell it out. You'll. Be. Dead. Get up and fight."

Don stubbornly stayed where he was. Niobe put her shotgun on the desk in the corner of the room.

"Fine. Have it your way." She jumped onto the edge of the bed. She was far enough away from Don to be able to avoid any leg sweep. This wasn't how this was meant to go. It was much easier to attack someone who was standing and on a stable surface. The bed was hardly an ideal base from which to launch an attack. She could jump and try landing on him with her knees, but if he was quick enough, he could swat her to the side while she was in the air. He was probably double her weight and nearly a foot taller, which led to one conclusion. Get in close. Make him think he had the advantage. Niobe began to kick Don's legs. She got in a couple of solid connections before he was able to sweep her. She fell on top of him. Don caught one of Niobe's arms as she fell and immediately rolled over and on top of her.

"Who was going to do what to whom?" Don gloated. "Don't you realise I can do what I want? Maybe I'll do you before we're through."

"Don, baby. You've already lost. If you're going to do me, it'll have to be as a zombie. Wait that didn't come out right."

Don sniggered. Niobe used the moment to strike with her free arm, *haito*, ridge-hand strike, to his temple. It made reasonable contact but wasn't enough to achieve more than a light stun. It did, however, have the effect of making Don grab her arm with the hand of his injured arm. He howled in pain, but held firm. Niobe now had him in her favourite position from which to defend herself. He couldn't really hurt her at this point, unless he went for a head butt. But that was a risky move, which she could counter by raising her head at the last moment.

"What're you gonna do now?" Niobe taunted. "You'll have

to strangle me." She knew people in a heightened state succumbed more easily to suggestion. Don took the bait, let go of her arms, and grabbed her throat with both of his hands. Without hesitation, Niobe pinched his adductor, right up by the groin. Niobe knew from experience this felt like a cattle prod touching you. She called it her cow pinch. As expected, Don leapt off her. As he did Niobe kicked him in the head as hard as she could, and he fell, semi-conscious, to the floor by the wall near the left side of the bed. Niobe leapt as high as she could off the edge of the bed and stomped down with her right heel onto Don's head. The sound would have been sickening for anyone else in the room, if they were conscious, but Niobe felt elated. She could tell she'd fractured his skull. Now, he was unconscious. Niobe jumped off the bed again and repeated the stomping kick. This time she clearly felt a piece of his cheek separate from his cranium. The emotional release it generated was unlike anything Niobe had felt. She couldn't stop smiling.

"Don, baby. How you gonna kiss me with that mouth?" Niobe said.

Blood oozed out of several places. A check of Don's carotid pulse and eye response confirmed he was dead. Niobe wiped her steel-capped boots on the carpet, retrieved her gun, and approached the unconscious woman.

Niobe started her *kappo* techniques on the woman. With some manual chest manipulation to force her to breathe, and further stimulation to her medulla, at the base of her neck, the woman started waking up. As the bean bag round had hit the woman in the temporal lobe, which was associated with facial recognition, it was likely she would have trouble recalling what Niobe looked like. Once Niobe was sure the woman was likely to wake up soon, she turned her attention to the bodyguard. He was easier to rouse, only requiring the manipulation of his carotid sinus. This stimulated his vagus nerve, slowing his heart and reducing blow flow to the extremities. A variation of the technique, in the right circumstances, could kill a person. Here it meant there'd be a better blood flow to his brain and vital organs. Within seconds the bodyguard groaned. He was also about to wake up. Niobe picked up the bean bag rounds and casings, wiped her feet again, and slipped out the door.

CHAPTER 8

Niobe snuck back into the castle via the drainpipe. It was a dangerous climb, but then so was the descent. She'd made it back to her bathroom within ninety minutes of leaving. A thorough shower washed off any blood. She washed her shoes and scrubbed them with a special paste to break down the haemoglobin in any residual blood to prevent its detection with luminol.

Niobe managed a few hours' sleep. It'd been hard to come down after the high of taking a life, but sleep had come, and with it a dream of using her power to fly over the ocean. When she awoke, she turned the TV on in her anteroom while she got dressed.

The bodyguard had raised the alarm about Don Azzure's death. It'd occurred too late at night to make the morning papers, but the television news programs were all over the story. They loved getting the scoop before the print media. Niobe flicked between channels. The headlines ranged from descriptive to prosaic: *Don Azzure taken out in mob hit. Don Done. Black and Blue.*

A breaking news alert appeared on the screen. Bodyguard speaks.

The morning show cut to the steps of a hospital, where the bodyguard was being released. Next to the journalist, Morgan Henry, he looked larger than Niobe recalled.

"This is being broadcast live," Morgan said. "Mr Wendall, can you tell us what happened last night?"

"I was attacked by Princess Niobe."

"You mean the queen?" Morgan sounded like she couldn't believe her luck. *The guy was delusional.*

Dammit, he saw me and remembered, Niobe thought. She sat on the edge of her bed to watch more.

"Yeah, she shot me in the head." To the viewers at home, and Morgan, this seemed far-fetched, as people usually associated the phrase with regular bullets and entry and exit points. Morgan couldn't help rolling her eyes.

"No, not like that. It must've been with rubber bullets or something. She killed Don Azzure."

"What do you say to rumours *you* killed Don Azzure? His skull was crushed. You're trying to say the queen, who must weigh less than half what you and Don Azzure weigh, single-handedly stormed the room, took you out, and killed Don. Is that what you're saying?"

Bless you, Morgan, Niobe thought. Mr Wendall looked confused by her question and tone of voice. "Yes. That is what I'm saying, and I can prove it."

Niobe jumped upright.

"How?" Morgan asked. Niobe was wondering the same thing.

"Don liked to tape his encounters with women. He had a camera in the room. I have the footage, and so now the police do. It records to a micro-SD card, which I have in my phone."

"You mean you can play us the video?"

"Yes."

"Go on then."

Shit. Shit. *Shit.*

Mr Wendall pulled out his large Android phone and brought up the video. The cameraperson was able to zoom in and get a decent shot of the screen. The resulting broadcast was a lot like a bootleg movie shot on a phone, but it was no less effective. The hidden camera was directly above the bed, so it didn't show her taking out the bodyguard, although it did provide the audio of her shooting the woman, which didn't come across well. It covered her asking Don for a fair fight and only shooting his arm when he pulled out the gun, which at least made her seem reasonable. The news censors weren't quick enough to obscure Don's genitals, which amused Niobe.

When Niobe jumped on the bed her face was obscured by her hoodie. Damn, she looked badass. Unfortunately, when Don was strangling her, there was a clear shot of her face. The camera caught her jumping off the bed, but her stomping on Don's head occurred offscreen because of the camera's tight focus. Joy surged through Niobe as she watched the scene. She couldn't wait to ask Patterson to get her a copy. She'd set up the request as though she wanted to see what the press were talking about.

"We apologise to our viewers for the explicit nature of the video, but it does seem like Mr Wendall was right about the attacker looking like the queen. Let's emphasise that. She looked like the queen. It's preposterous to think it actually was."

* * *

Somewhere in Europe, Gethan was watching the same video with an entirely different conclusion.

"So much for an early retirement," he said to himself.

Gethan thought over his friendship and service to King John. He was pleased the king had seen the folly of his plan to use his daughter as a weapon, rather than step up the training to nullify her deadly desires. He would have to deal with Niobe himself. No one else knew her well enough to do it. He would obey the final command of his king.

Gethan picked up his phone and called an old friend.

"Hi. I'm sure you've seen the news. I need you to convince Niobe to admit to the world what she's done."

On the other end of the line, Patterson sighed.

"Why would I do that?"

"Because it's the right thing for her to do. We need to stop this before it becomes habit."

"Do you disagree with her choices?" Patterson asked.

"Not the point. I'm getting the impression you're not sure, so let's take all the emotion out of this and consider it a return of past favours. You know how much I've done for you. I'd like you to do this."

"It's true you've been a great friend. I'm not totally comfortable about this, but I can see why you think it's a good idea. If she asks me a direct question about my motivation though, I won't conceal your request. That's the only way I can conscience this. Understood?"

"Thank you, old friend. Understood."

*　*　*

THERE WAS a knock on Niobe's anteroom door.

"Come in, Patterson."

He hurried into the room. "I don't know how you always know it's me. Ah, so you've seen the news."

"Yes. It's silly."

"Your Majesty?"

"A queen going around killing people? Who'd believe that?"

"After Alban, I would."

Niobe's heart beat faster.

"How'd you know?"

"I was your father's confidant for decades. We discussed all matters, including you. In fact, I think I was the one who suggested you be trained when you were five. It was why I guarded the entrance to the bathroom when you and Alban went in there. Although, in the case of Alban, it took Gethan to tell me how you'd done it. Just before he left the palace he asked me to keep an extra close eye on you. I didn't think you'd go … hunting again so soon."

Was she hunting humans? It was an odd thought, but Niobe acknowledged it fit what she'd done. What was really driving her? Did she have a need to kill? Out of the corner of her eye, Niobe saw the headlines change to a search for the queen's lookalike killer.

"You approve?" she asked Patterson.

"Of your choices so far."

"You think I'll do this again? I should do this again?"

"Won't you?"

"Maybe, I don't know. I wasn't intending to."

"Will you only target such people?"

"Yes. I have criteria they need to meet."

Niobe explained how she'd chosen Don. Patterson could be very useful if he was on her side.

"That seems reasonable."

"Thank you. We need to feed the idea that it's a lookalike or someone made up to look like me. Can you help with that?"

"Why?"

"Because we don't want people thinking it's me."

"Why?" Patterson repeated.

"Are you a four-year-old?" Niobe couldn't help herself.

"My point is that you cannot be prosecuted for the deaths. You have sovereign immunity."

Niobe thought of the Riddle of the Eye and the prison she'd created for herself. She hadn't compromised her morals by her actions, nor had she acted in any way that she hadn't felt justified in doing so. Why not accept scrutiny for that? Wasn't her public and private self meant to be the same now? There was only one concern.

"You mean 'come out' as an assassin."

"Yes. Haven't you been in the closet long enough?"

"That's absurd. I'd be crucified."

"Don't think too highly of yourself; you're just a queen."

"Why, Patterson, I don't think I've ever heard you display such humour."

"I did with your father, in private. He didn't like us serving class treating him like that in public. It sent the wrong message."

"I think that's how he felt about me too. I was allowed to be me within the palace, but in public I had to be a good little princess. Do you know how long it took Gethan and me to work out how to make that possible? The trick came through using meditation to give me a temporary mental frame from which to act."

"A while, I'd guess."

"A decade," she said.

"So, what now? Keep up the charade?"

"Well, duh. Yes. While I no longer feel the need to do it mentally, it would help maintain people's relationship with the monarchy."

"I've been a servant of this palace across four individual decades, long before you were born. I've seen so much go on behind these walls. And you know what, most of what would be considered scandalous here is just normal dynamics and

family behaviour. I'm tired of pretending things are so different, that we're so different."

"But in my case, we are."

"True."

"Are you trying to bring down the monarchy?"

"I don't think that will happen," Patterson replied.

"How could you think it couldn't?"

"Simple. It's you."

"What?"

"You feed off being in control."

Niobe hated that he could assert that with such confidence. How much had they spoken before her father's death?
Was it something her dad had seen and told him?

"Maybe."

"Not according to your father, nor from what Gethan and
I have observed of you. I'm just saying that given your nature,
you'd feel happier if it was your choice and your manipulation of the public which drove opinion. Getting ahead of the
whispers and innuendo will let you do that. And you also
won't have to wait until you are compelled to confess, when
you wouldn't be in control of the act. I'm simply providing
the advice I think, in the long-term, would make you happiest. That is what my role is—to act in your best interests. Not
Tantalia's."

"But what if they don't understand why I did what I did.
They only know about Don, not Alban. I'm not convinced
Tantalia, let alone the world, would appreciate the nuanced
and complex reasoning for my actions. What if they say I
think I'm above the law?"

"Aren't you an *ubermensch*?"

Niobe had been exposed to Nietzsche's philosophy by
Gethan a long time ago. He'd introduced the concept, and
she'd immediately felt a connection with the idea of some
people being above the rule of man, that they were able to

operate outside of social norms because they had their own higher code and higher mental state.

"That's a complex idea and a personal experience of the world. Most won't grasp it, or worse will say that's what Hitler thought, and I despise him."

"Then I guess the question it comes down to is how much do you trust your people?"

"Even if Tantalia accepts me, what about the rest of the world?"

"Which country do you lead? Which do you have responsibility for?"

"Tantalia."

"Exactly. We are a small country but have a strong sense of national pride. Shape the conversation correctly and they'll rally behind you."

"I can't believe I'm saying this, but fine, call a press conference so I can tell the world Tantalia has a sovereign who's an assassin."

She shook her head in disbelief at the phrase.

"It shall be done. Is 2.00 pm okay for you?"

Niobe nodded. What was she getting herself into?

"Make it a live broadcast," she said.

* * *

NIOBE SPENT the next couple of hours rationalising her course of action. On one hand, there was a coolness to stepping up in front of the world and having a Tony Stark moment. 'I am an assassin', was even bolder than 'I am Iron Man.' It would certainly make things easier in the future if she didn't have to bother concealing her crimes. On the other hand, there was the likely effect of her people revolting against her, and not to mention the potential repercussions for Tantalia's international relationships. The trade deal with

Australia could be thrown into chaos. But, as Patterson had pointed out, she had committed an act which deserved scrutiny. He'd tapped into the place where her feelings of being above the tiresome constraints of a social contract broke down; she still felt like she owed it to the Tantalians, as their queen, to have their acceptance of her actions. It was more a consequence of what Niobe saw the role of queen as being, rather than a need to subject herself to the rule of man. Besides, if she could control the narrative and make people accept her for who she was, how cool would that be? She'd be celebrated for her moral justice, and be feted on the covers of magazines. She might even get a parade.

THE PALACE'S media room was a large, oval room on the ground floor. Patterson had done his job in getting all the news services there for the afternoon briefing. It was far more packed than usual. Three TV stations had sent camera operators to complement the official 'palace vision'. Niobe recognised several journalists, including Morgan Henry from the *Tantalian Times* and Channel Six News. She had written a sympathetic article about Niobe after the king had died. In it, she'd shown understanding of the broader issues of being a royal while dealing with a very personal tragedy. She was also the journalist who'd interviewed the bodyguard that morning. Niobe also noticed Drysen Silic from the *Tantalia Sun*. He hadn't been as emotionally sensitive to the circumstances facing the new queen after the deaths of her parents. Instead, he'd openly questioned her ability to lead the country given her age and inexperience in state affairs. His editorial had attracted some attention, and he'd been invited on talkback shows to express his views. Combined with his articles on Don Azzure, Niobe wasn't a fan.

"My fellow Tantalians. I have called this press conference to address the footage screened this morning on Channel Six News. I know such a step is unusual, but these are not usual times." Niobe wondered why she didn't feel more nervous. Shouldn't this make her sweat? She guessed she could detect a slight scent of deodorant being activated but, overall, she felt normal. Niobe looked around the room, thrilling in the fact that regardless of how the room took her announcement, she was immune from prosecution. She was about to prove her dad wrong. The people could handle her. She took a breath and said, "The assassin in the video looked like me because it was me."

It was a full two seconds before any journalist found their voice. Whatever news they were expecting, this wasn't it. She caught Drysen's eye and he spluttered to life. "Are you saying you killed Don Azzure?"

"Yes."

"You took out his bodyguard and killed Don Azzure? With your bare hands?" Niobe wanted to scream at him that women were more than capable of hurting men, and maybe he should try her.

"It was a bean bag round fired from a shotgun which took out the bodyguard. I didn't want to kill him. Ditto for the prostitute Don Azzure was with. But, yeah, I killed Don Azzure with my bare hands."

"Why are you confessing?" Drysen asked.

"I can see you're confused. I'm not trying to get away with or conceal what I've done, or avoid punishment. But it is in Tantalia's best interests that I've done the things I have."

"Things?" Morgan interjected.

"Yes, I also killed Alban Crab."

There was more murmuring from the audience. She imagined that by now all the TV networks in the country had switched to coverage of her press conference.

"How were they chosen, your victims?" Morgan asked. Niobe wanted to hug her. She was giving her an opportunity to explain. Since Niobe's view was the first Tantalia would hear, it was more likely, due to the primacy effect, to be the one which stuck.

"I have five criteria. They met all of them. My criteria are that one, they needed to objectively be an arsehole." A ripple of nervous laughter spread through the room. "Two, they needed to have committed murder or incited it. Three, they needed to have shown no remorse. Four, they needed to have been tried for their crime but escaped natural justice on a technicality or their own interference with the trial. Like Don Azzure, who got off his murder charge because the key witness and her son were brutally stabbed the day before she was due to testify against him. And finally, five, their actions needed to have harmed Tantalia."

"So, if they weren't arseholes they'd be okay?" Drysen asked.

"Have you met anyone who meets the other criteria who isn't also objectively an arsehole?" Niobe replied.

Drysen went on the attack. "I guess not. But surely, someone being an arsehole is always subjective? I mean there were people who loved Hitler, loved Saddam—"

"They were likely arseholes too," Niobe said.

"Not the point," Drysen shot back.

"Okay. I guess there will always be a degree of subjectivity, but it is not without deep consideration I reach that conclusion. A remorseless killer will pretty much always be an arsehole though."

"But what if they've expressed remorse, but they were acting?" Drysen asked.

"Then they haven't expressed remorse. Remorse isn't just saying I'm sorry. It involves action. If they haven't behaved in a way which demonstrates remorse, then they meet that criterion. Let me be clear, you'd have to meet all the criteria. It's not a four out of five is enough. Five out of five only. Besides, you're talking about this as though I'm going to do it again. I've no intention of doing that."

"You say that now, but what if you decide to lessen the threshold later?" Drysen persisted.

Niobe noticed Morgan glaring at Drysen. "Won't happen," Niobe assured him.

"How can you be so sure?" Morgan asked. Niobe was grateful for the softball question. Another chance to explain.

"It's hard to be certain of anything. But I haven't surrounded myself with yes-men and yes-women—"

"You realise you meet two of your own criteria," Morgan interrupted. Damn, she was meant to be the nice one, although she did have a sly tone to her voice, which indicated she was confident Niobe would have an answer.

"Three, actually. I've committed murder; I'm not remorseful, and I've escaped justice because as queen I'm immune from prosecution. I guess you could call that a technicality."

"Who's next?" Morgan asked.

"Huh?"

"Who's your next target?"

Niobe didn't hesitate. "Let me repeat: I don't have one. It's not like I'm compulsive about this. It's only when the person is manifestly and unequivocally bad for Tantalia that I've acted. That's happened twice, and I can't think of anyone else I'd target, nor am I seeking another person." She was pleased with the speed of her response. While it was the truth, it was the certainty which would make her seem less sociopathic.

"But if someone came to your attention?" Drysen asked.

"Let me repeat. I'm not looking for targets. I don't want another target. That would mean the justice system isn't working."

"But if you were? How would you be sure they were worthy?" Morgan asked, with a glare at Drysen.

"Worthy? It's not a privilege to be killed by me. I've committed these acts. They deserve scrutiny. I'm not trying to conceal that fact."

"You might meet more of your criteria. By admitting what you've done, you might have harmed Tantalia. You might even need to add a sixth about those who undo their own father's life's work," Drysen said. Niobe managed to stop herself glaring at him again.

"Yes. It's possible I meet the harm to Tantalia criterion. I hadn't really considered that," Niobe admitted.

"So why aren't you subject to your own rules?" Drysen asked.

"If Tantalia feels I've harmed them, they can let me know. I feel the country is better now than it was a couple of days ago."

"How could they let you know? A protest march? A riot?" Drysen was determined to make a point.

"How about a plebiscite?" Niobe asked.

"You want us to *vote* on whether you should be allowed to assassinate people?" Drysen asked.

"We're a democracy, not a dictatorship. That distinction is important in what I do, what I might do. A plebiscite would establish whether I meet the fifth and highest criterion or not."

"And if you do?"

"Then I guess I'll have to end my life."

There was a collective gasp in the room. How could she suggest that? Niobe was just being logical, and inside she pondered if the height of morality would be ending your life because it meant acting in accordance with your beliefs. Or was that a paradox she needed to find a solution for?

"You can't be serious," Morgan said.

"Why not? I reached the criteria and decided to act upon them on the basis of vast introspection and thought. I determined my values and moral code. Even though my actions have come from love for my country, if they have hurt it, then I should face the consequences. Similarly, the consequences should be matched to the punishment I've delivered to similar transgressors. To do less would be unconscionable."

Patterson approached and with his back to the journalists whispered in her ear. He then returned to the side of the stage.

"Assembled guests, I've been informed the earliest date for a plebiscite would be seven weeks away. I will carry on the role of queen to the best of my ability in the interim, and won't kill anyone else. I know you have many more questions. You can direct them to my press secretary, and he will address them in a follow-up conference tomorrow. For now, that's the end of questions I'll be answering today."

Niobe needed to find a way to project a feeling of shyness. To bring to the surface her childhood before her parents got sick. To go back to a time when she felt self-conscious about being a princess because of the attention the world gave her when she was trying to hide her inner self. Back before she'd discovered her inner fire when meeting Alban for the first time. She softened her tone. "The plebiscite was an idea from the top of my head, and I think it should happen, but I need to talk to the electoral commission to confirm the timing. I'm sure details will be forthcoming. Thank you."

Niobe turned and walked slowly from the stage as though she were contemplating the weight of the world. Once out of sight she broke into a stride and headed for her bedroom. What the hell had she done?

CHAPTER 9

Niobe's little ruse had worked. A number of commentators noted her manner and body language. Niobe was delighted by the overall tone of the response—it was positive. A US presidential candidate had once said they could stand in the middle of Fifth Avenue and shoot someone, and they wouldn't lose any voters. It seemed the same was true for her, although she doubted her subjects were quite as loyal as the 'base' of that candidate.

The next morning, while Niobe was eating breakfast in her dining room, her Aunt Dahlia, the Duchess of Lower Scintilla, called to gently suggest she'd made a mistake.

"My darling niece. I'd hoped you'd outgrow such desires, but it seems that's not the case. Perhaps you could call off the vote and make a public apology? Then, maybe back to killing the odd animal on the royal farm, like when you were a child, instead of this, frankly, distressing course of action?"

"Aunty, I appreciated your concerns, but the action is set. I'm prepared for the consequences whichever way they go. If I need to abdicate and end my life so be it."

"That at least would be noble. But I don't want you to die,

none of the family do. Your cousin looks up to you so much, and she would be devastated. Haven't we already lost enough members of the family? Can't you do something for the family rather than only yourself?"

Even though Dahlia had stopped talking, Niobe was sure she'd wanted to add 'for a change'.

"Aunty, I'm content with my course of action."

"Can't you at least campaign for your survival? Why not sit down with Morgan Henry for an interview. At least she seems to like you, unlike that Drysen person. He'll never be satisfied until the monarchy no longer exists," Dahlia said.

"I've always had my public speeches limited and scripted so I don't reveal too much of myself. If I do an interview, I'm likely to unintentionally say something which makes things worse. I may be full of myself, but I'm not stupid. My best chance of swaying public support is to let the process take its course, thereby demonstrating I'm capable of self-control. Not to mention, it'll reinforce my desire for Tantalia to make up its own mind."

"What would it take to convince you?"

"There isn't anything."

"I'm sorry to hear that."

"I know, Aunty, and I do know you have my best interests at heart. Goodbye."

Niobe disconnected the call and stewed over the conversation while she finished her breakfast. Surely her aunt could understand the reasons behind Niobe's actions?

* * *

THE INTERNATIONAL REACTION from Tantalia's trading partners was muted in comparison to Niobe's expectation. She guessed this was due to their not wanting to condemn a head of state or spark conflict. Now that Tantalia was a full member of the EU, the EU was obligated to protect Tantalia under a mutual defence clause if a foreign military attacked them. As it was internationally recognised that Niobe was immune from arrest, any calls for detainment were moot. She couldn't be charged, let alone tried, for her confessed crimes. One downside was Australia declaring their trade deal would be put under review. There was surprising support from Russia and North Korea. Both countries congratulated her for taking a stand on her country's enemies. Their support made Niobe scowl. She wasn't removing people for personal reasons; she was doing it to make her country better, to improve the social landscape. Or was that what they thought they were doing?

However, those countries which were already not friendly with Tantalia declared outrage. Their neighbour, Autarchos, was particularly vocal. Autarchos' leader, Jork Dressov, appeared in an interview on his national TV broadcaster condemning Niobe for slaughtering a defenceless businessman in cold blood and saying she should've gone after someone who could defend themselves.

Niobe had said a quiet, "Fuck you," when she'd watched that one. Jork was probably just annoyed he'd lost a business partner.

Other articles opined that just because she'd cut off the head of Don Azzure's organisation, it wouldn't mean another wouldn't appear to take its place. Niobe didn't mind that so much, because for her it was irrelevant. The new head was unlikely to meet all of Niobe's criteria.

The interview which cut through her barriers and got to her was one shared by Drysen on the *Tantalia Sun* website. It was a video call of a man with a plain white wall behind him. It'd taken Niobe a few seconds to realise the man was Gethan, as he'd grown a beard.

"As the personal trainer of the queen, do you take some responsibility for her actions?" Drysen asked.

"Yes and no. And I'm the *former* trainer. I trained her according to her father's wishes and helped her develop the skills she used against Azzure. But I opposed her actions against Alban, which I only found out about after the act. I had suspected she'd try something, so I was keeping watch, but she outsmarted me to get to him, and for that I am sorry. I wanted her to respect her father's dying wish to make peace with Alban, not kill him. King John didn't want her to become a murderer and asked me to stop her should she try. I failed, which is why I left the palace. But that won't prevent me working on stopping her committing any further atrocities. I, for one, will vote against her in the plebiscite."

"A wise course of action. One I think everyone should take," Drysen said.

Niobe punched her mattress. "Journalists shouldn't editorialise," she said angrily. "No, it's not Drysen you're angry at, or not only him, it's Gethan," she added aloud. The worst feeling was having no idea how to deal with Gethan. He could be quite the destabilising force in the lead-up to the plebiscite if he so chose. He knew her secrets and vulnerabilities. If something as simple as the time he'd allowed her to trap, slaughter, butcher, cook and eat a rabbit was presented in the wrong light, he could almost single-handedly cause the vote to turn against her.

Religious leaders were also appalled. To them, no justification was sufficient to excuse a mortal sin. While she couldn't empathise with Gethan's position, she could empathise with theirs. They'd reached their conclusion based on the reasoning of their dogma, even if their logic was a throwback to a primitive way of thinking.

* * *

"Your Majesty," Patterson said as he served Niobe breakfast in her dining room the following morning.

"Yes, Patterson?"

"I just wanted you to know, I don't approve of what Australia's done. It's not like they don't remove prime ministers on a whim. Your actions, while more extreme, aren't all that different."

"Thank you. I agree."

"But if I may, it's a bit unfair to your mattress to take your frustration out on it."

"You've heard that?"

"And the language you used."

"Oh, sorry."

"It's fine, but you do have a dojo which was purpose-built for your training. You know, to control your tendencies."

"How long have you known? About my special interests I mean."

"Since it began."

"But you've never let on. I always thought I was a family secret."

Patterson smiled. "You were."

Niobe tilted her head. "You're family too."

"Is that a statement or a question?"

Niobe thought it through. She remembered the hot chocolate drinks he'd brought her without asking as she grew up, and the way he'd sneak away veggies her parents had insisted be on her plate, so she wouldn't have to eat them. They might not be blood-related, but he'd always treated her like a grandparent spoiling their grandchild.

"Statement. I hadn't twigged until now. Sorry."

Patterson beamed. "It's okay. I know your limitations to notice such things. But thank you for acknowledging it. Now, if I may offer you some advice?"

"Yes, of course."

"Show you're above all the naysayers by carrying on your role. I don't mean fight back in the press, but show that you're still queen, even for now. Business as usual, as though you were any other royal. It worked for that US president when he was impeached for lying about an affair, something unrelated to how he performed his formal duties. Unlike the more recently impeached president, where his high crime was directly relevant to his ability to be president."

"How?" Niobe asked.

"Well, the trade deal with the Aussies for one."

"Good thinking. There was meant to be a meeting next week. Let's get it back on."

"I'll get all the contact details for you."

"Thank you, Patterson."

* * *

A WEEK after her declaration of the plebiscite, she had her next meeting with the Australian Prime Minister, who was a different individual from the first meeting. The new PM, Kylie, had declared that Australia had taken and would continue to take a strong stand against violence, and cited their progressive gun laws as evidence. They added that, while they opposed Niobe's actions, it was important to have a strong trading relationship between the two countries, one they hoped might help the queen modify her behaviour. How a trading agreement could have such an effect was anyone's guess, but the conservative press in that country decided trade was more important than a few people's lives and supported the resumption of talks. Their editorials and articles tried valiantly to sway public opinion.

Kylie was visibly nervous at the start of the meeting, despite the presence of two Foreign Ministers and Zack.

Niobe delighted in letting her squirm for a few minutes before addressing it.

"Kylie, there is no need for you to be nervous. I'm not about to kill you."

Kylie's shoulders finally dropped. "Thank you for stating that. I don't know why I'm so nervous. Our countries have a good relationship, and my predecessor had made a good start to this agreement." Niobe was sure she heard Kylie mutter it was the only thing the previous PM had done well.

Niobe had to stop herself from adding 'or else' each time she stated what Tantalia would like the Australians to give her country. It would have been fun to see the PM nervously fidget some more, but international relations were hard enough without Kylie being reminded of Niobe's ability to kill whomever she chose. Fortunately, after what they'd been through to join the EU, Tantalia's Prime Minister and Foreign Minister were adept at such discussions, and considerable progress was made.

Despite this progress, two days later the newspapers reported the trade deal was being put on hold again by the Australians due to pressure in their country to show Tantalia, and the world, they disapproved of Niobe's deeds. As much as written text could be gleeful, Drysen Silic's article on the response was an over-the-top expression of support for Australia's action, even though he'd normally argue for the economic advantage of such a deal.

* * *

THE SATURDAY MORNING of the plebiscite was sunny and seemed to indicate an early spring was around the corner for the northern hemisphere. After trying for the 23rd of February, the date was pushed to the 8th March. Due to a leap day, this was two weeks later. In the interceding weeks,

Niobe's absence from the discourse stirred the conversation.

Both sides tried to argue her absence increased the validity of their arguments. Those who said she was in the wrong said she was insulting the people by not being part of the debate, whereas her supporters felt it was a proper dignified silence. The two main newspapers largely stuck to their unstated, but openly understood, ideology. The Tantalian Times were for Niobe being allowed to continue, while the Tantalia Sun were against her. There was a similar division on social media. Everyone seemed to have a strong opinion. There was a noticeable absence of judgements which could be described as neutral.

Gethan made a second appearance with Drysen Silic. He was asked what he'd like to see Niobe do. "Sadly, I've lost the ability to influence the queen. I'd like to see her put an end to all of this, and declare that her actions were selfish and in contrast to the expressed desire of King John. She should then abdicate. This has gone too far."

Drysen seemed to take pleasure from the response. He couldn't hide the smirk on his face. Niobe didn't bother punching her mattress that time, instead she summoned her instructor and made him spar with her.

After her instructor protested he was getting too bruised to continue and ended the impromptu training session, Niobe tried to call Gethan to discuss what he'd said to Drysen. All she got was that the number was "turned off or unavailable".

She tried again two days later, on her birthday, hopeful the occasion may change his response, but he didn't answer. She left the message: '*Populous me sibilat, at mihi plaudo Ipse domi stimul*, the public hiss at me, but I cheer myself when in my own house. Call me'.

Niobe missed Gethan's presence more than she cared to

admit. She was angry with him and wanted to punch him hard in the groin, but he'd always had such a calming influence over her that paradoxically she wanted to be near him, despite him being the cause of her distress.

* * *

THE NIGHT BEFORE THE POLL, two surveys predicted Niobe would lose the vote 51-49. Niobe hadn't thought much about what she'd do if she lost, but when the polls came out, she was forced to consider the consequences. She summoned Patterson to her room to discuss it with him.

"What should I do if I lose the vote?"

"Do what prime ministers do when they lose. Quit the leadership and snipe at your party from the sidelines."

"That sounds okay, but it's not easy for me to abdicate. I have no heir, and Uncle Jacques isn't exactly interested in world affairs, or thinking deeply about the direction of the country, even if Aunt Dahlia is."

"Maybe, but what choice would you have?"

"I could kill myself and let Tantalia sort itself out."

Patterson's expression grew dark. "Don't joke about such things, Your Majesty. I've already lost two of your family, who were my dear friends. I can't lose you too. I would never have agreed to try convince you to admit what you'd done if I thought that could be a consequence."

Niobe felt an uncommon wave of guilt flow through her. Patterson's feelings had never entered her thinking, but he'd *agreed* to it? That could only mean one thing.

"Gethan?"

Patterson lowered his eyes guiltily. "Yes. It won't happen again."

Niobe nodded. She needed Patterson to remain a friend.

"I know how he can manipulate. Never again though."

Patterson nodded. "Yes."

"Just so you know, Patterson, I wasn't joking. While I may not be an arsehole in my mind, I would still meet my criteria for removal. Plus, my crack at the coming out means I'd be subject to the fifth too. If they vote against me then I really have harmed the country and that means I should die. I accept that. I even know how I'd do it. I'd get a breathing mask attached to an air tank with air that only had 8% oxygen in it. Within five minutes I'd pass out, and within half an hour I'd die."

"Your Majesty." Patterson looked like he was going to cry. He seemed to need contact to reassure him, so Niobe reached out for a hug. Patterson accepted the embrace and squeezed her so tightly one of her ribs popped. It was the first time Niobe had truly appreciated the depth of his feelings for her. She knew Patterson and her father were close, but to know his affections extended to her too was a relief. His action with Gethan was indeed a one-off. She had an ally. One who'd now be extra vigilant to protect her interests.

"Don't forget we're asking the country to sanction not only the murders I've committed, but also acceptance of me committing more. I know the world's changing and boundaries of what's acceptable are being well and truly pushed, but still, it's a big ask. Maybe we'll be surprised?"

"I hope so."

"And, Patterson, I could always change my mind." The concerned look on Patterson's face softened. It was a kind-hearted lie, but a lie nonetheless.

* * *

PATTERSON BROUGHT Niobe her usual breakfast—a vanilla protein shake, and toast with scrambled eggs. The meal was designed to be high in protein to fuel her high intensity training. Depending on the day, the chef would add some smoked salmon, wilted baby spinach, or mushrooms. Normally, Niobe mindfully appreciated the chef's perfect sense of timing for cooking the eggs 'just right,' but today she barely tasted the food, despite its potential as her nearly-last meal. Niobe didn't want to die, but if she did, and it was for her country, then she'd take inspiration from the words of Nathan Hale: 'I only regret that I have but one life to lose for my country.' She spent the day wondering if she'd be required to give hers. If so, she decided it'd be a fair trade for the lives she'd taken.

Niobe filled her time with training. It was the one thing which could force her mind to forget about the external world. Flipping from bar to bar, practicing her thrown weapons, punching the training dolls and doing kata kept her occupied enough until the mid-afternoon, by which time she seemed to have run out of sweat. Niobe had made it clear to palace staff she didn't want to see a screen or hear any word of news about how the plebiscite was going.

At 6.00 pm the polls closed. Despite the lack of electronic voting for all but people with certain disabilities and fly-in-fly-out workers, the vote would be tabulated quickly as there were only three questions and two possible answers for each. With a population of four million, and roughly 3.4 million voters, it wouldn't take long to count. While there would still be scrutineering over the next week, the broad result would be known by midnight. Throughout the evening, Niobe allowed herself to look at the news. Several exit polls indicated a shift in the queen's favour. It was going to be neck and neck.

Just before midnight the chief scrutineer arrived at the palace and made his way to the media room. He smiled at Niobe as he entered. If he was pleased by the result what did that mean? Was he for or against her?

Niobe felt nervous sweat pooling under her arms. Had that ever happened to her before? Her life was on the line, so it wasn't an unreasonable response. The chief scrutineer stepped up to the lectern. Niobe stood a few metres away on the one-step tall stage, facing the audience.

"My name is Jorek Andersen, and I'm the head of the Tantalian Electoral Commission. The electoral commission fulfils an important role in elections providing scrutiny and oversight, ensuring the integrity and validity of the results. We've been doing this for nearly ninety years."

Niobe, like many of the assembled journalists and members of the palace staff who'd gathered in the room, tried not to roll her eyes. This was Jorek's moment in the spotlight, and it seemed he was going to use it to the full extent possible.

"In this plebiscite, we employed thousands of people to oversee the results I'm about to announce."

Niobe's temples throbbed.

"Before I do," Jorek said. Niobe groaned inwardly. Get on with it. "I'd like to say that the result did not go according to the pre-polls. This is not unusual. People will often say something publicly, which they think is the right thing to say, but then in the privacy of the polling booth vote differently. I'll give the results in rounded percentage terms. The exact figures will be released after scrutineering is finalised during the week."

Oh god, they've crucified me, Niobe thought. Why couldn't it go her way? Her 'justice killing' should continue; it made the country better. Couldn't people see that?

"Question one: Do you support Queen Niobe Ancora's actions in taking the lives of Alban Crab and Donald "Don" Azzure? Yes or No. Tantalia has voted 67% Yes and 31% No, with the rest invalid.

Niobe had to steady herself. The room erupted in noise. It

was so discordant it was hard to discern whether the mood was positive or not. Drysen Silic was clearly scowling. Morgan Henry looked relieved.

"Question two: Has Queen Niobe Ancora harmed Tantalia through her actions? Yes or No. 35% Yes, 63% No and 2% invalid."

"On the final question, question three. If it is found that Queen Niobe Ancora's actions are supported, should she maintain immunity for further actions? Yes or No. Tantalia voted 59% Yes, 37% No and 4% invalid."

Scattered applause emerged from the assembled crowd. Jorek suddenly realised he'd done his job and looked at a loss as to what to do next. He glanced at Niobe, who was a few metres to his right. She gestured with her head to the microphone.

"Uhh, Your Majesty, would you like to say a word?"

Niobe nodded and approached the lectern, trying to walk as though on uncertain legs. She had to play the part of the humble, chastised queen. As she approached, Drysen Silic yelled, "What do you think of the result?"

Niobe gripped the sides of the lectern as though to steady herself, and spoke directly into the microphone. "I'm grateful to Tantalia for accepting me, for both what I've done and who I am. I knew fifty-nine was prime, but hadn't realised it was a happy number as well. Thank you. Thank you, all."

"How have you coped over the last few weeks?" Morgan asked. Niobe appreciated her concern for her human side.

"Meditation and martial arts."

"And how do you feel about the international reaction?" Morgan asked.

"I've been surprised by the response. Mostly it's been accepting. I even had one country make a request for me to eliminate one of their bad apples, should this vote go my way."

"Which country? Who?" Morgan couldn't hide her desire to be the one who broke that story.

"I can't answer that."

"Are you going to do it?" Morgan asked. If she had subtitles, they would have read "and could you give me the exclusive if you do?"

"While the person met all my criteria, including damage to Tantalia, I'm afraid they're out of my jurisdiction, so to speak."

"As a member of the EU your sovereignty is recognised all over Europe and by most countries," Drysen said. "You can go and be a threat to people anywhere."

Niobe couldn't understand why he was still pushing the danger argument.

"There need to be boundaries. Tantalia's borders seem good enough."

"What about copycats?" Drysen pushed. Didn't he realise he'd lost?

"Other sovereign leaders have to make up their own minds about such things. This dialogue isn't going to a place I want to go right now. But let me just say that while there may be copycats, which I don't condone, I think this will lower such attacks in the same way Kurt Cobain's suicide triggered copycats, but also made the overall suicide rate drop in the aftermath, as studies in Seattle and Australia showed. I think the idea of me will help people avoid taking matters into their own hands. What I do want to say is thank you to my people for their trust. I won't let it be misplaced."

Niobe put her hands on her heart and mouthed a thank you. With a slight bow, she left the stage and retreated to the anteroom. Her breaths became so deep, she felt like she was breathing for the first time. *They accepted her.*

* * *

THE NEXT MORNING Niobe woke up to Patterson bringing in her breakfast. It was rare that he'd present it to her in bed rather than her dining room. Niobe must have slept through her alarm, which was not surprising, as she'd only managed to properly fall asleep a couple of hours before. The chef had made a face on the scrambled eggs. The eyes were spinach, the nose mushrooms and the mouth smoked salmon. It was smiling. Since the chef had never given her more than one side without her asking, the sentiment implied raised Niobe's already high spirits.

Half an hour later, Patterson knocked on her door again.

"Your Majesty, a Mr Jyons is here to speak to you."

"Who is he?"

"A TV producer."

"Send him away."

"He has a press pass for the building, and he's been here since we opened this morning. Says he's not leaving until he speaks to you personally. Something about getting in before someone else comes up with his idea."

Niobe assumed he'd want an interview or to do a special on her. At least an interview might help people appreciate her uniqueness.

"Ugh. Fine. Show him to the meeting room. I'll be there in fifteen, once I've had a quick shower."

Patterson shuffled out of the room to carry out the request. Niobe wondered whether they should change the access policy to the palace. It was too old school White House and not enough Buckingham Palace.

* * *

SIXTEEN MINUTES LATER, Niobe opened the door to the meeting room. It was a small, oval room, with a handful of leather armchairs arranged in a circle. Each armchair had a side table which could be placed beside the chair or put in a line to act like a coffee table. In the room was a man dressed in a black skivvy and pants. He was bald, but had an artfully trimmed beard and thick, black-rimmed glasses.

"Jim Jyons, at your service." He rushed over, shook her hand and bowed. He pronounced his surname as *Yons*. He produced an elaborate business card and gave it to her with two hands. Such was his theatricality, Niobe half expected him to kiss the back of her hand.

"You wanted a meeting with me? What for?"

"I have a proposal for you."

"I'm not interested in getting married," Niobe said firmly. If that's what he was here for, she'd have to have stern words with Patterson.

"That's not what I meant. What I'd like you to consider is starring in a reality TV show where you prepare for and, if you excuse the pun, execute your next kill."

CHAPTER 10

"*N*o!" Niobe couldn't believe the gall of the producer.

"Wait, you need to hear what I have to say," Jim said. He had a smirk which suggested he thought he could sell her on the idea.

"I don't."

"You *should* hear what I have to say."

"That's better. I have to address the country in half an hour, and I haven't read over my notes yet. You've got five minutes."

"That's all I'll need. Firstly, you've been given an awesome responsibility by Tantalia."

"True."

"Sanction to murder openly, and without fear of judicial repercussions, is a staggering burden."

"Yes. Get to your point."

"Wouldn't you like your people to understand how you reached the decision about your target?"

"Yes."

"Wouldn't you like your people to know how you're protecting them?"

"Yes."

"Wouldn't you like your people—"

"I know what you're doing. You think I don't know how you're trying to get me to say a lot of yeses in short succession so I'm more inclined to say it again when you slip in your target question."

Jim's eyes widened. He mustn't have been used to perceptive women. He probably cast women for their looks rather than their brains. Jim looked guilty for the briefest moment.

"Well, my technique doesn't invalidate my questions. So, one more. Wouldn't you like your people to feel a part of your journey? To give them the vicarious thrill and catharsis of what you do. It would make them give up some of their own violent propensities, because you helped them experience emotional release. You know the murder rate in this country is above the EU average."

"Only by a percent-and-a-half. I would like them to experience an emotional purge, but a reality TV show?"

"You don't have to hide; you are immune from prosecution. Not to mention the publicity it would bring for Tantalia."

"That publicity might also be negative."

"We have several hundred bloggers and influencers around the world who will promote what we ask them to or give a perspective we want them to."

"So? That's what, maybe a hundred thousand followers? That's not many."

"No these are celebrities with millions of followers. Ever wonder why Ms Kay mentions a particular brand in a tweet, or Ms other Kay mentions she loves a certain show. That's us. I can always tell when someone desires fame. I recruit such people, help them develop, then get them to help me when I need it. Our influencer pool has over two hundred million followers. For the most part we can control the narrative if it's needed."

"But?"

"We'll only activate the network if we need to. They cost a lot of money."

"Continue your pitch."

"We'd sell it as a limited series, a double entendre because 'someone's life is limited in this limited series'."

"Let's say I agree. What then?"

"We'd need to plan a three-to-five-episode story. You'd chose a target, and we'd show you training and preparing. Would you be open to flirting with a male instructor we bring in?"

"You want to put a love interest in the show?"

"It sells gossip magazines and generates social media traffic."

"No. You can leave now if that's a problem."

"Oh. That was going to give the show a subplot. We'll have to think of something else. Would it make a difference if it was a girl?"

"What is wrong with you?" Niobe asked incredulously.

Jim looked suitably embarrassed, albeit only for another brief moment.

"Listen carefully. I'm a straight ally, but I don't need a love interest to prove that."

"But it'll help you appear less … less…" Jim seemed to suddenly realise the hole he'd dug for himself.

"Say it."

"Butch."

"You're an idiot. I see how men look at me. I know I have a certain appeal. You don't have to worry. I know how to be a girly-girl."

Niobe took a hair tie out of her pocket, ran her fingers

through her hair, arched her back and tied her hair into a ponytail, making sure to raise her elbows as high as possible as she did so. This had the effect of pulling her chest up and emphasised her femininity. She'd noticed in the past how Gethan couldn't look away when she did it in front of him. Niobe wasn't surprised to see Jim look over her body.

"See?"

Jim cleared his throat. "Yes. Okay, no boyfriend then."

"You know, a year ago I would've jumped to have a love interest."

"But not anymore. Why?"

"A year ago it would've been good for my image, for the public's perceptions of me. But I don't need a man to validate me as a woman. It's not that I don't want a relationship, just not a manufactured one. I could be a mentor though. My cousin Ebony is of training age. Her mother mentioned how much she looks up to me."

"Now that's an idea. That could definitely provide a secondary story for us to tell. You know, your passing on the knowledge to the next generation—"

"She's only ten years younger than me. That's hardly the next generation."

"Close enough. Should also spark discussion about whether you should be teaching someone else your skills and whether someone else should have the same licence you do."

Niobe sighed. So much reality TV was manufactured to generate discussion.

"She wouldn't have immunity. She's not even next in line. That would be her father, Duke Jacques, and then her brother. She doesn't have any killer instinct either."

Niobe wanted to add that she was the only one with that particular quality in the family.

"We'll gloss over that."

"Why?"

"Ruins the narrative. And hey, we should also get some good discussion around the role of women in the 'me too' age. As you'll be talking about martial arts and assassination, you'll pass the Bechdel test."

"How do you know we won't talk about boys, marriage or babies?"

"You might, but it won't be all the time. Does she have a title?"

"I call her Ebony, or Ebs, but, technically, she's Lady Ebony of Lower Scintilla."

"Excellent. A title adds to the appeal of the show."

"If she says yes—"

"Between us I'm sure we can get her to," Jim interrupted.

"We? I haven't agreed yet, despite your inclusive language. Part of my training has been how to increase the chance of someone doing what you want. Like getting them to separate from a group, or go to a specific location."

"I'll be blunt then. This would be great for tourism for Tantalia. Imagine it, 'Tantalia, where the queen will kill to keep you safe'. Or, 'Come to Tantalia, our queen will protect you'. You could train in the mountainous region, by a lake et cetera. You could remove some of the concern about your actions by showing the justification and thought that goes into your kill, and you could raise a stack of money from the advertisements on the show, for your country, or a charity of your choosing."

"Why not pay me?"

"You don't need the money. But we could fund a school or something with what I anticipate the advertising revenue to be."

"I'm still not signed on, but let's ask Ebony and see what she says."

"Done."

* * *

NIOBE INVITED Ebony for tea the next day. They met in the second meeting room, which was reserved for more relaxed encounters. It had a few leather armchairs and couches, and several coffee tables. Ebony arrived with her mother, Duchess Dahlia of Lower Scintilla. Although in her late forties, the duchess showed no signs of grey in her perfectly straight, shoulder-length blonde hair. She wore rimless glasses and a thin, cream coloured woollen dress. Despite their conversation after the news reports, Niobe was fond of her aunt and had been grateful for her assistance during the funerals of her parents. Dahlia had been a whirlwind of organisation and brisk efficiency. Niobe had seen the behaviour for what it was: a way of delaying having to deal with the reality of losing a close friend through intense focus on an immediate task. At the time, Niobe had been jealous. She'd wanted that same luxury. Instead, all responsibilities and decisions had been made without her, so she could have time to grieve. Rather than deal with her grief in pieces, she'd been forced to deal with it all head on.

In contrast to Niobe's green eyes, brown hair and tan, Ebony was the picture of Nordic fairness. Her pale skin, blue eyes and straw-coloured hair didn't belie her heritage; Duchess Dahlia's family had been on the fringes of Norway's royal family for generations. Ebony was a decade and a day younger than Niobe, and, as a teenager, still growing into her body.

Dahlia and Ebony stood by the window which overlooked the palace's centre. Dahlia always seemed to like gazing upon the gardens.

Niobe called Ebony over to the couches she and Jim were seated on. Jim nudged Niobe as Ebony walked over. "She's perfect. That body and face. She can sell all the clothes, perfume and make up we can line up sponsors for."

Jim was so focused on Ebony that he didn't notice Niobe's look of distaste. Ebony was fifteen and didn't even have her full figure yet, but he wanted to hold her up as the standard? That was bananas.

Niobe hated the idea that the pressure on women to look a certain way came from themselves. Numerous studies showed men preferred the body shape of a twenty-three-year-old. In Niobe's mind it was women who put pressure on each other to be thin and hide their curves, effectively holding up the figure of a fourteen-year-old as the ideal. They were the ones who allowed the media to maintain this idea as the ideal. Niobe put this down to seeking a reproductive advantage. If you could get your competition to maintain a less desirable form, then you were more likely to be selected as a 'fitter' mate in comparison.

"Ebony, this is Jim. He's the producer and probable showrunner for a new TV show."

Ebony looked suitably impressed.

"What's it about?"

"About me and what I do as queen. But focused on my more recent, notorious activities. He's thinking it might be a good idea if you were part of the show too."

Ebony squealed in delight. "You mean I get to be on TV?"

"Yes, if you'd like," Jim replied.

Ebony looked across the room to the duchess. "Mummy, can I? Please?"

Dahlia took a last look at the garden, sighed and turned to her daughter. "Can you what?"

"Be on TV."

Dahlia took a seat in one of the armchairs.

"What are you talking about?" Dahlia asked, looking at Niobe.

"Niobe wants me to be part of her TV show," Ebony replied.

Dahlia kept her focus on Niobe. "You know I'm here for you, as is proper, and my duty. But are you sure you need this added burden right now?"

"You haven't even heard what it's about," Niobe replied.

"No. But you're new to your role, involved in something scandalous, albeit a situation you've handled rather well, but there's only so much people will tolerate."

"I haven't fully agreed to the show yet, so will bear in mind what you've said. Please hear what Jim has to say."

"As you wish, my queen."

Niobe winced. Dahlia never used titles with family members. Perhaps her aunt was one of those who disapproved of her vigilantism?

"Duchess, Lady." Jim looked from Dahlia to Ebony. "What we're proposing is a new reality TV show about the queen's next assassination—"

"Absolutely not," Dahlia replied sternly. "I was hoping that would be over and done with."

"Hear me out. What we'd like is for Niobe to have the opportunity to explain how she became the person she is now. We'd show her training; that would be the first episode. Episode two would be with Niobe as she chooses another target, and justifies her actions. Episode three would be filmed in a flashback style to show how Niobe got to this point, and the final episode would be her removing her target. Well, roughly that's what I'm thinking; it'll probably change a bit as the story develops. In the first episode we'd include Niobe showing Ebony what training she's gone through to be able to do what she does."

Dahlia arched an eyebrow. "You want my daughter to be trained as an assassin?"

Niobe was grateful Jim didn't hesitate. "No. We simply

want her to go through the motions to give perspective and show no one else can do what the queen does."

"At least we can agree on that. No one else can, or should, be able to do what the queen does, including the queen." Dahlia was firm. Niobe, once again, felt like she'd let her down. Dahlia had always seemed supportive of her in the past.

"What would you like me to do? This is a great opportunity to advertise our country. We can show me training in some of our forests, by the Paine River, maybe even at the Scintilla gold mine. Let's show off the country."

Jim glanced at Niobe. His look read as admiration for the way she was now using inclusive language to help persuade Dahlia to grant her consent. Niobe knew she needed to tread carefully to get that. Maybe a compliance technique was in order? Which should she use? Foot-in-door? Door-in-face? One of the other techniques? Door-in-face seemed like the most likely.

"How about we *do* train Ebony as an assassin? It would make for great TV," Niobe said. She noticed Jim's eyes widen out of the corner of her eye.

"I've already said no to that," Dahlia replied. The words gave Niobe hope, as they implied she was searching for a way to say yes. Equally, the no was expected. The request was meant to be refused. This was the door-in-face. Next was lowering the request a couple more times. This would give the impression Niobe had given something up and create tension within Dahlia, since she was offering nothing in return. It worked on the principal of reciprocity—if I give you something you should give me something in return. It didn't matter if nothing real was actually being exchanged.

"What if we have her train with me for the first two episodes, then just observe for the last two?"

"You want to put her in harm's way?"

Niobe could see Dahlia's expression shift, so she moved in for the final strike. "You're right. That wouldn't be wise. What if we just have her train with me for the first episode and then interview me in the second?"

Dahlia seemed about to say no again, then an idea seemed to occur to her and, with a slight twinkle in her eye and a deep sigh she replied, "Fine. But if she so much as gets a scratch, I'll … I'll … find some way of getting back at you."

"Understood. Thank you, Aunty."

Ebony squealed in delight and clapped her hands. "Thank you, Mummy. Thank you, thank you."

Jim turned to Niobe. "So, are you in, too?"

Niobe shrugged. "If a reality TV star can become president, why can't a queen become a reality TV star?"

EPISODE ONE

*S*CENE: A makeshift rifle range at the Scintilla gold mine. Mounds of rubble form the backdrop. A gazebo has been erected as shelter for the participants to shoot from. Enter Niobe and Ebony. Niobe examines the various weapons available on the gun rack, running her hands over them as she does so.

VOICE-OVER: Welcome to a very special television series. Over four episodes we will follow Queen Niobe Ancora of Tantalia as she prepares to assassinate an enemy of the state. Someone's life is limited in this limited series!

NIOBE LOOKED DIRECTLY at the camera. "When I was approached by Jim Jyons with the idea for this series, I was sceptical. I don't want to sensationalise what I've done or what I intend to do. However, it seems it would be useful for people to understand how and why I've killed two people and intend to kill a third. If you can see what it takes, hopefully, you'll understand that this will never be scaled up, nor occur without clear justification. The target for this series is someone who has manifestly and demonstrably harmed many lives in Tantalia. I wasn't seeking a target, but they've recently done something which means they now meet my criteria. On my journey, I'll be joined for some training by my cousin, Lady Ebony of Lower Scintilla. We're starting at a rifle range today to show you why I won't be using a gun."

Niobe picked up a rifle and went through some standard checks of the weapon. The ease of her movements made Ebony's eyes widen.

"You really know what you're doing!"

"Yes."

She guided the cameraperson and Ebony over to the firing station and set up the rifle on its stand. She lay on the ground and prepared to fire at a target two-hundred metres away. Niobe paused and, leaning on her elbow, propped her head in her hand, to speak to Ebony.

"The first time I fired a rifle I made a mistake. My mentor, Gethan, knew this would happen, but he let me make it. He knew it would help me develop a deeper understanding of the weapon. I pressed my eye to the scope as I aimed and fired at my target."

"So?" Ebony asked. She lay beside Niobe and mirrored her elbow propping stance.

"Newton's third law of motion states that for every action there's an equal and opposite reaction."

"But wouldn't that mean nothing could ever happen?"

"No, though that's a common misconception. The forces act on different objects. So as the bullet was thrust forward, the gun recoiled backward, resulting in me sustaining a deep cut from the scope, underneath my eyebrow. For quite a while, it bled like a dripping tap, but I learnt about forces that day. I also gained a deep respect for rifles; I even hit a target from a hundred metres away."

"Shouldn't Gethan have stopped you before you were hurt?"

How many times had Gethan hit and kicked her, made her bleed, bruise or dislocate? Too many to count. How to encapsulate their relationship? He was a teacher, mentor and friend, but also *master*. None of Gethan's attacks were done with the aim of abusing or controlling Niobe, just to help her develop her self-defence and self. It was difficult to convey to someone who hadn't trained before. Gethan had even knocked her out a few times, but in no way was it abusive, nor done with malice.

"His job was to train me to achieve a goal."

"And King John knew about it?"

"About what?"

"The plan for Alban."

Niobe wondered if her sharp intake of breath betrayed the answer. Would the microphones pick it up? Something about Ebony's tone also suggested it was a question she'd been asked to say. It was likely Jim was trying to stir controversy. He was obsessed with sparking 'conversation'.

"He knew broadly of the plan, but not the specifics, nor all aspects of what the training would involve. In his last months, he also made it very clear he wanted the whole idea stopped."

"But you didn't listen?"

"I was never interested in the plan because of Dad. I'd have come up with it on my own. The only thing he provided was extra training time with Gethan."

Niobe sighed. If Gethan were here he'd make this so much easier. Where was he? Why hadn't he responded to her calls? Surely, he'd watch the show. Assuming he would, Niobe decided to send a message to him.

"Gethan was a great mentor. He helped me learn about human nature and human physicality. I always treated him like a teacher, but he was a wonderful friend too. He was right to not support my actions, given his beliefs."

"Why? I thought you were proud of what you've done?"

"No, not proud. I'm pleased by the outcome, not the action. I'm not a sociopath." Niobe hoped that came across as true. Gethan would probably be able to spot the lie though. Niobe wished she knew how he did it. "I'm fully aware of the horrific consequences for the families and friends of my targets. It's why I've already secretly met with them and offered compensation. It's probably worth noting that Alban's family rejected the compensation but offered forgiveness. Don Azzure's family accepted it, but I'm not sure they'll forgive me."

"How did they take it? I mean—"

"Alban's family were quite friendly. It doesn't seem as though they were his biggest fans. His young wife appeared quite happy with what I'd done. She got the inheritance much earlier than she'd hoped. Don's family were very different. They would have tried to kill me on the spot, but for the security detail I had outside, and the certainty they'd be arrested."

"So, what did they do?"

"Took the money and told me never to be in the same room as them again. I think they'll leave me alone, but one day they may come for me. I guess I'll have to be eternally vigilant, but isn't that the price of freedom?"

Niobe knew she should get off the topic. If she kept talking it would be likely she'd inflame the situation with the Azzure family. "Let's see what this weapon can do. Do you see the target?"

"Yes."

"It's the length of two soccer pitches away. I'm going to shoot it. Do you think I can do it?"

Ebony shook her head. "No way."

Niobe put on her earmuffs and instructed Ebony to do the same. Ebony stood and backed a few steps away. Niobe took a breath and muttered her favourite grounding phrase about Ramona, with eyes of obsidian, shooting for her freedom. She aimed and gently squeezed the trigger. The rifle recoiled about 5cm. Just under half a second later splinters of wood flew into the air near the target's heart.

"Hmm. Sight's a little off." Niobe made a few small adjustments and fired again. This time the target was hit right on the heart. Niobe tried not to grin, but failed. It was always satisfying to hit a target like that. The intoxicating feeling of power that flowed from firing a gun and effectively hitting the bullseye, from such a distance, was a sensation Niobe knew was a large part of the reason why gun control stirred up such debate. Fortunately, Tantalia had never allowed rifles to be in private possession, though they were legal at gun clubs and for the military.

"Ooh, can I have a go?" Ebony asked, forgetting she was wearing earmuffs and so almost shouting. She seemed to bounce with enthusiasm for the idea. Even with her own earmuffs on, it was clear what Ebony had asked. Niobe took them off. Ebony copied.

"Sure." Niobe helped Ebony into the firing position and quickly explained the parts of the weapon. "Don't forget about the recoil. You don't want to get injured."

"But it's so much easier to see when I press my eye to it."

"Don't. I promised your mum I'd look after you."

Ebony moved her head back a little.

"Breathe. Aim for the closer target. It's seventy-five metres away. When you pull the trigger squeeze it gently. Any tremble in your hands or shoulder will muck up your aim. Try to clear your mind. When you're ready, let the weapon shoot the target, instead of you trying to shoot it."

Niobe replaced Ebony's earmuffs. Ebony took aim and a second later the rifle roared. A puff of dust appeared in the mound of dirt behind the target.

Ebony removed her earmuffs. "What happened. Did I hit it?"

Niobe laughed. "No, it was a complete miss. Use your shoulder to stabilise the butt of the gun more and breathe. Maybe talk to yourself so you're not focusing on shooting at all."

"Huh?"

"You'll shoot straighter if you don't focus on focusing."

"I don't get it."

"Just say to yourself, the supreme art of war is to subdue the enemy without fighting. It's contradictory to what you're doing, but it might work for you."

"Oh, I get it. If you can shoot them from a distance, you can win easily."

Niobe rolled her eyes. How could Ebony be so ignorant of the deeper meaning? Had Niobe ever been that naïve? She tried to remember her earliest sessions with Gethan.

"No. Just recite something as you shoot. Okay?"

Ebony took aim and fired again. This time the bullet hit the white background of the target. It still missed the silhouette, but was a much better shot.

"I hit it. I hit it!" Ebony was so jubilant, she didn't notice the thin streak of pink above her eye. She'd held her head just a little too close to the scope. Niobe winced and hoped the injury wouldn't be caught on camera. The skin hadn't broken, so there was no blood, but it was definitely a scratch. Dahlia wouldn't be happy.

"Go again."

Three shots later, Ebony properly hit the target for the first time. The bullet hit the silhouette's left shoulder.

"I did it! Look, I hit the target."

"Well done," Niobe said. "But for future reference, shooting someone is not a good strategy. They may have armour on, or be too well guarded, or in a crowd. The training is only good for what it teaches you about being relaxed in a high-pressure situation, demystifying guns and understanding physics. It's a coward's choice of weapon. Besides, from this distance, how sure can you be that you're aiming at the right person?"

Niobe knew this comment might annoy some viewers, but she had to get across that she wasn't a gun nut and wouldn't go around shooting people.

"Can we shoot something else? A watermelon maybe?"

"No. Let's go to the hall and do some martial arts. I'll show you *Jitte* kata. It translates to 'ten hands' and it's said that mastery of it will give you the power of ten men in combat."

"That sounds exciting! I'd love to be that strong."

Niobe wondered if she'd ever made Gethan feel like she felt now. Ebony was just so wet behind the ears.

"Strength has nothing to do with it. It's about being able to control your opponent or opponents. You know, take their weapons and use them against them."

"So, how many hours will it take me to master it?"

"Hours? It'll take decades."

"So, what's the point?"

Niobe felt an urge to slap Ebony on the cheek. How could she be so short-sighted? It was about the journey, not the destination. Niobe shook her head. "We have a lot of work to do."

CHAPTER 12

SCENE: Interior of Niobe's training hall at the royal palace. The polished wooden floors are half covered with padded mats. Niobe stands, alone, in the middle of the matted area. A camera focuses on her, zooming out from her green eyes to show the hall around Niobe.

VOICE-OVER: After training with guns earlier in the day, Queen Niobe meets with Lady Ebony in her training hall or *dojo*. Queen Niobe is about to demonstrate Jitte kata. Legend says it imbues masters of it with mystical power.

NIOBE STARED at the camera five metres in front of her and bowed. Her eyes shone as she moved through the kata's sequence of movements. A loud shout, called a *kiai*, resonated in the hall as she began and finished the kata. Her movements were sharp, and she felt the power flow through her as she let her hips drive her motion. Her bodyweight was behind each strike and, at the end, she was confident even Gethan would've approved of her performance. She suppressed a smile as she gave a final bow.

"That looked so cool," Ebony said, from her seated position near the camera.

"Thanks. I've worked hard at it." Niobe moved and sat cross-legged in front of Ebony, as the camera focused on her. It felt odd being the one in the mentor role, whilst sitting like she and Gethan used to.

"So how does it make you more powerful?" Ebony asked.

"Oh, Ebs, stop focusing on the mythology and look at the techniques. The opening move is to step back and perform arm movements which could be used to break an attacker's grip, or as a strike. Some karate styles do the first moves slowly, with *ibuki* breathing."

"What's that?"

"Controlled diaphragmatic breathing. You try and use your abdomen to breathe instead of your chest. You breathe audibly."

Niobe stood and performed the start of the kata again, timing her audible inhalation and exhalation with slower, more controlled movements.

"See? It's about coordinating your breathing with what you're doing. Exhale as you strike, inhale as you move," Niobe said.

Ebony's eyes showed a glimmer of understanding. "Like at the gym. Exhale on the effort phase."

"Exactly, well done, Ebony."

"So, is this what you do? Kata? For hours?"

"My normal day, before being made queen, was to do martial arts, including kata, self-defence, basics and weapons for a couple of hours, including up to an hour of philosophy and meditation. After mid-morning, it was regular education until I completed my master's degree in international communications a couple of years ago. Then it became free time unless there were royal duties, although I'd often do more training, particularly free-running and gymnastics. I love how they make me feel totally in control of my body, and that I can move in my environment in any way I wish. I've had less time since becoming queen. Now, my time is often spent in formal meetings."

"And that was your usual day for how long?"

"Twenty years."

"No wonder you're so good. Hey, um…"

"What? Ask me anything, Ebs. I'm an open book."

"How does that make you feel about Gethan? You must be in love with him to put up with him for so long."

Niobe laughed and again pondered how to explain their relationship.

"I miss him terribly and wish he'd return to the palace. I didn't realise how good a friend he was until he was gone. Although, I am upset with the way he conspired against me during the vote. I know he was loyal to my father, not me, and was just trying to follow King John's orders. But, yeah, I was a teenager for a decent chunk of our training, and he was a strong male role model. I fantasised about him a few times"—it was why she enjoyed targeting his groin. It was her way of punishing him for being unable to return her affection—"because he was my safe place. Even when he hurt me when we were training, there was always something behind his response to my pain. I guess you could call it affection, or love."

"He was in love with you?"

"Oh god, Ebs, *no*. Not like that. He was my teacher, my mentor. Even though I crushed on him for a bit, it would never, ever, come to anything." Niobe had the rush of an epiphany. "I just felt that he liked me, and that even if he wasn't my teacher, he'd still be my friend and hang out with me. That's why his leaving the palace is so painful. Why I'm unhappy he's gone. I just want to hang out with him again. I want to work on this with him, with him on my side."

"So, what's your happiest childhood memory?" Ebony's question seemed rehearsed. Had Jim fed them to her? She was smart enough to ask her own.

"When I was your age, Dad spent a lot of time training with Gethan and me. Having my two fathers help"—Niobe scrunched her nose as she searched for the right words—"refine? Mould me? I'm not sure how to describe it. It felt wonderful to have two role models so vested in my development. Mum trained with us too, at times, but the banter they had was always a little more freewheeling when Mum wasn't around. I liked that."

"And how would they feel about your recent actions?"

"They'd be upset I hadn't move beyond violence, in all meanings of that phrase."

"What other meanings are there?" Ebony asked as she scrunched her face.

"Krishnamurti wrote a treatise about moving beyond violence as being necessary for personal development and global change. For him, violence wasn't just physical confrontation, it referred to anything stopping you experiencing reality directly. So, even your memory of events is a form of violence, since memory is imperfect and reconstructive. In order to achieve transcendental peace, you need to free yourself from all violence and just be."

Niobe realised this was the goal of her decades of training. Perhaps she wasn't as advanced as she thought? She still craved violence.

"Sounds like an advertising slogan. Just be."

"It would work. Anything which helps ingrain the

concept in people's consciousness, regardless of whether it's being used to sell something or not, would be seen as being an agent of peace from that perspective."

"I'm not sure I get it."

"Language isn't just grammar and concepts, it's systems of meaning. Effectively, language directs your attention." Niobe sighed at the sight of Ebony scrunching her face. "Most ancient cultures didn't have a word for blue, because they had no blue dyes or blue products from nature around them. This limitation of their vocabulary altered their perception, not by altering what sensory information they received, but by what they paid attention to, and what their brain discarded. Thus, they referred to the sky as being white or colourless. It's only when we have a frame of reference, a mental concept of 'blue', that our brain pays attention to those wavelengths of light. The Himba tribe have no word for blue and really struggle to spot a blue square amongst green ones. Russians have separate words for light and dark blue, rather than a general concept, which is modified by words like light or dark, and they're much faster to notice a different shade amongst many blue squares. Their brains are more easily directed to the altered shade, so when they process colour, they process more of it than us.

"My training helps me learn to retain more of what my senses detect. I try to pay attention to the whole rather than components. This is why when I fight, I try not to focus on one aspect of my opponent. Not their incoming fist, nor their foot. I just react to the whole. In doing so, I am more likely to spot an opening or vulnerability to attack."

Ebony appeared to be stunned into silence. Niobe had the impression she'd grasped elements of the concept conveyed. After a pause, Ebony shook her head as though she'd worry about things later and blurted out her next question.

"So, do you think you let your father down?"

Niobe inhaled sharply.

"I betrayed his and Gethan's express wishes. Yes, I let them down. However, my father's purpose in trying to stop me from going through with the plan was to prevent me from becoming permanently shrouded under the personal and social consequences of my actions. My dad and Gethan didn't anticipate my comfort with what I wanted to do. I know I let them down. My father isn't able to forgive me, but Gethan can, and I hope he will. I hope he can understand how I'm both sorry for disobeying him, yet not sorry for the act itself."

"But how can you be content with killing someone?" Ebony seemed genuinely interested in the answer.

Niobe wondered how to express the process she'd gone through to obtain her state of mind. Few people were capable of such a degree of abstract thought and moral reasoning. Ebony wouldn't be able to understand, and she'd already been stretched enough today. Niobe wasn't sure her people would get it either. She wanted them to though, because it would aid their acceptance of her and reduce how much they would get in her way.

"It wasn't an easy decision. I'll work to help you understand, okay?"

Ebony nodded. Niobe felt like she hadn't got it, but was agreeing because she didn't know how else to respond.

* * *

GETHAN TURNED off the television at the end of the episode. Mixed feelings stirred within. Niobe had adhered to all their training and he was proud of her performance. She'd presented well and would probably have convinced people she was behaving reasonably and with restraint. However, there was still the plan to execute someone. Gethan hadn't been able to save Alban or Don. Maybe he could save the next target. It would be small recompense to his king, but at least he'd feel like he'd done something to uphold King John's command to stop Niobe killing.

CHAPTER 13

The next day, Drysen Silic published a lengthy article condemning Niobe. Niobe's revelation that King John had asked Gethan to train his daughter to kill Alban was for him not 'an' argument but 'the' argument to do away with the monarchy entirely. The disclosure was proof positive there was 'something rotten in the state of [Tantalia]' and the fact the rot extended to the prior generation was unforgiveable. He charged Niobe with staining the royal family and the legacy of her father who had worked tirelessly to improve the standards in the country.

Niobe wanted to point out the statement about the king contradicted Drysen's main argument. This was the problem with opinion pieces. They didn't have to make sense and could cherry pick the arguments, no matter how tenuous, which supported their perspective. Why couldn't the media be emotionless and present just the facts? They never were, of course, which was why Niobe felt compelled to read multiple papers. There was no other way to make sure she received enough detail to reach her own conclusion on the matter.

Even though they were published on the same day, there was also an article by Morgan Henry, which more or less countered Drysen's. In it she argued the revelation was the reason why Tantalia needed the monarchy. After all, it had clearly been a difficult decision for King John to have his daughter trained in such a manner, one he regretted at the end of his life. But, Morgan argued, Niobe was a special individual who had many years of training to be able to do what she'd done and cope with the complex repercussions. She was literally the only one capable of making the necessary higher order judgement. Plus, the criteria Niobe had created independently, Morgan added, was exactly why things wouldn't get out of hand. There was a strict code. Morgan wrote that if the code was broken, then she would join the chorus of people against the queen. She even volunteered to lead a protest march, although it was clear Morgan didn't think such events would ever occur.

"Bless you, Morgan," Niobe said to herself after reading that article.

Other reports were more focused on the show, which had been called *Sovereign Assassin*. It seemed the show had been watched by a large proportion of the population. They praised its production and noted the value of the extra insight into the royal family it gave. There were, however, several misgivings about what had been stated as the show's forthcoming conclusion. There was also some scepticism whether the murder would take place. Was the whole thing just a publicity stunt?

EPISODE TWO

SCENE: Ebony and Niobe are standing in a small clearing in the pine forest near the banks of the Paine River. The picturesque setting is contrasted by a range of bladed weapons lined up in a row on a table behind them. A further series of wooden weapons are in a stand next to the table. Niobe picks up the longest sword.

VOICE-OVER: The Queen and Lady Ebony are evaluating various weapons, which Queen Niobe may, or may not, use in her next assassination.

"THIS IS A *KATANA*. You probably recognise it as a samurai sword," Niobe said to Ebony, who nodded sagely in response. Niobe picked up a second slightly shorter sword. "This is a *wakizashi*. I like its smaller length. It suits my size better. When you're generally going to be smaller than your opponent, like I am, you have to train to fight in close to your attacker. A big sword makes that more difficult. I won't be using this with my target though. I prefer to be more hands on."

"Who's the target?" Ebony asked.

Niobe laughed, as did the camera operator and director. Even Jim, who was lurking nearby, leaning against a tree, was betrayed by the movement of his body. Like always the emotion didn't seem to last long and he went to his trailer a moment later.

"I can't tell you that. Let's just say it's not only someone who deserves what's coming to them, but also someone you've probably heard of."

"How will you do it?"

"Maybe we can finish talking through the options? There are various wooden weapons ranging from the *bo* and *jo*, which are two different staffs, and short sticks, also called *escrima* sticks. They're all good weapons but tend to be less lethal than bladed ones."

The word lethal seemed to make Ebony cringe, as though she was just catching on that this whole thing was quite serious.

"What about a knife?"

"I wouldn't take a knife to a gunfight. Actually, I wouldn't take one to a knife fight either."

"Huh?"

"A weapon weakens you. You tend to focus on attacking with it and neglect other attacks you have open to you. Besides, whatever weapon you bring, you better know how to defend against it. An experienced opponent may take yours from you. So, taking a more dangerous weapon, like one with a blade, is always a risk, which is why I won't be taking one. No knives, swords or stabbing instruments for me. I could try poison, but it was so … clumsy using that with Alban, and I couldn't even be certain he'd die. I'll leave that alone too."

Ebony scratched her head. "What does that leave?"

"There's an ancient martial art called *Marma*. Some say it can teach how to kill with a sound. I'm not sure that's anything more than urban legend. I mean certainly the right shout can temporarily stun someone into immobility, but for it to cause death, I think, is stretching it a bit."

"Did you answer the question?" Ebony asked. Niobe was pleased that Ebony caught the absence of an answer in her response, but she didn't want to reveal what she'd be using just yet.

Niobe smiled. "All hunters understand a golden rule; you have to know your prey. So, that means I have to know things about humans."

"Like what?"

"Humans are different to other species. We're the only animal which hunts for sport."

"I know that."

"Okay. But have you realised humans are the only animal that always shows the whites of their eyes, you know, when they're open? We use eyes so much as part of our communication. Partly, that's due to being an apex predator. We can afford to give more clues about where we're looking."

"That's cool. What else?"

"We're the only animal on earth that maintains secondary sexual characteristics throughout their lifespan."

"Huh?"

Niobe cupped one of her breasts.

"Breasts. We have 'em throughout adulthood. Other species only develop them around childbirth, and then they shrink back afterwards."

"Yeah. Never thought of that. Why though?"

"It means they're important for sexual selection. Size isn't the primary thing men care about with breasts; mostly they just want to see them."

Niobe was parroting something Gethan had told her. She knew Ebony wouldn't question the idea coming from her.

Ebony's eyes widened.

"Eyes are attracted to movement, particularly animal movement, but it goes deeper than that. We notice the movement of flesh more than clothes. Which is why people always notice when you display some cleavage."

"How can you use that to help you?"

"Easy. Wear a low-cut top when attacking someone and, particularly for women, let your natural assets distract your target during your fight. Use automatic, natural human behaviour to create a weakness, namely a lack of focus on fists and feet, to increase the success of your attack."

"You do know stuff."

"Gethan would occasionally bring in a naked man to fight me. He refused to do it himself, probably because he knew I was crushing on him when he started the practice. The first time, I must say the man's dangly bits made it difficult to fight. I lost that day. It's how I got this scar." Niobe lifted her top to reveal the scar on her side. This story was a better tale than the reality.

"Looks nasty."

"It hurt. We were using bladed weapons. It's another reason I don't like them."

"How old were you?"

"Sixteen."

"You saw a naked man when you were sixteen?"

"Yes, but I'd seen one before in my life-drawing class. This was different though, as this man was attacking me. That session was really training for what I might experience if someone tried to rape me. Even when I was just a princess, I knew how much I was photographed, and my image used in magazines. I've had stalkers since I was your age, an unfortunate reality of my role."

"How can you be so casual about that?"

"I've had a decade to get used to it. My father suspected it would happen, so he had me start training at age five. The training was usually only given to male heirs, but he broke the tradition since he knew it would be important for me. He wanted to be progressive, and after Mum's PND, I was always going to be an only child. Besides, with all the training I've had, I'm pretty confident I could handle a single attacker, as most stalkers or rapists would be."

"And if it was a group?"

"It would depend on circumstance. Pro-tip though. You can only attack one person at a time. So, if you have multiple opponents, focus all your effort on one at a time."

"What if you hurt someone you're not meant to?"

"That's where the other part of the training comes in. I've learnt ancient resuscitation techniques through studying *kappo*, and modern ones through paramedic-level training. The scholar warrior is a student of life. It's why I immerse myself in art and write poetry too. The arts help me appreciate life at a more meaningful level, and the martial arts and gymnastics give me the confidence to face life head-on."

"Is that why you're doing this show?"

"No. But, maybe, yes. In a way."

Ebony picked up a bo.

"Cool. Can you show me how to use this?"

"Sure."

Niobe spent the next twenty minutes showing Ebony various techniques with the weapon, including how to use it to strike, defend, parry or trap an opponent's limb or weapon. She then showed a bo kata from the Yamane-ryu school. The style was a dynamic and flowing take on the weapon. It was based on two principles; the bo should always be in motion, and you didn't need your little finger when using it. Legend had it the founder's little finger had been chopped off by a sword, so he'd adapted his weapon technique to not make use of it. Ebony's eyes lit up as she watched the kata—really just one half of a two-person exercise drill.

"That looked awesome. Can you teach me?"

Niobe began showing her the first movements. Jim came back from his trailer, holding the monitor he'd been watching the filming on, and called for a break.

"Great job, all. That should wrap-up the second episode really well. After the break we'll have Ebony ask a few questions in a more formal interview, then you can reveal what weapon you'll be using and how you're intending to kill your target."

Niobe and Ebony nodded their agreement and started walking towards the catering table in the nearby clearing.

"A quick word, Your Majesty?" Jim asked.

Niobe nodded, and she walked with Jim back to his trailer.

* * *

"Your Majesty, that was a fascinating insight into your upbringing, particularly about the public scrutiny and unwanted attraction you've faced and how you dealt with it. May I ask you a question?"

Niobe hated that phrase, since it was in itself a question, and since it'd been asked, the answer was self-evident; the inquirer had demonstrated that, yes, they were capable of the task. Niobe considered a pithy reply, but decided to nod instead.

"How is it you seem so unaffected by public scrutiny, when you are the most subject to it you've ever been?"

Niobe's mind recalled the emerald tablet, 'By this means

you shall have the glory of the whole world and thereby all obscurity shall fly from you'.

"I could be bonded in a nutshell and count myself queen of infinite space," she said.

Jim seemed confused.

"I've risen above such concerns."

More confusion.

"I pretend the cameras aren't there."

At last the producer's face cleared. Niobe sighed and felt guilty over dumbing down her understanding. If the exchange had been filmed they'd never have aired her first responses.

NIOBE WAS glad to have a break before more questions from Ebony and Jim, which would form the end of the second episode. The catering table was well supplied with pastries and her favourite food, sushi. Jim's question about how she coped with public opinion reminded her of the Riddle of the Eye.

As a child she hadn't killed a human because of the gaze from Gethan and her family. Such conduct wasn't becoming of a royal. So, she kept her true self hidden and fought to hide it. Now thanks to solving the riddle she was free from the constraints of the gaze. What would Ebony do if she was free from it too? She was only fifteen, after all. Would she turn against her mother? Turn against Niobe? Go and have lots of sex? Anything was possible, which was exciting. Should she try sharing the riddle or the revelation with Ebony? Would Ebony, a fifteen-year-old, be able to grasp the repercussions of it?

Recalling all the times she'd been frustrated by Gethan withholding information from her, and how pissed she'd been at him, made her feel guilty. It was hard not to give the answer. But, in doing so, when the solution was hit upon, it had a lot more personal meaning. Similarly, not teaching the next kata, piece of philosophy or mediation technique, until she'd mastered the previous one, must have been harder for Gethan than for Niobe. Gethan had been made to wait for over a decade before Niobe could start to have a conversation with him about techniques as something akin to an equal. It was nearly a decade after that when she'd truly felt like an equal.

GETHAN HAD WATCHED THE EPISODE, mostly because he knew he had to. If you were going to work against someone, you had to know them as best you could. He would have to leave Niobe with two things. But what would they be? Gethan wasn't sure, but he did know one thing—he would need to call his contact again as what they'd tried so far hadn't made Niobe stand down. If Niobe got away with this murder, Gethan was sure it wouldn't be her last. This madness needed to be stopped. Now he no longer had Patterson, he'd have to move on to his plan B.

CHAPTER 15

SCENE: The central garden in the palace. The fountain forms the backdrop, although its water has been turned off to stop any sound interference. Two chairs face one another, each with a camera pointing at them, so action and reaction shots can be continuously recorded. Niobe and Ebony each occupy a chair.

VOICE-OVER: We've seen the sort of training Queen Niobe has been through throughout her life. To end this episode, Lady Ebony interviews Queen Niobe about her life.

EBONY WAS DRESSED in a smart summer suit. Somehow, instead of making her look like an adult, it made her seem more like the private schoolgirl she was. Niobe wore a v-neck t-shirt and shorts, which went three quarters of the way down her thigh, long enough to not cause problems for the cameraperson.

The cousins sat opposite each other and smiled as the director counted them in.

"3, 2, …" The director pointed to Lady Ebony.

"My name is Lady Ebony of Lower Scintilla, and I'm here with Queen Niobe Ancora. Queen Niobe, thank you for agreeing to this interview."

Niobe had to suppress a laugh. Ebony was overacting.

"It's a pleasure."

"Tantalia has recently conducted trade talks with Australia. How are they going?"

That wasn't what Niobe expected to be asked. Jim must've wanted something to provoke online discussion. She inhaled slowly before replying.

"As you're probably aware, I'm not the main Tantalian involved in the talks. I've met with the Australian Prime, and Foreign Ministers in order to discuss the broad terms of a deal, so that if, or when, our Prime Minister says it's ready, I can give my assent to the agreement. I'm pleased with the progress to date. After all, the purpose of trade is not only to supply each country with the resources they need, but also to allow cultural information to be exchanged. It seems like we'll be able to agree to something mutually beneficial. Of course, the agreement will have to run through the EU to ensure it's not disadvantageous to any member countries. I don't anticipate that being a problem. We're grateful they let us continue these talks."

"Do you not anticipate problems because they'll worry you'll kill them?"

Niobe was stunned by the question. Her skin bristled, and she felt the beginnings of her cheeks flushing. Fortunately, she knew from experience that it would take a little more before it was visible. Jim must've anticipated Niobe's response to the question would be phrased in positive terms and prepared Ebony to pounce with the gotcha question.

Niobe's instincts kicked in. She would treat this like a real interview and not the anticipated chat with her cousin. That meant her mantra would be to keep calm and only show emotion if the response demanded it.

"Foreign relations are hard enough without the other leader thinking you could kill them at any moment. Any deal would have to begin and end with trust. I allow them whatever protection they feel is necessary for them to be safe, but to be honest, it hasn't been an issue. Their PM did seem nervous for a minute, but that disappeared the moment we started talking about the agreement."

"Do you feel above the law or that the law should change for you?"

Although Niobe felt like she was, in fact, above the law due to her mental reasoning and power, she was astute enough to know stating so on camera would be political suicide.

"No," she said as strongly as she could. It sounded convincing to her ear.

"What about the damage you're doing to the concept of royalty?"

"Symbols do die. Like Jung said, 'Why have the antique gods lost their prestige and their effect upon human souls? It was because the Olympic gods had served their time.' I'm simply using this quote for the way it describes symbolic change. The notion of what is royal is not fixed. The notion of what is acceptable for a leader to do can also change. These things can and will shift in accordance with the needs of society."

The blank look on Ebony's face betrayed her lack of understanding. It was clear she was asking what she'd been told to. Niobe's heart went out to her. Ebony's innocence and use as a pawn was both endearing and something Niobe decided she'd help fight.

"Mum said, 'A leader leads by example, not by force'. Do you see killing as something other than a show of force?"

With a start, Niobe realised Dahlia had fed Ebony the questions, not Jim. No wonder Dahlia had changed her mind about allowing Ebony to take part in the show when Niobe had mentioned the interview. She'd formed a plan to hijack the questions. Their pointedness reaffirmed Dahlia's unhappiness with Niobe's actions. Her aunt had been such an ally during the turmoil of her parents' illnesses, and Niobe understood Dahlia felt like Niobe had let her down. The recognition it was Dahlia trying to make her look bad made Niobe relax a little. She knew her enemy. At least it wasn't Gethan. He could have made the questions a lot more uncomfortable.

"That quote is from Sun Tzu's *Art of War*. It's one of the many martial art texts I had to study over the years. So, let me counter with another quote from the book. 'The art of war is of vital importance to the State. It's a matter of life and death, a road to either safety or ruin. Hence, it is a subject of inquiry which cannot be neglected.' As a king once allegedly said, '*L'État, c'est moi*,' the state is me. The people I've killed would have killed others and harmed the State. They defied justice. Rather than declare war on a crime family, like Don Azzure's, I cut off its head. In strategy terms, it's the least forceful way I could defend the State, and it was my obligation to do so."

"Okaaay." Again, Ebony seemed out of her depth with the level of response.

"It's also related to the weapon I'll be using to kill the target. It'll be the same one I used for Don Azzure. Anything else might come across as an unfair advantage."

"A shotgun?"

"That's misleading. I used *bean bag* rounds on the bodyguard and prostitute. When I attacked him, I was unarmed. So, the weapon I'll be using is me."

"But when you killed Alban Crab, you used poison."

"Circumstances conspired against me in such a way I had only that as an option."

"You still had the option not to kill him."

At last Ebony showed some independence of thought. Niobe recognised the pithy comment as one she might have made as teenager. After some of Ebony's statements about training and martial arts, it was good to see.

"You say that. I disagree. I know it seems illogical." Niobe thought about using an example from religion whereby the church had acted in accordance with its faith to persecute or kill unbelievers. But perhaps that wouldn't go down well.

"Let me put it this way," Niobe said. "You go to school."

"Yes." Ebony nodded.

"And there are rules you have to follow."

"Yes."

"What happens if you break them?"

"You get a detention."

"And if you keep breaking them?"

"You get expelled."

"And who makes that decision?"

"The principal."

"And what if there's an appeal, the student returns and they keep transgressing?"

"It undermines the system."

"Exactly. All I did was remove two people from our country who were undermining what we want it to be."

"But you killed them."

"Yes. And I regret that as being the necessary step, but the systems, the courts, had let us down. Though, like other countries which practice capital punishment, there was no pleasure in the act." Niobe flashed back to Don's skull crushing under her foot. It was one of the most satisfying events of her life. "That's why I reached out to their families afterwards. It's also why I'm working with the government to find ways to boost funding to prosecutors and police, as well as to increase the number of personnel in the judiciary. If the system worked as it should, it would prevent my feeling the need to take matters into my own hands again. I don't want to do it, but I will in order to protect our country."

Niobe recalled the first moments when the poison took hold of Alban and she knew it would be lethal. That smug grin was wiped off his face and transferred to hers. Why couldn't Tantalia get entirely out of her way so she could do it again?

Niobe hated sounding like a politician, but it was all she could come up with, on the spot, to avoid the slippery slope of arguing she was the best arbiter of determining who should live or die, and that her morality was superior to everyone else's. Those arguments wouldn't go down well with the public, no matter how true Niobe felt they were in private.

"Let me tell you a story which explains how I really want to treat people. It's an event from when I was fifteen..."

* * *

Niobe had felt the blood pumping through her after a vigorous training session, which had finished with a couple of rounds of sparring against other students Gethan had brought in. It was something he often did when she'd been angry—his way of getting her to work out her aggression. She'd been hostile towards him for the last week, ever since he'd told her parents she'd snuck out of the palace to meet a boy. It had worked too. She felt much less frustrated now she'd burnt through some stress hormones. But Niobe still wondered why he'd betrayed her trust and gone running to her dad. Was he jealous of the boy she'd gone to meet?

It always seemed odd to Niobe that Gethan often made her meditate immediately after exercise, but then part of the aim was to teach her to control her breathing in any circumstance.

His voice guided her into a relaxed state and bade her to reflect upon the story of LiLi from her *Bagua* manual. This Chinese martial art was known for its circular forms and conditioning of the body of its practitioners. Its manual contained an oft told story of LiLi, a tempestuous girl who hated her mother-in-law. She went to the local wise man and asked for some poison. The wise man listened to her tale and prepared a potion for her. He told LiLi they couldn't use a fast-acting poison to kill the mother-in-law as that would arouse suspicion. It would need to be one that would take many months to act. He said, 'It is best that you prepare meat and fish for her every day, and put a small amount of the poison in the dishes. In addition, in order to keep others from suspecting you when she dies, you must act respectful towards her and obey her. Do not quarrel with her either.' LiLi promised to do as he said and rushed home to implement her plan for murder. Every day, she cooked special dishes for her mother-in-law. To avoid suspicion, she tried her best to control her temper and obey what she was asked.

In a month, LiLi found that she did not get angry as easily as before, and she no longer had disputes with her mother-in-law. Her mother-in-law's attitude towards LiLi also changed, and she began to love LiLi like her own daughter. By two months, the mother-in-law started singing her praises to her neighbours, relatives and friends, and said LiLi was the best daughter-in-law in the world.

After three months, LiLi went to get help from the wise man again. She said, 'Please help me stop the poison. I do not want it to kill my mother-in-law. She has become a good woman, and I love her like my own mother. I do not want her to die because of the poison.'

The wise man smiled. 'You can rest assured. I never gave you any poison. Those herbs are to nourish the body and will only improve your mother-in-law's health. The only poison was in your heart and your attitude towards her. It is fortunate that your hatred has been washed away by your love for her. In this world, resentment cannot be eliminated by poison. Only love can wash away the grievances in your heart, allowing you to live in harmony with others.'

Niobe thought through the story for half an hour. First she picked apart all the holes in the tale, but then she focused on what it said about human relationships. Gethan had only acted in accordance with his duty. He had not gone out of his way to betray Niobe. She would have to forgive him for their relationship to continue. It was clear he'd already forgiven her for her response to his tattling on her.

* * *

"AND THAT, Ebony, is how you can have a richer life. Don't try to make enemies. Be above the pettiness of little squabbles which cause division. Be the bigger person and be kind to your enemies. Even with Alban, I offered him the opportunity to make amends." This was a lie, but he'd had plenty of opportunity over the years. "Over time, it will make your opponents look worse, and people will see them for what they are: small-minded fools."

Ebony nodded sagely. Niobe wondered if she was acting rather than reacting.

"Who's your next target?" Ebony asked suddenly.

"I can't say that on TV. They'd know. I will say that they are a serial killer. The legal system has let the public down, and this person is free to continue living their life. They are doing so in a way which harms our country. That's all I'll say, since any more detail will alert them I'm coming."

"So, you're really going to kill another person?"

"Unless they kill me. That's a possibility."

"What does it feel like?"

Niobe recalled the surge of power she felt with each assassination. The god-like feeling of determining someone else's fate. It was a rush she'd never be able to replicate through other means. It's what made her fear the tide of public opinion would turn against her if they knew she was a sociopath. Tantalia wouldn't let her continue.

"I mourn the loss of life, even though I know the world is better off without them. They squandered their opportunity for redemption."

"But what does it feel like?"

Niobe realised Ebony was sharp enough to know the question hadn't been answered.

"It's horrible. I want to throw up afterwards. Feeling someone's skull crush under your foot is sickening. I don't know how people could think it was thrilling." Niobe was grateful for the training she and Gethan had done on her emotional control. In the moment she spoke, she believed the lie she told, so it appeared as truth. But she couldn't hide the goosebumps created by the excitement of the memory. Thankfully, a long-sleeved shirt concealed them.

"Wow. I guess I hadn't thought about it as being difficult for you."

"It is." That, at least, was true. The training and process were hard. Niobe struggled to maintain her serious expression. This exchange would be gold for swaying opinion.

"So, are you afraid?"

Niobe looked directly at the camera.

"As Sun Tzu says, 'If you know the enemy and know

yourself, you need not fear the result of a hundred battles. If you know yourself but not the enemy, for every victory gained you will also suffer a defeat. If you know neither the enemy nor yourself, you will succumb in every battle.' I have a healthy level of concern about how the encounter will go, but I'm not afraid of the battle."

"Thank you."

"You're welcome. It's been great to have an interview where I'm not asked about marriage or babies. Bechdel would be proud."

Ebony nodded, but Niobe was confident she hadn't understood the reference.

Jim Jyons bounded up to Niobe after the interview. He was beaming as usual. "That was great."

"Uhh. Thanks?"

"I liked the way you handled Lady Ebony's questions." Jim's expression shifted to one of concern. "I had no idea she was going to be that tough," he said earnestly. Niobe wondered if he was lying. Spotting lies from others was something she'd struggled with throughout her life, and Gethan had refused to teach her how he did it with her.

"It's fine. I know Dahlia fed her those questions. She may not be as on board with this as you think. You might want to schmooze her, not me."

"I love that you see through me. I'll do that."

Niobe rolled her eyes. Why was everything with producers twisted into a positive? Their guile was extraordinary. Or was it just this one?

"You should know the ratings for the first episode were unbelievable. We had two million in Tantalia alone. That's half the population! We also broke the record for most pirated downloads in twenty-four hours. The European distributor says it's raking up hundreds of millions of views."

"Oh. That's a lot more than I was anticipating." Niobe's mind once again flashed the thought, 'You shall have the glory of the whole world and thereby all obscurity shall fly from you'. She was certainly the opposite of obscure now.

"I know. It's amazing. I think we're going to have the most watched show ever!"

"Hmm." Niobe wasn't happy. This was getting beyond a bit of fun and the chance to plug Tantalia. Now it was moving into the realm of a world-changing experience.

"I was thinking it would be great if you recounted a key piece of your training. Maybe we could even stage it as a flashback with a re-enactment? You know, show from where to here."

"Why not? You'll just need to film me at the palace this afternoon. How about we make it of the day I turned sixteen?"

* * *

As she'd walked to the training hall, Niobe had been excited about her birthday. Now she was sixteen, Gethan had promised to start teaching her a new kata, one she'd been wanting to learn for years—ever since she'd heard about its claim to empower masters of it. The hall looked like it usually did from the outside, grey and lifeless. Niobe was often amused by this, as it was here she felt most alive. Even when the hall was freezing cold in the middle of winter, it was still a warm and welcoming place.

Gethan kept his word and acknowledged Niobe's birthday by showing her a new kata: Jitte. Niobe was immediately drawn to the middle steps where the arms were raised at right angles, since they seemed to imply holding a bo above the head. Gethan showed her how to use her hips to generate power in her strikes, rather than using only the muscles in her arms. The subtle change in emphasis meant if she did have a bo, she would generate much more power than if she thrust only with her arms, as her bodyweight would be added to the muscular power of the strike.

They'd previously spoken about the ball which would be held in her honour that weekend. Niobe was excited as it could be a chance for her to meet someone special. Gethan warned her what they'd be after and reminded her of defences against someone attempting sexual assault, which were different to the defences used on a regular attacker.

Niobe smiled. So far this had been a great birthday. Jitte was something Gethan had spoken about a few times, and she was fascinated by its mythology. At last she was getting to learn it. Their talk about sexual predation had been awkward, not merely because Niobe kept imagining herself in the role, but because, as she realised after a few minutes, Gethan was using gender neutral terms because he wasn't sure of her sexuality. They'd discussed sex and relationships before, but this was different, since the king and queen had now agreed to let Niobe start dating.

"I'm mostly straight, you know, so you can talk about boys rather than 'a person' who is attacking me."

"Mostly?" Gethan raised an eyebrow. Niobe enjoyed the response. She'd provoked his interest. Nothing could ever happen between her and Gethan, but at least she could have some fun.

"Gotta leave some room for negotiation."

Niobe laughed. "Yeah, on the odd occasion, I fantasise about girls, but ninety percent of the time it's boys, so assume that's who we're talking about."

"Okay," Gethan had replied. He'd never brought it up again.

* * *

Jim interrupted her recount and got the cameraperson to stop recording. "Are you sure you want that to go to air?"

"Yes. Why not acknowledge that sexuality is a spectrum?"

"If you're sure. Be warned though, the fact of who you are and your role means there will be a significant response."

"As we've established, I don't care."

Jim's eyes lit up. It was clear he was contemplating the discussion and ratings such a revelation would bring. He nodded to the cameraperson to start filming her again. The re-enactment would be filmed that afternoon to match the voice-over.

* * *

"I can't wait to wear my dress. It makes my breasts look great." Niobe liked to mention her breasts in front of Gethan since it always made him squirm. There was a line she was on one side of, and when she forced him to cross it, however briefly, he was made uncomfortable. The line's existence made Gethan her safe place. He would protect her, and she could turn to him if she was in trouble.

"Someone's coming," Gethan said. "Actually, three people. Your father, Patterson … oh, and your mother."

"You must show me how you do that," Niobe replied.

Patterson opened the door and announced the king and queen's presence.

Niobe smiled as her parents entered the hall. It was rare that they trained as a family. This would be a welcome birthday treat. Something seemed off though. They weren't in training clothes, nor did they look happy. Patterson closed the door and stayed outside. The unseasonable near-freezing temperatures wouldn't bother him in his thick cashmere overcoat.

The king went to the storage area and pulled out two chairs. After placing them opposite each other near an electric heater, he returned and got two more. The king and queen sat next to each other facing the two empty chairs. They motioned for Niobe and Gethan to sit in them.

"My darling daughter," Queen Marigold began. "I can scarcely believe you're now sixteen. You're becoming such a beautiful young woman—the perfect accompaniment to your best asset: your intelligence." For someone giving a compliment, her mother sounded sad.

"What's wrong?" Niobe asked.

"We have some news. It's not good," King John replied.

The queen seemed sad. "You know how I've been coughing a lot—"

"Yes," Niobe replied.

"Well, the scans came back this morning. It's definitely mesothelioma." Her mother dropped her gaze, but Niobe could see tears welling.

"Isn't that what that Crab guy was spreading through his asbestos company?"

King John nodded. "You're oversimplifying it. But yes, he knew it was causing health issues, covered up the evidence and actively campaigned for its increased use. It seems that when your mother and I went to his factory a few decades ago, his publicity stunt of spraying us with the dust was enough for your mother to become sick now."

"What does it mean?" Gethan asked.

"They've given me eighteen to twenty-four months," the queen said.

"To recover?" Niobe asked.

"To live."

Niobe slumped in her chair. No one spoke while they waited for her response. It took over a minute.

"What's going to happen to Crab?" Niobe asked.

"What do you mean?" King John replied.

"How long will he go to jail for?"

"He's been through the courts. He's not receiving a sentence," Gethan said.

"Why? I thought he was guilty."

"There was a technicality. I agree, it's wrong though. I mean, there was a mountain of evidence that even when we were there he'd known about the health issue for a few years," King John said.

The queen scowled. "I won't live to see my daughter get married or meet my grandchildren because he traded lives for money. We should have him executed."

"I feel the same," King John replied.

"Are you serious?" Gethan asked. Niobe thought her parents were joking, but Gethan seemed to think they were actually considering the idea, and he was always much better at spotting lies than her. The monarchs looked at each other and shrugged.

"I guess we are," the queen replied.

"You can't. It would ruin the monarchy," Gethan said.

"We can't," King John agreed.

"We could. It wouldn't be hard to get someone in the military to do it," the queen said.

"That would leave a trail and other people knowing. I mean, what would happen if they told someone. I know they're trained for discretion but, even a drunken hint could let everyone know what we've done. I won't let that be our legacy," King John said.

Queen Marigold scrunched her face. "I hate that you have a point."

"I'll do it," Niobe said.

The queen studied Niobe's face.

"I'll do it," Niobe repeated.

"No," Gethan said.

"No." King John was firm in his response.

"Please, Dad."

"No. I can't use you as an instrument for my revenge."

"What if we waited until after Mum dies, when it truly is regicide. That would give me time to train, and you could see if you still want it to happen."

The queen continued to stare at Niobe. "She could, you know. I think we all admit; she's quite capable of it."

"Gethan, could you train her for that?" King John said. "Your military and martial art experience should've given you the required knowledge. It would only mean a slight difference in focus to what you're doing with her now."

Niobe felt her nerves firing with anticipation. It would be awesome to be able to do it, especially with her parents' approval. That would mean they were embracing her tendencies rather than trying to hide them.

"I could, Your Majesty. Are you sure I should?" Gethan appeared to have misgivings.

King John stroked his chin. "Yes. I think you should."

"This is a mistake," Gethan protested.

Niobe was floored. It was the first time she'd heard Gethan oppose her father.

"Maybe I should leave. It's not—" Gethan said, before King John interrupted.

"Gethan, you know me. So you'll know how I'm feeling about Alban and what he has done to my wife, and how I'm feeling about Niobe losing her mother at such a young age. Plus, we're not the only family so affected. There are literally hundreds of others. They deserve justice, which has so far escaped Alban, too."

"It's not how the monarchy should behave," Gethan said.

"Would you rather us use the military?" the queen interjected.

"No."

"So, let us do this ourselves. Don't quit. Train my daughter as I'd like you to," King John said.

"As you command." Gethan bowed his head.

* * *

NIOBE SHIFTED her focus from the distance back to Jim. "My specialist training began the next day. My mother was one of only seven percent of people who survived for five years. She lived for one month past that milestone. It was only her stubbornness which saw her live that long. From a daughter's perspective, those last three years were horrible. She had no quality of life. Let me repeat, for three years she could barely interact with those around her. Fifteen minutes of talking to me was all she could manage before she'd either descend into coughing or require medical intervention. She'd have fluid drained from her lungs once or twice a week. Her fluid build-up was worse than Dad's. He wound up being diagnosed a month before she died. He never told her."

Jim looked pleased. He must've felt the narrative would help keep the weight of public opinion on her side.

"Well before I was born, my parents thought deeply about what sort of world they wanted a child of theirs to live in. They looked around Tantalia and realised if it was to stand on its own feet as a country, it would need to improve its standard of living and join the EU. They made it their focus to improve the country, to make it worthy. My father, in particular, was driven in this regard. He thought membership of the EU would bring Tantalia acceptance on the world stage, and it has. My hope is that my actions haven't undone that. The evidence to date indicates it hasn't, which I am grateful for. I wasn't meant to get caught, so none of this was meant to happen. At least I can try to turn that into a positive and show off the country through the show."

Jim nodded. "What does it mean to take a life?"

Niobe shook her head. Jim frowned and motioned for the cameraperson to turn off the camera. When the light was off, Niobe replied.

"That's not an easy question to answer."

"Why not?"

"Off the record?" Niobe asked.

"Off the record," Jim replied.

"There are so many layers. In two thousand years, no one will be talking about it. But for now, it's significant. What it means to me is something else, and I'm already on record about how I feel about killing. While I like to discuss ideas and the idea of personal meaning behind taking a life, the arguments don't sound good to people who have a conventional level of morality, where there is the view that if one person gets away with breaking the social contract or law, everyone will; a view which is based on social conventions, and a sense of duty to obey the laws of the land. Any further comment about having risen above such concerns will make me look like a twat, and I already feel weird enough about being on this show. I mean, the ratings from the first episode and those streaming numbers are insane. Nearly a quarter of a billion people have watched the episode. Is it because they're getting vicarious pleasure from the thought of having someone take an action they agree with, but could not take themselves? The meaning of taking the life I intend to has changed significantly in the last week. Suddenly there's a lot more consequence to it. It almost makes me not want to go through with it."

Jim looked horrified. Niobe guessed he was concerned that would ruin his ratings. Probably, his reputation too.

People might think the whole premise was a scam to promote Tantalia. Niobe enjoyed Jim's expression, but kept her own neutral. No need for him to know she was just making sure he thought she was normal rather than a sociopath.

CHAPTER 17

After filming the flashback, Niobe retreated to her bedroom. She called for Patterson to bring her an Irish Cream hot chocolate. Even though it was officially springtime, it was still cool enough for Niobe to look forward to the extra pleasure from the drink's warmth, and the smoothness of its flavour. After she'd changed into her pyjamas and received the drink, Niobe curled up in her armchair and sipped her drink contemplatively. What should she do now? The ratings were well beyond reason. That brought a shift in perspective. As much as Niobe felt she was above the gaze of the public, and her own actions were independent of it, the reality of her situation was that she was in a position of immense influence. Undoubtedly, there would be copycats whose imitation would lead to 'murders and executions' or should that be mergers and acquisitions? Only Patrick Bateman would know. While Niobe knew she could not prevent such acts, she could take action to minimise them. She took out her phone and recorded a video.

"Hello, world. My name is Queen Niobe Allison Andrea Ancora of Tantalia. Recently, I've gained some notoriety for committing two assassinations in defence of my country. The reality show which is recording my preparation for another such act has gone beyond my expectations in terms of its reach. I mean, the producer has told me it's at over half a billion viewers now. I think that's exaggerated the idea of what I'm doing to the extent of misrepresentation. The disclaimer at the start of the show is there for a reason. This is a one-off. I've no intention of repeating the act or targeting anyone else. The third target is the last person who meets the criteria I established, and I hope no more people wind up doing so, because feeling like I have to murder for my country sucks. I know people will think if I can do this, they can too. That is not true. I have immunity; you don't. I have two decades of training; you don't. Leave it to me, or maybe I'll come out of retirement to target you."

Niobe stopped the recording. She'd run it past Jim and get him to upload it tomorrow. Hopefully, the response from Tantalia—her people—would be a call for her to continue.

Niobe sipped her drink and was soon disappointed to see she'd finished it already. There was a knock at her door.

"Come in, Patterson."

Patterson opened the door and gave his usual nod-cum-bow.

"Your Aunt Dahlia is here to see you."

Niobe felt her skin prickle as her hairs stood on end. What could her aunt want? The unexpected meeting could only be to argue a point. Niobe quickly worked out a plan to wrong-foot the duchess.

"I'll meet her in the formal lounge. Please bring me another one of my drinks and whatever she'd like. I'll be there in five minutes, once I've changed into smarter clothing."

Niobe changed from her pyjamas into a pair of leggings and a long-sleeved polo shirt. She bypassed the lift and skipped down the flights of stairs to the fourth floor. A short weave through the maze-like corridor and she found herself outside the formal lounge. The room was brightly lit inside. Usually, the light well leading to the garden below was the source of illumination, but since it was the evening, and the sky dark, special lighting which mimicked daylight would be on in the room. Niobe entered, navigated to an armchair and sat. The room's configuration was designed for flexibility, and the arrangement of chairs was altered according to the guests using the room. Tonight, Niobe and Dahlia's chairs were facing each other, exactly how she'd asked Patterson to arrange them. Each had a coffee table beside it. Dahlia was already sipping a black coffee as Niobe settled into her chair. Dahlia was wearing a form fitting woollen dress. Its medium-brown colour complemented the fairness of her features.

"Thank you for seeing me." Dahlia appeared to be holding her breath. She put the china coffee cup back on its saucer and leant forward with her hands crossed on her knees. Niobe recognised the defensiveness of the position. Dahlia was nervous.

"Of course, Aunty, but also thank you for coming."

Dahlia raised a questioning eyebrow.

"You wouldn't come at this time, uninvited, unless you had something urgent to discuss. Thank you for doing it face-to-face rather than over the phone. It makes it easier to resolve issues when you can see body language as well as hear what someone is saying."

Dahlia visibly exhaled. Niobe was pleased her strategy had worked. "Astute as always, niece. I'll come right out and say it then. I'm unhappy with your TV show. Jim is manipulating you for ratings, and you're putting a very dangerous message out to people that it's okay to kill."

"It can't have been easy for you to make the decision to

come here, so thanks again. As it turns out, I agree. It's gone too far."

Dahlia smiled, and in what Niobe guessed was an unconscious move, opened her arms.

"So, you'll put an end to it?" Dahlia asked.

"I'm certainly considering that idea."

"Considering, or have reached the decision?"

"Considering."

"How can I help you make up your mind?"

"I need time to think. My sticking point is that if I abandon the project, it will cause people who've aligned themselves with my way of thinking to take matters into their own hands against anyone *they* perceive as meeting the criteria. That could be worse than if I go through with the act."

Niobe's argument caused Dahlia to cross her arms again.

"If you kill someone on TV, you'll destroy the monarchy and everything your family has worked decades for."

Something in Dahlia's tone irritated Niobe, and she fired back. "I might remind you I have already killed someone on TV, so I'm pretty sure your conclusion as to the consequences are wrong. Are you more concerned about the monarchy or about being caught in the flack and having your own reputation tarnished?"

The pause before Dahlia's reply told Niobe she'd struck a nerve. Niobe cursed herself for inflaming the situation. What did Sun Tzu say? 'It is the unemotional, detached warrior who wins, not the hothead seeking vengeance, and not the ambitious seeker of fortune.'

"I'm sorry that was uncalled for," Niobe said sincerely.

"You're a perceptive girl. Yes, I'm concerned about my reputation, but my focus is on Ebony, which is why I allowed her to do this, despite knowing I'd cop some flak for allowing my daughter on such a show. She adores the attention she's receiving at school because she's on TV. We've tried to downplay her royal connection, so she can make better friends. While I knew this would bring attention, the level is beyond imagination." Dahlia paused as if considering whether to say more. With a sigh, she said, "She thinks you're the greatest, and her admiration is leading her to feel like she can stand up to people, as you do."

"So, she feels empowered." Niobe felt a warmth spread through her heart. She was inspiring someone. "Isn't that a good thing? Or do you mean she's violently standing up to people?"

"Empowered," Dahlia said reluctantly.

"Don't you want Ebs to be a strong woman?"

"Sure, when she's an adult. As a fifteen-year-old, I want her to be obedient, not defiant."

"Seems reasonable. I can remember the grief I put my parents through when I was her age. I snuck out of the palace a few times to meet boys. It didn't end well. I thought I knew what I was doing and couldn't possibly be wrong. I was, of course, but at fifteen you think you know the world better than your parents."

"She wants to train now."

"To be an assassin?"

"Martial arts and weapons. But I'm fearful it could lead to that."

Niobe shook her head. "She's not the type."

"And you can be so sure?"

"She doesn't have it in her. Gethan's brought in hundreds of people for me to train with over the years. Only a handful had that real killer instinct … they were the ones he brought back."

Dahlia shifted in her seat.

"Ebony doesn't have it in her," Niobe reinforced. "You've raised her well."

"Stop complementing me to curry favour. It makes me think you aren't going to cancel the show."

Niobe took a sip of her drink. It was going cold. She slugged the remainder. "I don't have free rein—"

"Actually, that's exactly what you do have," Dahlia interrupted.

"What I mean is, despite my immunity, I can't just go around killing anyone I choose—"

"But that's what you're doing!"

"No, otherwise I'd be hounded out of my role as queen. We're an established enough country that there are still checks and balances on my power, as there should be."

"But you're killing with impunity."

"No. There are significant consequences to each life I take. They are weighed carefully, cautiously. I expect repercussions because of what I've done. I even expected the vote would go against me; I was intending to abdicate and be tried, and quite probably end my life."

Dahlia rolled her eyes. "Oh please."

"I was prepared for that result. What you don't understand is that I committed the assassinations, as they've been called, despite that."

"Why?"

"Alban and Don Azzure didn't uphold their part of the social contract and were making this country worse. They deserved to die, especially given they had multiple opportunities to atone for their sins. I had the skills and opportunity. That placed the onus upon me to make it happen."

"Which you did," Dahlia said pointedly.

"I did," Niobe acknowledged.

"But you don't feel guilty about it. You broke the law."

Niobe felt sorry for her aunt. Morality, and indeed the world, was not as black and white as she thought. But if Dahlia wasn't capable of understanding an abstract way of thinking about right and wrong, how could Niobe convince her the assassinations were the right thing to do?

Niobe thought about how to help Dahlia realise there were alternatives to her perspective on what was right. The best way she could think of was to use Kohlberg's story of Heinz.

"They were violating human rights. Something I hold dear. Let me tell you a story, then you can ask a few questions."

"Fine."

"Heinz's wife was dying from a particular type of cancer. Doctors said a new drug might save her. The drug had been discovered by a local chemist, and Heinz tried desperately to buy some, but the chemist was charging ten times the money it cost to make the drug, and this was much more than Heinz could afford. Heinz could only raise half the money, even after help from family and friends. He explained to the chemist that his wife was dying and asked if he could have the drug at a cheaper cost or pay the rest of the money later. The chemist refused, saying he had discovered the drug and was going to make money from it. The husband was desperate to save his wife, so later that night he broke into the pharmacy and stole the drug. Do you understand?"

Dahlia nodded.

"Should Heinz have stolen the drug?" Niobe asked.

Dahlia glared at Niobe, then spoke assertively. "The law prohibits stealing, making it illegal. However, a husband should protect his wife and *vice versa,* and he's doing it from a place of love, not with evil intent. Heinz should steal the drug for his wife but also take the prescribed punishment for the crime as well as paying the chemist what he is owed. Criminals cannot just run around without regard for the law; actions have consequences."

"I say Heinz should steal the medicine, because saving a

human life is a more fundamental value than the property rights of another person. Here's a thought for you: Would it matter if he didn't love his wife? What if the dying person was a stranger?"

"I don't think that changes the punishment he should receive. Although, in my mind, it would mean he shouldn't steal the medicine. It's breaking the law for the sake of it, not for someone he loves."

"I see. I'm all out of my drink. How about you? Would you like another coffee?"

"I'm fine."

Niobe pulled out her phone and sent a text to Patterson to bring her another drink. She decided to try a different course with Dahlia.

"What do you think should happen to the chemist? Should the chemist be arrested if the woman dies?" Niobe asked.

"What do you mean?"

"Surely the chemist is culpable if the woman dies. They've been offered a fair, but not market, price for their drug, even offered a payment plan, but they've refused and someone they could have saved has died. Don't they have a moral obligation to act, to save a life? By not acting, shouldn't they experience repercussions too?"

"They haven't broken the law."

"So, they shouldn't be punished?"

"No."

"Hmmph. Okay. Well, as contradictory as it sounds, I see the protection of life as more important than breaking the law against murder," Niobe said.

"You think your assassinations protect lives."

"Exactly. They protect others."

"Doesn't make it right."

"I'll try a different approach. Is being good about reducing suffering and causing the most pleasure and happiness to the greatest number of people, or is it about perfecting your character and developing virtues like fairness, honesty and kindness?"

"How do you see it?"

"Both. I try to reduce suffering whilst developing virtues."

"But if that means taking a life then I don't think you really are," Dahlia said.

"Even if taking a life reduced suffering by many times that which the life caused?"

"You shouldn't kill."

Niobe realised that was Dahlia's fundamental belief.

"I don't think we're going to change each other's minds. Our truths are not the same and are seemingly fixed. I'm sorry we couldn't reach a middle ground. I'm going to go through with the show," Niobe said.

"What? You were seeming against it."

"True. But you helped me realise how important it is for women to feel empowered and, equally, why people need to see me complete the act. Yes, there will be copycats, but I think there will be fewer people than if I didn't complete the project. Besides, you signed the paper for Ebony, saying you wouldn't interfere. Jim won't let you get out of the contract."

"So, you're really not going to stop?"

Niobe's mind flashed to her childhood and her parents giving her permission to kill a rabbit, then later a sheep, 'to get it out of her system'. She added thoughts of Gethan setting her meditations about killing with the stated aim to give that part of her some catharsis.

"Why does everyone keep thinking all I need is a bit of this or a bit of that to get it out of my system? No, I'm not going to stop."

Dahlia scowled. "I will see you have a comeuppance, young lady."

Niobe returned the scowl. "I've got better enemies than you. I'm sorry it's come to this. You were an ally. I hope we can be allies again. Until then you may refer to me as Your Majesty."

Niobe nodded to the door. Dahlia took the hint and left in a huff.

EPISODE FOUR

*J*im seemed anxious when Niobe appeared in the dojo the next morning. As soon as she entered, he rushed across to her.

"I heard Duchess Dahlia came to see you last night."

"She did."

"And?"

"And what? She's my aunt. She's allowed to visit."

"But what did she say about Lady Ebony? Will she prevent her from appearing again?"

"What do you mean? She's finished recording for the show. The episodes have even gone to air."

"Yes, but what if we decide to film more episodes, or another season?"

"This is a one-off. There will be no season two."

Jim's face fell.

"The ratings alone demand it. Not to mention the need for your process to be documented for fairness. It might be worth doing something similar for each future attack. Besides, your fandom will need it."

Niobe thought of the incredible numbers the papers had said watched or commented on the show.

"My fandom? You mean the social influencers you paid to shape opinion?"

"You don't understand. We never activated them. This is all organic."

Niobe caught her breath. What if that was true? She didn't think Jim had lied to her face before, so it was possible.

"Jim, stop it. It's not going to happen," she said after a pause.

Jim turned and walked away, seeming flustered. Niobe was sure she heard him mutter something about her contract under his breath. Niobe told herself to ignore him, as she had to prepare for the assassination, which was planned for that night.

* * *

THE USUAL CAMERAPERSON followed Niobe around for the day. After a short meeting with the Australian and Tantalian Foreign and Prime Minister to help get the talks back on track, Niobe went through her usual training session: basics, partner work and gymnastics. Her new training partner, Nathan, was heavier and taller than Gethan, which made for some useful refinement of her technique.

Niobe ate a couple of sandwiches for lunch. Between mouthfuls, she spoke to the camera. "I normally eat three sandwiches for lunch. I exercise a lot, so need fuel. I'm having one less today, since I'm nervous about tonight." Niobe was really eating less as mild hunger had been shown to boost mental acuity, a throwback to when our ancestors hunted, and hunger meant you might have to get creative to obtain food. "Any coward can shoot someone from a distance, which is why I'm choosing to go in unarmed tonight, even though I can't guarantee my opponent won't afford me the same luxury of eschewing guns, razors and knives. I'll see you in a few hours when my target is likely to be heading home."

"And clear," the cameraperson said after shutting off the recording.

"Thanks."

Niobe and the cameraperson ran through how to setup and use her shoulder camera that evening. Niobe thanked them, asked them to meet her later and then requested to be left alone. Niobe spent time intermittently sitting by the fountain and strolling around the interior garden. It was such a peaceful place and always seemed to help her still her mind, though today she was too excited to feel calm. After an hour, it was time to leave and make further preparations.

* * *

Niobe put the camera in her backpack. It had been designed to film stunts from close up. The lens had image stabilisation built-in and 4K resolution. It was capable of recording two hours of video and had an inbuilt transmitter which would broadcast the video with a fifteen second delay. When the camera was turned on it, the footage would transmit to the broadcast centre and then to live TV. Niobe had told Jim to prepare for her only using the camera for a few minutes here and there as she made her way to her target. The concern was a non-stop broadcast could alert the target, and they'd hide or seek reinforcements. Niobe was only after one person and didn't want any collateral loss of life.

Niobe was driven out of the palace in the seventh of eleven studio cars. Anyone watching the palace wouldn't be sure which car she was in. She was driven towards Tantalia's capital city, Biopolous, but didn't enter the city before two swaps of vehicle. She was dropped off in front of one of the many Biopolous skyscrapers. Niobe slung her backpack over her shoulders and pulled her hoodie over her hair. From the front of the building she could see the cameraperson who'd filmed her that afternoon on the other side of the street. They nodded at her. The target was at home. Niobe held up one finger then two. The cameraperson held up one. The target was alone. Perfect. Niobe pointed to the building behind her, one of the taller buildings in Biopolous, and received another nod. Niobe gave a salute as the only thanks she could think of, then went to the front desk of the building she was in front of. The building manager there was, apparently, an outspoken fan of Niobe's. He told her he'd already unlocked the door to the roof for her as he guided her to the service elevator. He seemed thrilled, rather than scared, when she warned him she'd come back and hurt him if he told anyone or posted anything about his help until after the show. Within a moment, she was alone, heading to the roof of the skyscraper.

* * *

ONCE SAFELY ON THE ROOF, Niobe took the camera out of her backpack and placed it on the small wall which bordered the roof. She turned it on and looked at the lens, while unpacking her backpack.

"My target tonight is someone who has killed five women. It's probable he's killed others. Two of the women he killed were his wives. Each asked for a divorce. Rather than grant it, he beat them to death—a fate that now awaits him. Two of the other women he killed were business rivals, and the last was the prosecutor who brought charges against him. His trial was short, as you can imagine, due to no witnesses being willing to testify. Ample evidence was presented, but without a witness, the trial was abandoned after the court couldn't conclusively demonstrate when the skin cells were deposited on the victim. My target has bragged about getting away with murder and even threatened he'd kill others, like he did his wives."

Niobe began putting pieces of equipment together.

"What I'm assembling here is the zipline I'll be firing and sliding down in a few minutes. Although it's only a distance of fifty metres or so, I won't have a safety harness due to how I need to climb off at the other end, so if I fall, I'm dead. I'd better grip tightly."

Niobe calmly picked up the projectile launcher which would shoot the rappelling hook to the building over the road.

"When they do this in the movies it's always shown as someone shooting a gun or an arrow, and the hook sticks into the side of a building and they get pulled up. That violates reality. If the building is made from concrete, then it's more likely to chip the surface rather than imbed. If it has cladding on it, it may sink in, but it's unlikely to hold the weight of a person. The cracks created around the bullet or arrowhead create a weakness which wouldn't hold a person. Basically, there isn't enough grip of the embedded object to hold the weight. That's why I'm using a hook which is fired to my target building, but securely attached to this one. If the grip fails, I'll swing in an arc against this building. Assuming I'm not too far across, it'll hurt, but if I don't let go, I'll survive. In a best-case scenario, I'd be able to hit the building feet first. I may break an ankle or shin from the impact, but I'll be okay."

Niobe shot the rappelling hook towards the other building. It arced beautifully and landed on the roof, which was about fifty metres lower than the one she was on. Niobe pushed the button on the launcher which drew the cable back. After a moment the anchor 'caught' the building and the line went taut. With a fifty-metre run and fifty-metre drop, it'd be a fast fall to the other building. Niobe clipped the trolley to the cable.

"Here goes nothing!" Niobe picked up the camera and confirmed the image stabilisation was on and set to maximum level. She attached it to the specially designed clip on her shoulder. Her backpack's lower strap clipped around her midsection. She took a small brick of gymnast chalk, the size of a matchbook, from her pocket, and crumbled it in her hands. Its scent brought flashes of her decades spent training in gymnastics. Niobe was pleased she'd brought it as her hands were sweatier than she'd anticipated, but then she was about to do something life-risking. She swung her legs over the side of the building. Gripping the trolley, she took a few deep breaths, reached with one arm under the cable to the grip on the other side, and prepared to drop, knowing there'd be a jerk as her body swung from above the grips to below them.

Niobe felt her grip temporarily loosen as she launched. The chalk was a lifesaver. The ease of the 'drop and go' of the zipline reminded Niobe of the flying foxes she'd been on as a kid. Those had safety harnesses and you simply ran the length of the wire until you hit the block at the end. You'd swing back and forth a little and then someone would help you down. No one would be there to greet her when she reached the building opposite, and the building itself would prevent her from swinging back and forth at the end. All she had as a safety mechanism was a brake.

The brake was activated by pushing a button on either side of the grip. Her heart picked up its pace, just like she did, as she zipped to the other building. Her senses were heightened by the potential consequence of her falling. Niobe counted to control her emotions. One. Two. Three. Four. She pressed on the brake and the trolley came to a stop a few metres short of the building. Niobe released the brake, and the trolley ran until she hit the wall. The thud was relatively gentle. Niobe used her legs to walk up the side of the building until her feet were on top of the edge. Pressing down through her right heel, she swung her left foot around the cable next to it. With both feet on the edge, she shuffled until her bottom was pressed against the polished stone of the top edge of the building. Having spent thousands of hours practicing gymnastics, Niobe was able to swing her body round so the front of her thighs were now face down on the buildings edge, and her body was on top of the wire. She stared at the ground below and told herself it was just an illusion she was up so high. The ground was merely a metre away. Niobe noticed someone nudge the person they were with and point up at her. She smiled as she shuffled back until she was on the rooftop. Hopefully, the diminishing light would mean they'd question what they'd seen.

Niobe located the door leading from the roof into the building. It was one of several doorways, but identifiable by lettering that read *LS1*. The door was locked, and the lock was too sophisticated to be picked easily. Niobe opened her backpack.

"Phew. I'm glad I didn't fall. I think someone saw me, but hopefully they won't raise the alarm. Anyway, as you can see, the door is locked. I can't pick it, so I'll have to use explosives. I'll reimburse the building's owners for the cost of repairs later."

Niobe took out a small wad of plastic explosive and moulded it into shape around the lock. She attached two wires and took backward steps until she was seven metres away. Niobe held up the controller.

"This is the detonator for the explosive. When I push the button, the door will be badly damaged. The aim is to effectively cut out the lock. You can see how I've made a rectangular shape around it. I probably don't need the line in the door jamb, but I'd rather be sure it works first time. I won't have a heap of time from entering the building to reaching my target. He lives in the penthouse below. I should point out, this door doesn't lead to a stairwell, but rather his personal lift. I'll be dropping onto the elevator, using its manhole to enter it, and then pressing the button to open the doors. I'm fortunate that Mr. Gladwell's lift is one that stays at his floor when he's used it. It opens directly into his penthouse. No one else can use it." Niobe realised her slip. "Oops, did I just say his name? Oh, well, if he's watching, he'd better get ready to die."

Niobe hoped the fifteen second delay would give her enough time. She pressed the detonator and there was a loud explosion. When the dust cleared the door was still in its place. Niobe raced over and kicked the door. It didn't go crashing in, instead it rebounded a few millimetres: an equal and opposite reaction. Gripping the edge of the door with her fingernails, Niobe was able pull it towards herself. Jumping through the opening led to a two-and-a-half metre drop onto the top of the elevator. She opened the manhole and dropped to the floor inside the elevator carriage. A quick push of the open-door button and Niobe pressed herself against the back of the elevator. She was primed to push off the wall and launch.

As the door opened, she threw a small flash-bang through the gap and pounced. Unfortunately, it either had taken her more than fifteen seconds, or Mr Gladwell was concerned enough he might be a target that he had anticipated the attack. Bullets raced towards her. Instinctively, Niobe counted the shots. One. Two. Three. The gunman kept firing until his gun was empty. The first three shots were panic firing, and with the distraction of the flash-bang, missed her.

The fourth and fifth hit her in the gut, the sixth hit the clip attaching the camera to her shoulder, so the camera fell along with Niobe. The camera skidded behind Niobe and spun while it broadcast Mr Gladwell's evil grin as he approached. It also showed Niobe's body slumped on the floor with blood pooling underneath it.

CHAPTER 19

When the first bullet hit her, Niobe felt it like a punch. The third, which hit the camera, she barely noticed, but the second caught her just under her ribs on the right side of her body, heading directly for her liver. Dropping to the floor because of the pain wasn't just a reflex response, it was also to take cover. The smell of her own blood flooded her olfactory receptors. She barely noticed Mr Gladwell grab her wrists and drag her into the penthouse. The camera broadcast an image of her blood smearing across the floor as she was dragged from the elevator onto the tiled floor of the penthouse and out of sight.

The pain in her abdomen was strong, but Niobe knew it wasn't life threatening. She'd have some pretty horrible looking bruises for the next couple of weeks. If her liver was bruised too, she'd have to avoid alcohol for a while. The armour she was wearing had done its job. Niobe had always hated when movies showed someone getting shot and flopping to the ground only to get up a few minutes later as though it was some kind of revelation or resurrection. Then the hero would lift up their shirt to reveal a bulletproof vest.

People bleed. There were five litres of blood in the average human. It should've been obvious to the gunman in these movies that the person wasn't dead. A week earlier Niobe had withdrawn just under half a litre of her blood, the amount given in a standard blood donation, and used it to make a vest. The vest held thin sponges, which had been saturated with her blood and a preservative. When the cover was burst by the bullet, a small amount leaked out. Once she fell onto her stomach, more was squeezed out, leading to the pool of blood. It was an effective ruse and would work whether she was shot or stabbed, both of which she'd reasoned were possibilities.

Niobe waited for Mr Gladwell to drop her arms. While she was being dragged it was hard to spring up and surprise him. It was harder to conceal her level of excitement. She was sure her heart was beating loudly enough for him to hear. This was it, the anticipation of a kill, the moment just before the ecstasy of the act.

The moment he let go of her arms, Niobe pressed down and launched herself upwards at him. She shouted a *kiai* as she did so, hoping the tone would resonate in his body and slow his reaction time.

It worked. Niobe's fist caught him in the jaw. She was sure it snapped. She hit him five more times with a flurry of fists. As he stood, dazed, she used her strongest kick, a *mawashigeri* roundhouse to kick him in the head. He crumpled to the floor. Niobe remained standing as the body beside her, badly injured and disfigured but not yet dead, fell to the floor.

After a while, he regained a level of consciousness. Niobe knelt beside him, and he tried to focus his gaze on her. "What are you doing there?" said he at last. "I knew long ago the devil would trip me up. Now he drags me to hell. Will you prevent him?"

"No," Niobe answered, "but there is nothing of where you speak. There is no devil and no hell. Your soul will be dead even sooner than your body. Fear nothing anymore; be at peace as you die."

Mr Gladwell looked up distrustfully. "If you speak the truth, I lose nothing when I lose my life. I'm not much more than an animal who's been taught evil by this world."

"Not at all," Niobe said. "You made hurting women your calling. Now you perish by your calling. For what it's worth, I'll bury you with my own hands."

Niobe felt the now familiar adrenal surge as she felt for Mr Gladwell's carotid pulse on both sides of his neck. She moved her fingers just behind the points and began massaging. This stimulated his vagus nerve causing his heart to slow and, with the technique she used, partially blocked the carotid artery, reducing the fresh blood supply to his brain.

Within twenty seconds, Mr Gladwell lost consciousness. After two minutes Niobe stopped. She waited a few moments then checked his pulse again. Its absence confirmed what his dilated pupils had already told her. He was dead.

Niobe exhaled as she realised she'd been holding her breath. She looked around the penthouse. It was a more luxurious and ornate dwelling than the palace. It seemed so over-the-top.

A sudden noise, the elevator whirring, made Niobe remember the camera and the fact it was still broadcasting. She ran to the elevator, but it was already heading down to the lobby. Emergency services must have called for it. Viewers must have realised where she was and either called help for her or Mr Gladwell.

Niobe returned to the body to check the scene. The broken jaw would make an uncomfortable sight for viewers, but to Niobe it was an expression of her art. She checked him over. It'd only been a couple of minutes, but she swore his body felt cooler. There was a ding as the elevator arrived back at the penthouse. Niobe ran and stood to the side as the doors opened.

"Queen Niobe!" a voice called, sounding panicked. A male paramedic ran past Niobe and into the room.

"I'm here," she said.

"Oh, thank god. I thought he'd killed you." Two female police officers and a second male paramedic exited the lift behind him.

"No. Still living."

"I was watching it on my phone. How aren't you dead?" The paramedic reminded Niobe of a young Gethan. He had the same eyes and build. Was it wrong to feel an immediate attraction?

"I had a bulletproof vest on. I put some blood pouches in front of them so if I was shot it'd look real. It worked too."

"But the TV showed you being dragged out?"

The camera! She'd forgotten about it again. Niobe raced into the lift. The second paramedic handed it to her. She held it out in front of her.

"Uh, I'm okay. Uh, as you can see. Gee, it must have looked horrible. Sorry. Sorry."

One of the policewomen asked what had happened to Mr Gladwell.

"He's around the corner. He's dead," Niobe replied, pointing towards his body.

The woman nodded, and she and the second paramedic went in search of him, while the first paramedic stayed with Niobe.

"What's your name?" she asked him.

"Devin."

Niobe offered her hand. "Pleased to meet you."

They shook hands. Niobe placed the camera on the gurney the paramedics brought with them, removed her armour and placed it next to the camera, leaving the top half of her body covered by only her bra and a crop top. Niobe started to remove the last items.

"Uh, Your Majesty. Umm."

"Really? I thought you guys had seen everything in your line of work."

"But you're the queen. And you're on camera."

Niobe eyes widened as she realised how quickly she wanted to disrobe in front of Devin.

"Fine, I'll just take off the crop top," she said with a wry grin.

Once it was off, the paramedic seemed to hesitate as he looked her over. He's eying me off Niobe realised with a surge of adrenaline. He's attracted to me too. Finally Devin seemed to switch to professional mode and made an assessment of Niobe's injuries. After a minute he said, "You look okay. Those bruises are dramatic, but I don't think they go deep enough to affect your liver or other organs. Short version, no heavy lifting for a week or two while you heal. The bruises will look worse in a day or two, then change colour from purple to yellow."

"I've often wondered why they do that."

"The initial red colour is your blood. They'll then turn a purple colour as the haemoglobin breaks down and changes its structure. This then gets recycled. Some bits more quickly than others; bilirubin, a yellowish pigment, is slowest. Since that's the last to go your bruise ends looking that colour."

"Cool."

The paramedic smiled. Niobe returned the smile and winked at him. "You'd better join your colleagues. I'll say a piece to camera and sign off."

As Devin left, the elevator doors opened to reveal the cameraperson Niobe had met earlier. A red light meant their camera was also broadcasting live, with the feed being switched at Jim's whim. The cameraperson passed Niobe to film Mr Gladwell.

Niobe looked into her camera. "Hi, Tantalia, and, I guess, the world. I nearly died tonight. Without twenty years of training, I would have. I want you to know the meaning of life is found in every moment of living; life never ceases to have meaning, even in suffering and death. My target tonight at his end was concerned by this concept. Mr Gladwell's psychological reactions to dying are not solely the result of the conditions of his life, but also from the freedom of choice he always had, even when causing suffering. I promised I'd bury him, and I intend to keep that promise. I'll be reaching out to his next of kin to ask permission to dig him a grave. The palace will cover all funeral and legal costs associated with what I've done. Actually, scratch that because I should clarify, the money will come from my personal bank account, not the palace."

Niobe paused. Should she say more? What the hell; why not?

"Something I've been thinking about for a while is the meaning of violence. With what I've done, I know what I'm about to say may sound hypocritical. So, I ask you to study a transcription of what I'm about to say before casting judgement. One view of violence is that it is only physical, that an emotional consequence of it cannot be predicted. Evidence for this is shown in how different people will respond to the same act differently. For example, I'm calm now. I'm not suffering for killing another. It's logical to expect me to suffer within for the violence I've committed. Instead, I'm placid because in my mind one thing happens and then another. That's all that ever happens. We can only react to our present circumstances, so that's where I choose to live my life—in the present. This exact moment. Taoists call it *wu wei*."

Niobe thought back to when Gethan had introduced her to the concept. She'd nearly wet herself laughing at twisting the phrase to be 'the way of *wu*.' It had become a running joke between them for a few years. She remembered Gethan showing her a kata when he was in the moment versus when she was thinking about other things. The difference was subtle but perceptible. When Niobe realised how hard the demonstration was to perform, to be able to switch modes that efficiently, it was the moment she realised Gethan was a true master. She'd started taking his training more seriously afterwards. She'd been seventeen at the time.

It suddenly hit Niobe how much she missed Gethan. Where was he now?

"Sorry, I'm getting off track. Another view of violence is that it demonstrates human frailty. For all our sophistication as a species, for all our progress: social, spiritual and techno-logical, we still succumb to this most basic and base response. Others say this fact alone means it's part of human nature and should be embraced and trained so it can be controlled. My view is this: it's something that exists. Full-stop. If I try to give it more meaning than that, I'm distorting what it is and that distorts the concept. Sorry for the repetition. I know I'm rambling a bit. What I mean to say is it becomes something else, something harder to respond to, harder to put an end to. It stops you directly experiencing the reality of the situation, of the act. I'll shut up now. I'm sorry if anyone was alarmed when it seemed as though I was dead. Goodnight."

Niobe turned off the camera. She took a deep breath, winced with the pain from her abdomen, and exhaled, suddenly feeling extremely tired.

CHAPTER 20

Niobe stuck around while the scene was analysed by the police. She answered all their questions, even though it was unequivocal what had happened, and they couldn't charge her anyway. She even helped the building manager patch the door, so it would be secure until it could be fixed. She enjoyed a chat with Devin, who was also hanging around. He told her he was a fan of the show and appreciated what Niobe was doing. He seemed to understand her reasoning for killing Mr Gladwell. Devin wrote down his phone number for Niobe, arguing it was simply so she could contact him with any follow-up questions about her treatment. This was amusing. Surely he knew how transparent he was being?

When Niobe arrived back at the palace she went straight to bed. As she fell asleep she found herself with a half-smile as she recalled her conversation with Devin. He really reminded her of a young Gethan.

* * *

AWAKENING the following morning after a small sleep-in, Niobe wandered down to the dining room rather than calling for Patterson to bring her breakfast. She was surprised to see Jim waiting for her. How had he known she would go there? How had he got in? Niobe remembered the pass he'd been allocated gave him access to much of the palace. She held her bruised stomach as she gingerly sat down at the metre square dining table. Years ago, she'd asked for it to be brought to the room, and she always chose it when dining alone. The main dining table was huge, and she felt silly sitting by herself at a table which could seat fourteen people. Jim immediately brought over a seat from the main table and sat opposite Niobe.

"Geez, Jim, I haven't even had breakfast or coffee yet. Can't it wait?"

"No."

"Remind me why I gave you a special pass?"

"You like me."

"I'm tired, hurting and hungry. You know my skill set; do you really want to piss me off?"

Jim smiled and proceeded as though what she'd said meant nothing. With a sigh, Niobe realised his behaviour reminded her of herself at sixteen. It was how she'd treated Gethan. It was only now she realised how much it must have annoyed him. He'd hidden it well.

"When people thought you died, social media lit up with support for your actions. People really wanted you to succeed. They love what you're doing."

"So what? A thousand people say, 'go for it my queen,' and you think that's a big deal. Go away and let me have my breakfast."

"No, Your Majesty, it was millions, sorry, tens of millions of people. You're a global phenomenon."

"Ughh. I repeat, so what?"

"You have to do another show."

"An aftermath dissection? No thanks."

"But people want, or rather need, to know if you and Devin are going to work out. Really great of you to give in on the love interest thing."

"What on earth are you talking about?"

"Your flirting with Devin. There was a twitterstorm and Instagram tsunami in response. People think you'll make a great couple. You're a meme now."

Niobe picked up her knife. "I said no to a love interest. Don't make me stab you. Go away."

For the first time Jim seemed to hesitate.

"Now," Niobe said in her most commanding voice as she pointed to the door. Niobe watched Jim's body language slump as he stood and turned to walk away. She was sure it was an act, but acquiesced anyway. "Come back in half an hour," she said.

Jim immediately straightened his shoulders and sprang out of the room.

* * *

EXACTLY HALF AN HOUR LATER, Jim returned to the dining room. Niobe had just had enough time to read the three newspapers waiting for her and eat her eggs on toast. Today the chef had added smoked salmon, spinach and mushrooms. He must've thought she needed extra nourishment. The newspapers were filled with the story of Niobe's third assassination. Some of the reports, as well as the editorials, seemed to be written from the perspective of approval. The most noticeable exception was Drysen Silic. He wrote another lengthy op-ed criticising the queen and calling for his readers to boycott royalty by not celebrating any royal event or national day, and he encouraged them to write to their local parliamentarians to protest against her actions. When Patterson collected the newspaper from her he said, "I won't bother sending Drysen a warning from you."

"Why not?" Niobe replied.

Patterson pointed to the fresh dents in the table and to her knife. "You've stabbed him enough times already."

* * *

Niobe was surprised by the social media reports, which were largely positive, and she wondered if Jim had started rigging the system. Somehow, the papers had already collected several 'your say' messages and compiled them into a half-page spread. A recurring theme was disappointment in not being able to see the actual kill and only glimpses of Mr Gladwell afterwards. There were several comments suggesting Niobe must've been 'hot to trot' when meeting Devin, so hot she had to take her top off to cool down. Niobe liked the play on words, although it did give her pause. Was she interested in Devin in that way? They'd got on well with each other, and both had used long words when talking to each other. Gethan had shown her research which concluded that men speaking to women in that way were trying to impress them with their intelligence and therefore suitability as a mate. But women only did that when they thought their date was a long-term prospect, otherwise they played dumb and used small words so their date wouldn't feel threatened.

While it was an entertaining study, Gethan had meant it as a means of discouraging Niobe from trying to get time alone with the boy she liked back then. He pointed out that when he'd chaperoned their first date, Niobe had sounded nothing like the fiercely intelligent young woman she was, and that concerned him. He didn't want her going too far with the boy, as he saw it as being her equal and opposite reaction to the news of her mother's diagnosis. She had enough to worry about without adding an unintended pregnancy or scandal to her list. Niobe reminded Gethan he wasn't her father, and snuck out anyway to meet the boy. He was the one who'd tried to rush things and suffered the consequences. She felt guilty for not listening to her mentor. The next day Gethan had noticed something was wrong straightaway. He asked if there was anything he needed to know. She told him it hadn't gone how she'd hoped, but that the boy wouldn't bother her again and there was nothing to worry about.

Gethan had given her that look which said are you sure?

"Fine, I kneed him in the groin, hard, and hit his sternum and neck. He walked away. Okay? I restrained the urge to break a bone or two. At worst he'll have a bruise on his neck. He'll probably say it was a hickey. I wanted to do more, much more, but I didn't. I don't think he suspected how much danger he was in, okay?"

After a shrug from Gethan, they started training and that was the end of it, although Gethan had told her parents, who'd had a long talk with her about the need for her to conceal her predatory desires, both sexual and homicidal, to protect the monarchy. "Boys," Gethan had told her, "could be your undoing." What would Gethan make of the way she interacted with Devin? Niobe frowned. She still wanted Gethan's approval, and that irritated her. Wasn't she above that now?

Jim approached Niobe's table and sat opposite her. He immediately ordered a coffee from Patterson as though at a café. Niobe wondered if he ever changed his behaviour in accordance with his surroundings.

"You know what, Jim? It's just occurred to me the paper barely reported on how we're going with negotiating the trade agreement with Australia. That should be front page news."

"Ah, my dear, but that would mean you wouldn't be! And that would be a travesty since you've broken the record for the most watched show in television history."

"Surely you care about more than ratings? I mean someone died."

Jim looked properly ashamed for the first time Niobe could recall. It was brief, and almost immediately replaced with his usual smirk, but it was there.

"How do you remain so grounded?" Jim asked.

"If you'd had my training, you'd realise it's not optional for me."

This seemed to strike a nerve with Jim, and he was quiet for a moment. "Something you said when Lady Ebony interviewed you struck me."

"What?"

"That you couldn't announce the target before the kill."

"Yes?"

"I can't stop thinking about it. How awesome would it be if you announced the target in your first episode?"

"This was a one-off."

Niobe realised his silence a moment ago was actually due to him needing to change his plan for what he was about to propose. He was so used to dealing with starlets he probably thought she'd be caught up in the fame and that's how he'd sell her on the second series. It was like he had only just realised she'd lived her whole life in the spotlight.

"Yes, but think about the challenge. What if they knew you were coming? What if they had a chance not only to defend themselves in a fight, but beforehand to state why they shouldn't be a target, or maybe even confess to their crimes? It would counter all the criticism of you as a self-righteous executioner."

Niobe couldn't help herself. The idea *was* intriguing. What if this target had a formal chance to repent?

"This was meant to be a one-off." She heard her voice waver. Was that because she'd, once again, enjoyed the rush of killing? "Besides, I don't have any targets in mind."

"I do," Jim said quietly.

Niobe felt her face ask the question her mouth didn't: who?

"How about Jork Dressov?"

Jork was the president of the neighbouring country of Autarchos, which had a population of around two million people. It was separated from Tantalia by a section of the Paine River. Niobe recalled the PM talking about how her father had wanted to make peace with Jork, but had been rebuffed by the dictator.

"That's another country."

"I know, but he's a brutal autocrat and responsible for the deaths of tens of thousands. NATO haven't been effective in curbing his power through sanctions. He'll kill again to protect his regime. The fact his country borders yours means it does affect Tantalia. He meets all your criteria, including being an arsehole."

"But interfering with the government of another country is an act of war."

Jim seemed surprised. "I'll admit I hadn't thought of that."

"No, you only thought about the TV ratings his profile would bring."

Jim shrugged. "But will you do it?"

"You are incorrigible. *It's war.*"

Jim grinned. "I'm not hearing a no."

"*No.*" Niobe shook her head for extra emphasis and pointed to the door. This time Jim went straight out.

CHAPTER 21

Niobe entered the graveyard with some trepidation. Not because of superstition, but because she was there to meet Mr Gladwell's family. The exclusive cemetery cost upwards of half a million per plot, and Mr Gladwell had three next to each other. He was survived by his sister, Elaine, and seventeen-year-old son, Taschen. Both were estranged from him.

Niobe met them at the burial site. Elaine displayed the timidity of a lifetime of being bullied by her brother. Something she'd never resolved. Taschen was an interesting looking kid. To Niobe's eye it seemed as though there was some fire there, but that it might take some getting out. Niobe introduced herself to them.

"Uh, we know who you are," Taschen replied.

"She was just being polite," Elaine said.

"I know, Aunty, I just thought…"

Taschen seemed to get on about as well with his aunt as she did with hers.

"Please. It's okay. I'm sorry to bring you here under these circumstances. I know it's my fault," Niobe said.

"Look, we're not upset with what you've done. But we can't condone it either," Taschen said.

"I understand. I promised your father I'd bury him. I'd like to volunteer to dig his grave."

"His funeral is not for another week," Elaine said.

"I'd still like to do it," Niobe replied.

"Now?" Taschen asked.

"Whenever suits. It can be now, or another day some time before the funeral, so it's ready."

"You mean so the media can be alerted?" Taschen said.

"No. This is between us. I haven't told anyone I'm here. This is a private moment."

"Hmph." Elaine uncrossed her arms. "Can I watch?"

Niobe tilted her head. "Sure." It seemed an odd request.

"Would you do it now?" Elaine asked. "I need to imagine him in the ground. I need to be able to picture exactly where he'll rot."

Niobe shrugged. "Okay. Give me a couple of minutes to find someone to get a spade. I know they usually use a digger for it, but a spade seems more fitting."

Niobe left and went to find a groundsperson.

RETURNING TO THE GRAVE, carrying a bag with a water bottle and sandwich in one hand, and a shovel in the other, Niobe was surprised to see Elaine and Taschen hadn't moved. They remained huddled next to each other. Elaine nodded to Niobe. Niobe knew it would take her around seven hours to dig the grave, more if there was a lot of clay. She started her work. The first few minutes hurt a lot due to the bruising on her abdomen, and Niobe wondered if she'd be able to complete the task. The pain mellowed as she went on, or at least that's what she told herself. The truth was, it was probably more like she got better at tuning it out. Elaine and Taschen stood silently watching her for half an hour before they went to get a coffee. They offered to get her one too.

The next two hours after that were relatively easy. Niobe was thankful she was highly athletic and had enough stamina for the job. It became harder the more time passed. Niobe tried a mindfulness meditation while she worked, but found the more tired she became, the more her thoughts turned to Devin. Should she contact him? He would be useful to tend to her injuries, since she was sure all this activity was making them worse. Perhaps he could check to make sure she hadn't.

By the time she finished the hole was deeper than her head. Elaine and Taschen had come and gone a few times. The last time they thanked her for her show of penance. Niobe was grateful to observe Taschen sneaking a couple of photographs of her at work every hour or so. She'd not alerted the press to her actions but hoped word of her deed would get out. Surely someone would notice the royal car out the front? This was a story she wanted the world to see as it would reinforce her stated desire for peace and make her seem like an amazing human being.

It'd taken Niobe another hour to finish. By the end she'd really felt for those people in centuries past who'd held the job of gravedigger. It was damn hard work. No wonder Shakespeare's gravediggers in *Hamlet* told jokes. It'd be the only way back then to distract you from the physical impact of the job.

Niobe stopped to think about how she'd climb out of the hole. She could call her security detail who were in the car out the front, monitoring movement into and out of the cemetery; she could just reach up to the edge and pull herself out. Both would be boring. Instead, she placed the shovel lengthways across the narrow edge of the grave, stood with her back to it, reached her arms up and with an underhand grip, raised her legs and torso, so they flipped her over the edge. Her hair brushed against the side of the grave. It was already so covered in dirt that she didn't care. She nearly got stuck part way as her arms barely had any strength left in them. As she struggled with the push, she recalled Gethan once lining up thirty people for her to fight for a minute each. By twenty minutes she could barely breathe, let alone move, but she found a way to keep going. One of her proudest moments in martial arts was when she knocked out her second to last opponent, a man who was bigger than her and who hadn't seen her flailing *haito*, ridge-hand strike, until it was too late. With a loud *kiai* shout, Niobe forced her way out. When she was safely out of the grave, she burst out laughing. What was she trying to prove by doing that?

THAT EVENING, after a hot bath and having taken a couple of painkillers for the first time in years, Niobe felt like she was becoming human again. For the last hour it'd felt like she'd run a marathon. It helped that she'd called Devin. He was going to visit to check her injuries, even though that was normally a doctor's job.

Niobe was in the meeting room when Patterson brought her an Irish Cream hot chocolate. He lingered after handing it to her.

"What's up?"

Patterson smiled and pulled a phone from his pocket. "I rewound the news and paused it here for you." He pressed play and handed her the phone.

Morgan Henry was interviewing Taschen outside the cemetery.

"We have here the son of the person our queen removed

from our society yesterday. Taschen, why don't you tell us what has happened here today?"

Taschen appeared awkward in front of the camera. He maintained his focus on Morgan, so Niobe assumed there were no other journalists around.

"Queen Niobe asked to meet us here, at our family's plot. She said she told my dad she would bury him with her own hands, and so she offered to dig his grave for us."

"You mean she meant what she'd said? But we're only here because we recognised her car. She hasn't alerted the media," Morgan said.

Niobe delighted in the question. There was only one possible response, and it would make her look good.

"Yeah. She was really focused on this being between us. She stuck to her word about digging it, and was humble and sorrowful for the whole day."

"You mean she spent the whole day here?"

"Digging the grave. Yeah, she did … I even caught some on video."

"Can you show us?"

"Sure." Taschen brought up the video on his phone and played it for Morgan. It was from towards the end of the day, so Niobe was practically underground. She was covered in dirt, sweaty and dishevelled, but her muscles rippled as she dug, and there was a particular attractiveness to her appearance. From a PR perspective it was TV gold.

Morgan looked delighted. It was the second time she'd been given such a scoop on the queen.

"The whole day?" Morgan repeated.

"Yeah, she's been here for six or more hours now. She's still going too. She barely let up in her digging. It was amazing to watch. She really is repentant. We'd already forgiven her for what she did to my family but do so doubly now."

Morgan beamed as the report ended. Niobe mirrored the action.

"Patterson, did you tell Morgan about my work today?"

Patterson allowed his smile to betray him, then exaggerated his response. "Why, Your Majesty, weren't you watching the video? The palace had refused to release details of your whereabouts today. How Morgan came to know exactly where you were is anyone's guess."

"Thank you. It will help the narrative that I'm a normal woman driven to extremes," Niobe said, returning his phone.

"You mean rather than an extreme woman who is creating a new normal," Patterson said with a grin.

"Exactly."

"Well, let's just keep that between us, Your Majesty."

"Thanks. I probably haven't said it enough, but your support means a lot."

Patterson's expression was pleased. A buzz sounded and he looked down at his phone.

"The fact you've registered I'd like hearing that shows me how much you do, in fact, acknowledge my support. Thank you. Now, I need to go let someone in to see you. I'll return soon."

Patterson shuffled out of the room.

* * *

WHEN THE DOOR opened and Patterson entered, Niobe smiled, waiting for him to introduce Devin. Instead, he announced that Jim was here to see her. Niobe scowled and reminded herself to cancel his access to the palace now the series was over.

Jim grinned as he greeted Niobe, but she wasn't sure if it was devious or self-satisfied. Maybe both?

"Your Majesty." He greeted her with a slight bow. He definitely wanted something, as he wasn't usually so formal.

"Jim, cut the act and cut the crap. I'm stiffer and sorer than I've been for years after digging a grave for Mr Gladwell today."

Jim's face fell. "Please tell me you took a camera and got some footage?"

Niobe realised he hadn't seen the news yet. She decided to pretend that was also the case for her, so she rolled her eyes. "It was between me and his family. Not for the public. Tell me what you want."

Jim took a deep breath. Niobe saw the intake and told her brain to fire up. He was about to launch into something.

"I made some enquiries today that have yielded some fantastic results. I think you might be interested in what they might mean. They relate to our conversation about Jork Dressov."

Niobe pointed to the door. "I'm too tired, Jim."

Jim didn't bat an eyelid. "I spoke to Jork's personal secretary, basically his version of Patterson. I met her a few years ago when I did a sci-fi show set on another planet. We filmed at the Autarchos' copper mine. It looked other-worldly. In my call I emphasised this was an off-the-record and private conversation between myself and her. In other words, I didn't bring you into the conversation."

"I don't like where this is going."

"All I did was say I was the showrunner for *Sovereign Assassin,* and I was wondering if Jork might consider fighting you to the death. You know, since he likes to post all those judo videos of himself and portray himself as a killer."

"You did what?" Niobe's voice had an icy edge she rarely heard herself use. She'd trained with Gethan to conceal it.

"Jork's secretary called me back and said he'd do it."

"That's because killing me would cement his power."

"But it won't because you'll beat him."

"Jim, listen to what I've just said. If he kills me, no one in his country will rise to overthrow him. He'll also rally other dictators around him. It could start a war, not just with Tantalia, but world war three. You're a lunatic."

"No. It wouldn't come to that."

"Sorry, but that's bullshit, and I suspect you know that."

"But you'll win."

"That's not the only possibility. As Sun Tzu said, 'defeated warriors go to war first and then seek to win'. I win by not going to war."

"But you will win. I've seen how hard you train."

"As Musashi said, 'the ultimate aim of martial arts is not having to use them'."

"My contact says Jork is willing to provide assurances that whatever the outcome it would simply be a contest and regardless of the outcome he would not pursue further action against Tantalia."

"That's all well and good, but what about his regime?"

"Them too. But when you win, the regime will change."

"But someone will replace him."

"And you can apply a pressure on them no one else can."

Niobe admitted to herself the idea was tempting. It could have huge benefit to the region. The EU and NATO had been trying to oust Jork for nearly a decade. It would be a near-bloodless coup and avoid the consequence of war if handled well.

Niobe shook her head. "Leave now. Or I will hurt you."

"I'll go if you promise to think it over."

Niobe sighed and pushed her feeling of frustration with Jim down. "Fine."

Jim left immediately, seeming to skip out of the room.

*　*　*

NIOBE COULDN'T STOP THINKING about Jim's proposal. She knew how hard her parents had tried to draw international attention to some of the atrocities Jork had committed. He'd had two opposition leaders executed and had sent their grieving families to jail. Other dissenters had disappeared or been jailed. He'd suppressed free speech and promoted the killing of babies with deformities. He certainly was an arsehole.

Niobe took out her phone and looked him up for further details. He'd had more military experience than she realised and was in good shape for someone in their mid-fifties. There were several recent clips of Jork displaying prowess in judo. He seemed like a larger, uglier version of Gethan. Her previous victims hadn't seemed like such a trophy. Only Don had experienced proper fights before, but he certainly wasn't trained, and she'd caught him off guard. How awesome would it be to take on someone like Jork. Someone as cold-blooded as she was?

For the majority of her training with Gethan, Niobe hadn't understood why she'd been made to memorise great chunks of martial art texts. One day, Gethan had explained that the purpose was twofold. The first was to expand her mind. "Research," Gethan said, "has shown that you can increase your working memory through memorising many long passages of text. This gives you the ability to consider more ideas at once, make links others can't and improve your critical thinking." The second reason was to make their wisdom accessible to guide action at any point in time. The words of Musashi came to her. 'You must understand that there is more than one path to the top of the mountain', and 'Do nothing which is of no use'. Fighting Jork would be useful if she succeeded, because it would solve decades of impasse in generating change in Autarchos.

There would need to be iron-clad assurances on both

sides to prevent war, though. Niobe wasn't sure what form they'd take. Maybe a commitment to a new election in Autarchos, overseen by NATO, regardless of the fight's outcome. If Jork won, he'd likely secure the majority of the vote without having to use his military as he had at the last election eight years ago, so that could be a selling point. Niobe wondered what Jork would demand in response.

CHAPTER 22

Niobe took a sip of her drink. It was cold and unappetising. Patterson knocked, entered the meeting room, and announced Devin had arrived. Devin trailed behind him. Niobe felt her heart rate increase as she admired Devin's physique. She guessed he was in his late twenties. His hair was a similar brown colour to her own, and his face was quite symmetrical with warm, hazel eyes. She was, once again, reminded of the version of Gethan she'd met as a child. Devin seemed equally pleased to see her. He smiled and held their handshake for just a fraction too long, as though wanting the physical contact.

Patterson guided Devin to the chair opposite Niobe. Niobe looked at her mug on the coffee table and asked Patterson for a new drink. He nodded and asked if Devin would like anything.

"What are you drinking?" Devin asked.

Niobe told him.

"Sounds good. May I have one too, please? I've not had one of those before. It'll be a new experience."

Niobe admired the manners he'd used and that he'd

ordered the same drink as her on a whim. Patterson dutifully turned and left to get the drinks.

"Thank you for inviting me here. I was hoping you'd call."

"Oh yes?" Niobe raised an eyebrow.

"To see how you were healing," Devin said with a sly grin.

"Well, let me show you." Niobe stood up gingerly. Despite the soothing bath, she was still worn out. She lifted her top to reveal her abdomen. Most of it was purple from bruising. The effect highlighted her scar.

Devin carefully examined her. "That looks worse than before."

"I spent nearly eight hours digging a grave for Mr Glad-well today. I may have aggravated the injury."

"I'll say. There's fresh blood mixed in there."

"It had to be done."

"Are you sure?"

"Yes."

"Today?"

"Maybe not, but yes."

Patterson returned with their drinks and they both returned to their chairs. With a shy smile, Devin offered up his mug for a toast.

"To new experiences," he offered. They clinked mugs.

"To new experiences," Niobe replied.

* * *

DEVIN ASKED Niobe about various injuries she'd had. She described all the accidental cuts and contusions she'd acquired, particularly from weapons. She showed him her scar and told him it was from a sword training accident. That was her worst injury, so far.

"I'm fortunate not to have broken any bones. I've only had

bad soft tissue injuries. Enough of me though. What about you? What are the worst injuries you've seen?"

Niobe leant forward in her chair. This would be exciting. He must have seen some extreme things. Niobe recalled some of the images she'd been shown when she'd completed parts of the paramedic course. They were graphic but not as extreme as she'd hoped.

"The absolute worst was a man who was high on PCP who'd punched through a mirror."

"Why was that so bad?"

"He picked up the broken glass and started cutting his skin off. By the time we got to him he'd flayed most of a forearm, part of one leg and was just making a start on his cheek."

"He wouldn't have called the ambulance though, I mean if he was high?"

"No, but his Shih Tzu was going nuts barking, and a neighbour from the next apartment went to knock on the door to see what was up."

Niobe wanted to interject and tell Devin how since she was a little kid she hadn't been allowed to have a pet because she couldn't be trusted with one, but she bit her lip to make herself stop.

"The door was ajar and when they pushed it open they could see blood pooling under the bathroom door. They didn't even open it, just ran back to their apartment and phoned the emergency line."

Niobe had to know. "What did it look like?" Thankfully, Devin didn't seem concerned by her question.

"It was horrific, and that's not a word I think I've used in a sentence since … well for a very long time. There was blood everywhere. He resisted us too, but after the exertion of pushing us away and trying to go back to peeling his face, he passed out. It wasn't as though he'd just hacked randomly at his arm either. He'd made some deep cuts and peeled the skin back like—"

"Oooh, like skinning a rabbit."

Devin looked at her quizzically.

"Biology class," Niobe said quickly. She'd nearly said too much.

"It was so hard to know how to treat. I think that's what made it stick with me so much, that rush of decision making. I'm used to deep cuts, or even amputations, but this was something else. Was I meant to pick up the skin from the floor and do something with it like an amputation? Put gauze on the open wound, which just seemed an odd thing to do that deep inside the body. We put gauze over skin not under it. It just seemed like any option wasn't ideal. In the end though, that's what we did: gauze, compression bandage and green whistle."

"Green whistle?"

"An Australian invention which contains methoxyflurane, a pain reliever. Half a dozen breaths on the whistle relieve strong pain almost instantly. It's good for half an hour, just enough time to get the person to hospital for proper anaesthesia. Your trade deal was going to make them cheaper."

"It's being resurrected. The PM has sent their Foreign and Trade Ministers to meet with Zack next week. Apparently, the public opinion of me in Australia has changed with the show. I hate to admit it, but the guy who talked me into it was right."

"Awesome! So, will you do another show to improve things further?"

Niobe told Devin about Jim's efforts to get her to fight Jork Dressov.

"He's a legitimate killer, though," Devin said.

"I know. All the people I've faced so far have been untrained. He would be a challenge, if I accepted."

"Why wouldn't you? I think he meets your criteria."

Niobe realised this meant he'd followed her since before the show. The criteria weren't covered in detail on *Sovereign Assassin*, since they didn't want to promote the idea that if you thought someone met them you should execute them.

"It could start a war," Niobe said.

"It could also prevent one. Eventually, the EU will up sanctions and force Autarchos to up its relationship with other despotic countries. At some point, one of them will declare war against someone, and the others will back them up, since they really have no choice."

"An interesting take on things."

"If you remove Dressov though, you can help shape the new regime."

"I think you mean our PM can do that with me in the background."

"Okay, but let's say war is inevitable. If you remove Dressov and open up relations with the country, then you can at least reduce the despotic presence in this region. Who knows? Best-case scenario, you might cause other countries to change their ways. I mean you'd become the bogeyman, er, woman. You know. Change your ways or the Sovereign Assassin will get you."

Devin laughed. Niobe liked the way he did it. She found herself thinking how charming he was. He had a point as well.

"Food for thought. So, while I ponder it, why don't you tell me about yourself."

"I'm twenty-eight. Favourite colour is blue. Cats not dogs."

Niobe concealed a frown. She remembered something Gethan had told her about ways of judging people you're thinking of letting close to you. *Always go for dog people.* Be cautious about cat people. This wasn't to say don't let them in, just to be aware they won't form bonds as easily. The reason, he explained, was that dogs naturally release five times the level of oxytocin, the hormone that promotes bonding, compared to cats. That was why dogs were always pleased to see their owners; they really did feel love for them. Gethan's theory was that people prefer the animal they're most like. So, if a person preferred cats, they may not be as eager or able to form the long-term bond of affection a dog person could. It was just a theory, Gethan had said at the time. Something for Niobe to think about.

"Uh, favourite pastime is to go kayaking on the Paine."

"Why?"

"I like the solitude and the challenge of some sections. I really like the silence. That may not make sense, but what I mean is the lack of man-made background noise. No cars, music, computers and so on. It's peaceful."

Niobe nodded. She felt the same way about her time in the central garden. It was as though her brain stopped trying to interpret speech in everything it heard and relaxed, which helped switch off the hypothalamus, pituitary and adrenal response to her environment.

Niobe smiled. "I'll drink to that." She held up her mug and they clinked them again. Gethan seemed to be wrong about cat people. Devin was clearly someone who appreciated the odd bit of quiet time that a young dog would prevent through its constant demand for walks and playtime.

"So, what's your happiest memory?" Devin asked.

"It occurred about a year ago…" Niobe began.

* * *

NIOBE AND GETHAN had completed their training for the morning and were sitting down for their usual philosophical conversation and meditation, when Niobe's father entered the dojo. Patterson helped him make his way over. Niobe was pleased to see her father well enough to make the journey from the palace to the hall. It was uncommon these days.

Niobe ran over to give him a hug. Afterwards, she led him by his hand to where they'd been seated. "Will you join us?"

"If I may?" The king looked at Gethan, who smiled.

"I'm at your command. It would be an honour."

A nod from the king was sufficient to get Patterson to wait outside. Niobe was amused at Gethan's formal tone, which he always adopted with the king when other people were around. It often struck her as being odd as the two were close friends. She'd asked her father about it once, and he'd said Gethan dropped the formality in private, but only then.

They sat cross-legged facing each other, in a triangle.

"Gethan, Niobe, I'm curious about your response to something I've been puzzling over," King John said. "Really, it's just two questions, but the answers I have seem paradoxical. The first question is this: Can your perception of reality ever not be subjective?"

"No," Gethan said. "All stimuli are converted to electrical and chemical signals, which are then filtered and combined in the brain before we perceive them. We don't experience the raw signal directly, so we don't experience reality directly. We run a simulation of reality in our minds, which is the best bet our mind can make as to what that should be. That's why we can't perceive impossible colours. Reality isn't the illusion, our perception of it is. So, it is always subjective. The goal is to reduce that subjectivity as much as possible by eliminating our biases and retraining our brains to make them process more of the incoming stimuli."

"A fine answer and one which I'd also considered." The king looked at Niobe. "My 'Bee, did you follow what Gethan said?"

Niobe nodded and felt herself roll her eyes just a little bit.

Of course she knew that. It had formed the basis for chunks of her training.

King John addressed Gethan once more. "Okay then. The second question is this: If you could experience reality objectively, what would that mean?"

"You'd go from running a simulation of reality to direct interaction with it. What would change? I think—"

"The purpose of much of my training is to find meaning in the smallest thing, while also trying to eliminate thought biases which might otherwise colour that meaning, effectively trying to remove personal meaning," Niobe interjected. "Your argument supposes objectivity and subjectivity contradict or better yet contraindicate each other. I'm not sure that's right. I mean when Gethan punches me, I feel it. My body moves from the impact. That's objective. The meaning I attach is the subjective bit. I might be angry with him for it, or myself, for not parrying it, or I may not react at all."

"In that model are reflexes then a response to objective reality? And the pain signal reaching the brain when it becomes subjective?" King John questioned.

"Yes. So, you can have both. But I think you're both missing something."

King John smiled at his daughter. "What's that?"

"The question 'If you could experience reality objectively what would that mean?' is unimportant. I think you're not asking the right question, and the right question is why is the subjective experience of reality universal? Wait let me phrase that better. Why do we add subjectivity to what could be an objective experience?"

The king and Gethan looked at each other. Niobe wasn't sure if it was in amusement or admiration.

"To my mind, it's universal because as per the rules of evolution, it confers a survival advantage, so is selected for. A direct experience is therefore inferior."

"Go on," Gethan said.

"Subjectivity leads to diversity, a key criterion for evolution, greater adaptability, which is also important, and could theoretically help drive speciation."

"How?" the king asked.

"A lot of animals display fixed action patterns," Niobe replied.

She tried not to smile at the recollection of when her biology teacher had taught her about them. He kept referring to them as FAPs, apparently not realising that was a slang term for masturbation. Niobe had laughed a little too much when the teacher had said, 'It's thought that humans don't have any FAPs', and been told off for her behaviour. She'd not been able to bring herself to tell the teacher why she was so amused, although she'd told Gethan about it the next day. She'd loved that he hadn't known where to look as she spoke about masturbation. Teasing him was so much fun.

"If the subjective interpretation of the pattern differs then some members of a species are more or less likely to be mated with, because the female finds one display subjectively more appealing than another. Which can lead to division within a population—some attracted to some movements versus others. Assuming two populations are separated then over time, and generations, the division could be large enough that the groups are no longer able to mate with each other as their action patterns would be too different for them to feel an attraction to start mating. Similarly, being able to see a stick and see it as a tool for getting termites out of a termite mound to eat, or a building tool, versus it being just a stick, could confer a survival advantage. Therefore subjectivity drives evolution."

"I think you're getting the hang of Musashi's maxim: 'Think lightly of yourself and deeply of the world,. I'm impressed," King John said. With some effort, the king stood.

Niobe and Gethan did the same. King John held out his arms and Niobe leapt up for a hug. "I'm so proud of who you're becoming. I love you," he said softly into her ear. Niobe relished the evident truth of the statement.

Niobe squeezed him more tightly. "I love you, too."

After a moment, the king had held out his arm. "You can come in here too. I'm sure you're just as impressed as I am." Gethan had joined in, completing Niobe's feeling of being deeply understood and richly appreciated.

* * *

"AND THAT's my happiest memory. I'd made my two fathers proud of me. That's all I'd wanted for so long," Niobe said.

"That's a great story. I really like the idea too," Devin said.

"Okay, my turn. Why being a paramedic?"

"I like the rush of the big calls. You know when you have to make a lot of decisions and assessments in a super short time frame. Each of which has serious consequences. It makes me feel alive."

Niobe felt the same way about fighting, the split-second decision on what move to make, the thrill when a strike connected, and the ecstasy of knocking an opponent to the ground and making them submit. Not to mention the intoxicating hope they wouldn't, so she could go further.

"I guess the drive to become a paramedic came from when I was fifteen. My family was driving home from one of my inter-school basketball games and we were the last car in a four-car pile-up. My dad had braked hard and we barely touched the car in front of us, but we couldn't leave. When we got out of the car, my parents kind of just stood there. Dad called the emergency services on his mobile. It was one of those ancient ones that couldn't even take photos. We heard the sirens a few minutes later. While we were waiting, I got to see the other people's injuries. The driver in the second car hadn't worn a seatbelt, and even though the airbag had fired, he'd still hit his head on the windscreen, so he was bleeding badly from that, and his legs were crushed by the car, although it was kinda hard to see what that actually looked like, but I could see enough to imagine it. It was so fascinating I couldn't look away."

Niobe felt herself smiling at Devin. Maybe he had a darker side too?

Devin caught her eyes. "I mean, I … the paramedics who jumped out of the ambulance were amazing. So assured and in control. The opposite of my parents. I decided then and there that I wanted to be like them, so when I finished school that's what I went on and studied."

"Cool. Being queen was always my destination. I think with all my training, I'd have to become a philosophy teacher or something similar if I hadn't been born who I am. What do they call it? An accident of birth. Much of my life has been shaped by being born into royalty. I was fortunate to have Gethan to keep me grounded. If I acted up too much, he'd just drill me in basics and kata until I was too exhausted to think about anything other than what I was doing. He used to say it was the oddest thing: The more tired I got, the better my technique became. I think it was because I stopped trying to control my movement, and I just let it happen. My body would follow its natural path."

"I get that. I used to be terrible at free-throws. My coach said to stop overthinking it. Bounce the ball a couple of times and pretend you're just having a shot with some mates. It worked too. Once I stopped trying so hard to control the ball, I made so many more baskets."

Devin had a great smile. She wondered what it'd be like to kiss him. What would his skin taste like? Would he let her bite down on him? How far would he let her go before he said, "Too much"?

Patterson knocked on the door and informed Niobe the palace was closing to visitors.

"I guess it is that late," she said reluctantly. She and Devin stood and walked to the door.

"I'll show him out," Patterson said.

"Okay. I'll just say a goodbye." Patterson took the hint and walked over to the door.

"Thank you for coming to check on me this evening. I've really enjoyed talking to you. Maybe we can do it again soon?"

"I'd love that."

Niobe stood on her toes and gave Devin a peck on the cheek to see how he'd respond. He placed his long arms around her and went in for what became a long and enjoyable kiss.

Niobe let him go with a sigh, as Patterson escorted him out.

CHAPTER 23

*N*iobe went to bed and fell asleep quickly thanks to her exhausted body overriding her buzzing brain. The next morning, when she awoke, she smiled at the memory of her kiss with Devin.

The chef seemed to know she'd exerted herself the day before and served an extra egg and slice of toast. Niobe loved that such things just happened for her. It made focusing on grander things so much easier. So many people she met just wanted to discuss other people or, if she was luckier, events. But the best ones shared Niobe's enjoyment of discussing ideas. Having the little things taken care of made it easier for Niobe to occupy that headspace.

Niobe was unsurprised when Patterson returned with her second coffee of the morning and announced that Jim was waiting to see her. Niobe nodded and a few minutes later Jim strode into the room with his usual swagger.

Niobe was shocked when Jim told her that overnight he'd spoken to his contact again and had told her about Niobe's condition of democratic elections regardless of the outcome of the fight. Jork had agreed to that term, on the proviso

Niobe would commit to Tantalia changing its laws, so the monarch could be charged with murder. It would mean an end to her assassinations. Niobe found it an interesting request. She was having more of an influence than she'd realised. If he wanted her to stop, it wasn't just himself he was afraid for, but his allies too. That was telling.

"Would you consider that outcome?" Jim asked.

"Sure. But I can't pass laws relating to my powers myself. That would fall to the government. I would, however, direct them to do so. I'm sure the PM would comply."

"Yes, I'm sure he'd agree to that."

"Speaking of agreement, I haven't agreed to any of this yet."

"You said that last time. But I think you'll be interested to know"—Niobe scowled. How could a man be so utterly shameless?—"I spoke to Duchess Dahlia earlier this morning. She has already agreed to Lady Ebony being part of the show. The duchess would even like to be on an episode herself!"

Niobe was shocked. Dahlia was so against the show and what Niobe was doing. Why would she want to take part? What was she playing at? Curiosity about this alone made it worth signing up for.

However, the idea of an enforced end to her killing made her uneasy, although it was appealing that it would give her one further chance to show herself as a reluctant killer. An enforced end to *Sovereign Assassin,* supported by a statement from her saying she'd only ever acted the way she had due to her unique position, should improve Tantalia's international relationships. Australia had said that while the talks on their trade agreement had resumed, they wouldn't sign a final version unless Niobe would guarantee she'd stop killing. What better way than this? But she'd have to stop. No more rush from taking someone's life. No more feeling like she was making a meaningful difference to the fabric of her country. But was she really killing for her country? Or for pleasure—satisfying the dark side of herself that her parents had tried to contain for so long?

The choice seemed out of her hands in some ways. That the idea of the fight had already been raised with Jork and he'd agreed pointed to only one possible outcome. She would have to fight him, even though she'd never had him in her scope as a target. No negotiations between the countries could proceed while this idea was hanging in the air. What was it Devin had said? It could 'reduce the despotic presence in the region and prevent a war'. Both were appealing ideas. It would give her a chance to honour her parents, by finishing what they'd started, and would, in her mind, make amends for disobeying her father. King John had often said for Tantalia to truly shine, it needed strong, stable neighbours. This would be her way of starting to make that a reality.

"Fine. I'll do it. At least it will end things once and for all." Niobe was pleased the decision didn't make her feel any immediate regret, but then she still had the fight to look forward to. Though, maybe she wasn't as compulsive a killer as she'd thought? After all, she had waited eight years to kill Alban.

Niobe told Jim to leave. His assistant could make arrangements through Patterson. Niobe sent Devin a text to say she'd enjoyed their chat last night and that she'd agreed to the next fight. He texted back a love heart and smiley face emoji.

Niobe wondered why he hadn't called, or at least said more, then realised she was behaving like a teenager, over-analysing every interaction. This was probably just the way Devin communicated. Why couldn't men just say how they felt?

* * *

NIOBE ASKED Patterson to tell her instructor, Nathan, she wouldn't be training that morning, and to bring her three books from her personal library. He agreed to get them and, appearing reluctant, added that on the way out the night before Devin had been a little rude to him. He wasn't going to mention it, but since Niobe was forming a bond with him, he thought he would. "He probably just didn't want to leave," she said. Patterson bowed and left to get the books.

Two were on the *Onna-bugeisha*. The *Onna-bugeisha* were literally the women who practiced martial arts. They were female samurai who fought alongside men as equals and members of the Japanese nobility class. One such legendary woman, Empress Jingu, had used her skills to produce economic and social change. Although what was known about her was more myth than reality, she and other *Onna-bugeisha* would provide Niobe with inspiration and, she hoped, a strategy she could use. The third book was on legends of the samurai. It was a series of short stories, which broadly canvassed aspects of the way of the samurai. Niobe ordered a third coffee, her last for the day, and settled down to read, hoping a path to victory, or a novel strategy, would reveal itself.

* * *

FILMING for the new series of *Sovereign Assassin* would occur throughout the week. As the highest rated TV show of all time, the broadcast network was keen to ride the wave of momentum and produce the second series as soon as possible. After all, the buzz appeared to be peaking, so if they waited too long people would move on and find something else to talk about. If POTUS 45 had taught the world anything, by continually going from one controversy to another without pause, you were always relevant to the public discourse.

* * *

THE FIRST EPISODE aired a week later. During the week, Niobe had enjoyed two dates with Devin. On one, they'd been to see the latest superhero blockbuster at a cinema the palace had rented out. Niobe had secretly torn apart the reality of the fight scenes in the movie but told Devin she enjoyed them. The thing which annoyed her the most was how the villain gave the hero time to take stock and find the will to overcome them during the climactic fight. That was ludicrous. In a fight to the death, there was no rest and no mercy, no matter what. In Musashi's words, 'You must achieve the spirit of not allowing the enemy to attack a second time'. They didn't adhere to that and should have been defeated. Instead, the hero regrouped and overcame their foe. Niobe wouldn't make the same mistake.

SCENE: After a montage of Niobe training, she is revealed to be present in the press room of the palace for an announcement. The room is filled only with the crew of the TV show. No journalists are present.

VOICE-OVER: Queen Niobe has achieved some notoriety for being an assassin who cannot be arrested for her actions. As such, she doesn't have to conceal what she does. After people felt robbed of vision of her killing due to her camera being shot off her shoulder, she has agreed to another series of the show. This will be different, folks, as within a few minutes we will announce who her target will be!

NIOBE WAITED while another montage sequence played. She felt excited, but the uncertainty she'd be able to find the right tone for her presentation was making her anxious. For the first time in recent memory she was sweating, not the fresh sweat of a workout, but the odorous sweat of a stressed body.

A minute later, the director held up his hand. He started counting down with his fingers. Five, four, three, two, one. He pointed to Niobe.

"Ladies and gentlemen, I don't want to be here tonight. But an opportunity has arisen to make a meaningful difference to the social fabric of our region," Niobe said.

She inhaled. "Last week, the producer of *Sovereign Assassin* reached out to a contact he knew in Autarchos to float the idea of a fair fight between myself and Jork Dressov."

Niobe paused as she imagined the gasps in living rooms around the nation and beyond.

"Jork welcomed the opportunity before I'd even been consulted about this possibility." Niobe couldn't hide the scowl which crossed her face.

"When the idea was put to me, I had to consider what it could mean. I'm pleased to say that Jork has acceded to my demand for a new election in Autarchos, overseen by NATO, regardless of the outcome of our fight. This will be a significant event for the region and something the international community has been trying to achieve for decades."

Niobe paused and took a sip of water. She always hated when presenters did that, but she wanted to give the audience time to let the information sink in.

"I imagine you're wondering what I needed to agree to in return. Jork demanded Tantalia pass laws which would see the monarch charged with murder for events after the fight. I've spoken to our Prime Minister, and he's agreed to put the legislation to parliament to amend our constitution. Which means this will be my last attempted assassination. Well, unless I decide the crime is worth the time."

Niobe longed for a shower to freshen up. The director gave the signal for her to wrap-up the speech, so they could play a pre-recorded clip.

"Jork has agreed to fight me, in a fortnight, at a neutral

location, still to be determined. Here's a video of his response."

Niobe was able to watch Jork on a monitor. He was seated at an ornate desk, in a room which was clearly modelled after the famed oval office.

"Queen Niobe needs no introduction at this point. She is a menace whose unfettered abuse of her power has caused instability in our region."

Niobe had to admire the blatant hypocrisy of the statement. Jork had done more harm than anyone. She was surprised she couldn't detect him lying. Did he think that was the truth?

"Such abuse cannot go unchecked, so I will put my life on the line on behalf of Autarchos and the world." Jork paused, as though wanting the nobility of his sacrifice to sink in. He stood and placed his hands on the desk. A commanding stance.

"Queen Niobe has managed to create an aura around herself, which I intend to expose. Sure, she's killed some people, but let me ask you this. Did we see her actual kills on screen? No. Do we have any proof she was actually the one who killed the victims? No. Could someone else have been with her? Yes. All we have seen is her doing some fancy gymnastics, and all we have heard is her spouting martial-art philosophy as though it's something profound. Well, I see through you, Queen Niobe, and when I defeat you the world will too."

Jork sat back down. "Autarchos has agreed to the terms of combat. There will be no consequential hostility whatever the outcome, and we've agreed to the demand for NATO to supervise a new election in five months' time. Now let's see if Queen Niobe has the guts to go through with the fight. She won't be fighting an untrained person this time."

Jork sniggered. Something about his final thought seemed to amuse him.

The video ended, and the director pointed to Niobe.

"That was the first time I've seen that. I'm not about to back down. I will say this to Jork. I'll pre-pardon you if you manage regicide. If he thinks all I have are gymnastics and fancy, impractical moves, he will lose faster than I anticipate."

The director mimed winding a thread with his fingers.

"I'm getting the wind up, so enjoy the rest of tonight's episode."

"And clear," the director said. He thanked Niobe and left to go to the press room's adjoining biobox-cum-TV mixing studio.

As they walked to the hall to do some filming for the next episode, Ebony turned to Niobe. "Hey, cuz, I just wanted to say I'm sorry for the touchier questions during our interview. Mum made me ask them. I'd never be like that otherwise."

"Thanks for saying that Ebs, but it's okay. I know what it's like to have to do something you don't want to for your parents. After all, that's why I behaved 'the royal way' in my public appearances growing up."

"So are we okay?"

"Yes. Let's train."

A few moments later, they were doing a few running laps of the training hall to warm up. Despite Ebony and the cameraperson's presence, the training hall felt empty. It just didn't feel right practicing without Gethan or Nathan. In contrast to Dahlia's earlier scowls, Ebony seemed thrilled to be back on TV. After some stretching, Niobe nodded to the cameraman to start filming.

"Lady Ebony, it's great to have you back in the dojo with me. I thought it'd be worth going through some partner work together." Niobe pointed to two dummies standing upright against the wall at the side of the room. "This is Bob 1 and Bob 2. They're anatomically correct models used for target practice. As you can see, one is shaped like a physically fit man"—Niobe's brain flashed to Devin. He had a similar build. The thought made her want to smile—"and the other is of a less fit, let's just say out of shape, man. Certain regions of the body are more vulnerable than others. By using these we can train to hit the right spots more often. If we came up against some man mountain, we might not be able to hurt them with a regular strike to the abdomen or chest. This training helps us cope in such a situation."

Niobe ran through two drills with Ebony. The first involved a series of pointed strikes: a right hand under the left ribs into the stomach, left hand to the right carotid sinus, right hand into the left carotid sinus, left hand into the liver, right hand to left temple and *vice versa*. If you could get inside your attacker's defences to deliver the strikes, they would rapidly incapacitate the victim. Niobe demonstrated the moves a few times. Her body twisted with each strike so that her weight was behind each of the six strikes and it wasn't just her arm muscles generating power. The speed, accuracy and strength of her strikes was apparent.

"That looks cool," Ebony said.

"Your turn," Niobe replied. She spent a few minutes guiding Ebony through the drill on both dummies, pointing out the differences in anatomy and how they impacted the strikes.

Once Niobe sensed that Ebony had become bored with the drill, Niobe handed her a pair of thick gloves and two short sticks. The second drill would involve them doing several patterns of hits. Niobe explained the moves were related to what they'd just done, even though they might be in a different order. What both drills aimed to achieve was an increase in left and right side coordination of the body as well as general awareness of the attacker and or movement. Combined they would help a person launch a series of fast attacks against an opponent. It was vital to strike several times when attacking. First time fighters tended to throw a single punch and pause to gauge its consequence before throwing the next one. It was an often fatal mistake.

"Attacking is a different art to defending, and harder too. Virtually all martial arts are based on being struck first. As Funakoshi said, 'There is no first strike in karate', but there are times when you need to strike first. *Ninjustsu* covers some direct attacks since its practitioners, who you'd call ninjas, were on occasion used as assassins. It's one of the arts I've studied."

Ebony nodded. "Ninjas are cool. Do you have the throwing thingies they use?"

"Yes, I have *shuriken*, the throwing stars. But you'll be disappointed to learn that they, and smaller, or lighter throwing knives, aren't that effective as weapons. They don't always 'stick' either. A thrown star will rarely penetrate a leather coat deep enough to really hurt someone, for example. However, they are excellent as tools to distract your enemy while you make up ground and get close enough for proper strikes. They're also good for helping you develop aim or driving an approaching enemy backward."

Ebony's face fell a little. Niobe knew she'd taken the fun out of the idea for her.

"Tell you what though, how about we have a go with them. See those cork targets on the wall over there? We'll chuck them at those, okay?"

Ebony grinned and clapped her hands. Niobe laughed and went to get the weapons.

* * *

AFTER THE TRAINING, Niobe and Ebony were in the change room adjoining the hall. Niobe was pleased to have the opportunity to chat to Ebony without cameras or Dahlia being around. So far, their relationship had always seemed so formal, but *Sovereign Assassin* was giving them a chance to get to know each other better, and Niobe was appreciating the opportunity. Plus, it gave her a chance to make sure Ebony stayed on her side rather than her mother's.

"Hey, cuz. I just want you to know I'm here for you always. Okay?" Niobe said.

"Yeah, I know. Thanks for showing me all this stuff. It's really cool."

"What do you like the most?"

Ebony put a finger on her chin as she thought.

"I guess the punching. It's nice to feel like I'm able to defend myself." She waved her hands palm down across each other. "Not that I could yet. Just that I think that would be a great feeling. I dunno, I guess I see why you do it."

Niobe smiled.

"Can I ask you a question?"

"You just did," Niobe said with a grin.

"Ugh. So lame, cuz. You're the queen now. What does that mean for boys? How are you going to meet anyone now?"

"I don't need a man to be complete. But since you asked, there is someone I'm kind of seeing!"

Ebony clapped her hands in excitement. "Tell me everything."

* * *

THE LATE-EVENING NEWS was filled by reaction to Niobe's announcement of her target. The countries which sided with

Autarchos were appalled. The others ranged from neutral to supportive. The latter included nearly all EU countries, the US, the UK and Australia. Drysen Silic once again wrote a piece criticising her decision. He worded his article carefully, so Niobe appeared like a worse and more brutal leader than Jork. Niobe's hackles were raised further by what seemed to be a new quote from Gethan which said, "I welcome the end to the queen's killing. I only wish it didn't have to come with the ending of another life."

After her evening meal, Niobe was joined by Devin for a dessert date. With the schedule leading up to the fight being filled, Niobe had to shoehorn in some royal duties during her dinnertime. This only left a small window each evening to see Devin, especially given Niobe's recognition that she needed extra sleep and a strict bedtime until after the fight.

Niobe felt her heart jump around as Devin was shown into the dining room for their date. Over the last week, they'd kissed a few more times and Niobe found herself increasingly enamoured with Devin. They seemed to have so much in common. Niobe wanted to start a sexual relationship with him, but the logical part of her knew it would complicate things too much before her fight. Still, her sexual side rarely let her forget it wasn't being satisfied. The energy it provided was good fuel for training.

"So, anything much been happening?" Devin asked mischievously.

"You saw the episode?"

"Yes. I can't believe they film, edit and release it all in a day. It seems incredible."

"It is. But since it's documentary style, they don't need to add digital effects or such things. Each setting is set up for filming and miked up, so they don't need to do a lot of tweaking to the video or audio. It's no different to filming a football game or evening news bulletin really. Throw in a few pre-recorded segments and you're good to go."

"I guess so."

"So, how do you know Jork's being honest? That he'll run and won't interfere in the elections?"

"A whole bunch of sanctions have been contingent on such elections for ages. He'll reignite his country's trade by having them. Personally, I think he's been wanting to do it for ages, but was afraid of looking like he was giving in to the 'foreign powers'. He knows he'll win an election anyway, since his people will assume that somehow they're being watched."

"So, what's the point?"

"He needs supplies his country can't produce. This gives him a way of getting them without losing face … oh, you mean of pushing for the elections. It's something my parents wanted for ages. It'll be a step in the right direction to bring Autarchos back to the international community. Jork agreed; I'm sure because it'll increase his stature in the community. Not to mention he'll be able to say he saved the world from the menace of me."

"That's if he's alive," Devin said with a smile.

"Yes. I'll work hard to make sure that doesn't happen."

"I know."

"Which leads me to a favour I'd like to ask." Niobe tipped her head and looked up at Devin.

"What?"

"Will you be there for the fight? I can't think of anyone I'd rather have in my corner, so to speak. Plus, since it's likely I'll be hurt during the fight, regardless of the outcome, I could use your special skills. But mostly, I'd just like you there because … because you mean a lot to me."

"It would be a privilege. I'll do it."

Niobe smiled with satisfaction.

"There's something I should tell you though—" Devin began.

Patterson knocked on the door, interrupting the conversation. "Your Majesty, the PM apologises for calling so late, but he'd like a quiet word with you."

"Thanks, Patterson." Niobe turned to Devin. "Can you tell me later?"

Devin nodded.

"Patterson will show you out. Patterson can you transfer the call here?"

Patterson gave a slight bow. Niobe was amused by his formality. He'd never relented with it, but it seemed to step up when Devin was at the palace. It was as though he was trying to model appropriate respect to Devin. Niobe stood when Devin did, and despite Patterson watching, went over and gave him a long kiss goodnight.

Patterson frowned at Niobe, which puzzled Niobe. For some reason he didn't approve of Devin. Devin for his part had seemed resistant to the kiss, but then they were in front of someone else.

SEASON TWO, EPISODE TWO

The following morning Niobe found a few new texts from Devin. The first was timestamped just after he'd left the palace the previous night. *Jim knows we're, err, meeting regularly. He wants to interview me for the show. I'll only do it if you say it's okay. Would you mind?* So that's what he'd wanted to say. The second was from later that night. *Thinking of you.* The text ended with a love heart emoji. The final text was from earlier that morning. *I hope you slept well. Can't wait to see you tonight.* It also ended with a heart emoji. Niobe quickly typed, *Go for the interview.* She ended it with a thumbs-up, sent it, and then sent a separate message of a heart emoji.

After a vigorous workout, some of which had been filmed for the show, Niobe showered and changed before making her way to the palace's media room. Jim had told her they needed to film another segment for that night's episode. On the way she received another text from Devin. He'd completed his interview but was still at the palace if she was free? Niobe told him to meet her in her dining room. She'd get there as soon as she could after filming.

* * *

WHEN NIOBE ENTERED the oval-shaped media room, from its main doors, she was surprised to see Dahlia and Ebony already there, on the stage at the opposite apex of the room. They were seated behind a large desk, which had been covered with a white tablecloth and dressed up with some flowers. There was a jug of water, and the Duchess and Lady each had their own glass. A fixed camera was pointed at them. A second camera was held by a mobile cameraperson. Despite advancement in technology, it was still shoulder mounted. Niobe had been told that was just to help with ease of filming. The camera itself was very lightweight.

A couple of taped crosses marked the floor in front of a door to the side of the tables. The door led to a hallway where Niobe usually entered the room from. Niobe had seen such markers on sets before. They indicated where to stand at certain points for filming.

The cameraperson remained focused on Niobe. It was the person who'd filmed her on the day of her previous assassination. She'd become used to having a camera pointed at her throughout her life, so she easily ignored their presence. Jim was lurking near where Niobe had entered the room. What was he stage managing here? Niobe felt her senses tingle with anticipation. Ebony's scowl, which seemed directed at her mother, did little to reassure Niobe all was well.

"Duchess, Lady Ebony. How wonderful to see you," Niobe said cautiously.

"Hello, my queen," Dahlia said with a sly grin, making Niobe wonder again what was going on. "I have a surprise for you."

A surprise? Niobe was dumbstruck. Dahlia had been working against her, hadn't she? Surprises were usually good things, weren't they? Ebony seemed oddly downcast though, especially in contrast to Dahlia.

Dahlia stood and walked to the side of the room and stood on one of the tape crosses on the floor. It was the perfect spot to open the adjacent side door to the room, without blocking the view.

"And here it is." Dahlia opened the door to reveal Gethan, dressed in his usual gi uniform. Niobe's heart surged, and she ran and hugged him. He'd returned in her hour of need! Gethan responded stiffly to the embrace, and Niobe felt her confusion show.

"Gethan is here because he will be training Jork Dressov for his match against you," Dahlia said as she studied Niobe's face.

As Dahlia's plan revealed itself, Niobe was reminded of Sun Tzu's words. 'Let your plans be dark and impenetrable as night, and when you move, fall like a thunderbolt.' Niobe certainly felt like a thunderbolt had struck her.

She looked at Gethan for confirmation. He nodded. "It's the only way I can honour your father." Was that sadness in his tone? Guilt? Niobe's head was spinning so much she couldn't tell. She went to shoot a look of hatred at Jim, but only saw his back as he slipped out of the room.

Dahlia shut the door on Gethan. Niobe wanted to throw her aunt out of the way and go chasing after him, but she couldn't get her body to move.

"That is the last time you'll see Gethan until the fight. We want to be certain you'll be stopped then, if you don't call off the fight first, which is what we really want."

Niobe felt so broken and hollow she was sure the merest breath of air could knock her over.

She fell to her knees and cried with frustration. The thought that, somehow, she'd let her father down and this was what he had warned her about, left her unable to breathe. Niobe mentally encouraged herself to overplay her reaction. Tears rolled down her cheeks and snot dripped down her nose. She hadn't cried so hard at her father's funeral.

"You. How could you?" Niobe yelled at Dahlia when she'd regained enough composure to form words.

Dahlia regarded her calmly. "You need to understand there have to be limits. Remember the words from the Temple of Apollo at Delphi? *'Meden Agan,* nothing to excess.' You took things too far. That needs to be corrected. You opened some floodgates which need closing. Gethan agrees. Come, Ebony, we're leaving."

"But *Mummm,*" Ebony protested. An icy glare shut Ebony up, and she dutifully follow Dahlia out of the room, although she mouthed the word 'sorry' to Niobe on her way past.

Niobe remained kneeling on the floor as the cameraman backed away, lowered the camera, and almost ran out of the room. Her tear-stained cheeks and look of absolute rage must have scared the life out of him.

* * *

A SHORT WHILE later there was a knock at the main door. Devin's head peeped cautiously into the room. When he saw Niobe crying he ran over to her, knelt behind her, and cradled her in his arms.

"Dahlia said you were in here and needed me."

Niobe realised Ebony must have told Dahlia about their blossoming relationship.

Niobe took comfort in Devin's strong arms. He kissed the back of her head every few moments.

After a while she turned and kissed him lightly on the lips. "I don't get it. Why are they so against me?"

"I don't know. I thought Gethan was like a father to you.

Maybe Dahlia put him up to it. Was there anything going on between them?"

Niobe sniffed.

"No. I mean he's at most palace functions. She's here a lot, too. They've always been friendly, but I wouldn't have thought anything more than that. Besides, she and Uncle Jacques always seemed like a happy couple. But I dunno, maybe."

"What are you going to do?"

"What can I do? I still have to fight Jork." She sniffed again. "I'll have to find someone new to train with. Nathan's style is too much like Gethan's. I'll have to work to be unpredictable. I'm not sure how much I can adapt in a week, but I guess I'll have to try."

Devin hugged her.

"Thanks. Thanks for being here and understanding."

"No place I'd rather be," he said.

Niobe lifted her head upwards and gave him a deep kiss. After a few more minutes of quietly holding each other, Niobe told Devin she needed to sort some things out. She asked him to come back tomorrow. She needed to be alone tonight to think things through, and Devin would prove too much of a distraction.

AFTER DEVIN LEFT, Niobe had Patterson meet her in the media room where she informed him of the updated circumstances.

Niobe felt like she might break down again as she described the betrayal.

"Can you please revoke Jim and Dahlia's access to the palace? Gethan's too, if that hasn't been done already."

"Certainly, Your Highness. Anything else?"

"Could you find a new trainer for me? Someone who teaches a style I haven't studied."

Patterson raised his eyebrows.

"Yes, I know I've studied most of them. Just whoever you can find. Tell Nathan he can have a couple of weeks off."

"As you wish."

Patterson seemed unusually hesitant to leave.

"What is it?"

"It's just that it seems so unlike the duchess and Gethan. Are you sure there isn't another explanation for what they're doing?"

"No. It's betrayal, pure and simple." Niobe felt tears well. "I don't know how I couldn't see it coming."

* * *

LATER THAT AFTERNOON Patterson sat with Niobe on the edge of the fountain in the inner garden.

"How do I stop them, Patterson?"

"If I may Your Majesty, you don't need to."

"But I could leak that Gethan and Dahlia are having an affair and make it too scandalous for Gethan to remain involved."

"That wouldn't be wise. It would take everything from them."

"You know about the rule of two?"

"What rule?"

"Don't worry. You have a point though. Why do you think I don't need to stop them?"

"When you defeat Jork, they'll have nothing over you. They're trying to get you to stop now, but after Jork you won't be able to kill anymore. They won't be your adversaries then, because their cause would be redundant. The best thing you can do is keep training and make sure you win, not least because I don't want to see you hurt or worse."

"Thanks, Patterson. I see why my parents considered you wise counsel."

"You didn't before?"

"You know what I mean."

Patterson smiled. "Of course, Your Majesty."

Niobe had a restless night. She tried meditating to help get to sleep but found no matter how hard she tried she couldn't dismiss the thought of what Dahlia and Gethan had done. She also couldn't help but think she was at real risk in her fight. Her previous victories had been against untrained people. Jork had been in the secret police. There were rumours he'd personally killed dozens of people. He was a formidable foe without being trained in Niobe's fighting style and now his trainer was the sole person who knew it better than Niobe herself. By 6.00 am, Niobe gave up trying to get a decent amount of rest. She went to her dining room and ordered breakfast. Fifteen minutes later Patterson entered with her tray of food.

"Your Majesty, Jim's been waiting at the palace gates for an hour," Patterson said as he placed Niobe's breakfast in front of her.

"Let him in, but warn him he may not walk out of here. Remind him I'm still pissed he didn't tell me about Gethan."

"Of course, Your Majesty."

A few minutes later, Jim burst into the room with a rush of energy.

"Great news!" he said. "Italy has offered use of the Colosseum for the match."

Niobe was unsure where to begin. It wasn't a match, it was a fight to the death, and she still hadn't rebuked him about Gethan, and there was more.

"I don't know if I want to go through with the fight."

Jim was stunned into silence.

"But it's the Colosseum. Icarus Air has even offered first class flights for you and your entourage."

"Jim, stop. You are…"

"Oh, yeah, right. I'm sorry I didn't warn you about Dahlia's plan and Gethan's appearance. But I needed to get your honest reaction."

"You knew about it?" Niobe asked, wanting confirmation.

"Sure. I encouraged it," Jim admitted with a shrug.

Niobe picked up her knife and pointed it at Jim. "Jim, I'm struggling to contain my desire to take this knife and make you hurt in ways you can't imagine."

For once Jim looked like what Niobe said had an impact on him. He was clearly imagining a few of the ways.

"Let me explain. Getting you to show your vulnerability and human side is crucial for shaping public opinion of you. Great characters need to show emotion and that there's a personal cost to their action."

"You know I've spent my whole life learning to control my emotions. Even to remove my thoughts from them."

"Yes, we covered it on the show. That's why it was so important to show you still had them. Otherwise, you'd just be a cold-blooded killer. That wouldn't sell at all."

"Sell?"

"It all feeds into the show. Did you know we have sponsors lining up to be involved? This may be the most profitable show in television history. All we needed was to make the story a little more compelling."

"You're sick. You know that, right?"

Jim smiled. "I've been called worse."

"I may need medical attention after the fight. Can I bring Devin? You'd need to get him a separate room."

Jim's eyes lit up. "Sure, I'm certain we can manage that. By the way, the Colosseum will be great. We can sell a couple of hundred seats—"

"I thought it held fifty-thousand."

"That was when it was built. These days there's only a small amount of seating. We could have sold out a boxing stadium or something, but that wouldn't have the same appeal of such a historic place. Plus, we can set up our own rig, so there's no chance of cameras missing out on the action. We'll even set up two drones, so the audience can get an unprecedented view of the event. It'll be the TV event of the decade."

Niobe couldn't tell if Jim's enthusiasm was for the event, or the fame he'd receive from being associated with it.

"We've had a very quiet request from the US to topple other dictators, if you're successful. They appreciate the expediency and less politically damaging fallout from what you do. It's all so much easier when you don't have to conceal the act," Jim said.

"True, but you're forgetting Tantalia will be changing its laws, so I can be charged if I kill again. That's the agreement."

"You'll honour that?" Jim seemed to deflate a little.

"Absolutely. The bill has been drafted. It's got a week of debate before a vote after the fight. After this, it's over," Niobe said with a certainty she found oddly comforting. Having her people accept her for who she was, for who she would have always been if her parents hadn't spent the better part of her lifetime trying to control her desires, was freeing.

It was so cleansing she believed she could be content with the new reality. Sure, she'd have the odd pang, but it was a bearable situation. It was a more meaningful conquering of herself than she'd achieved before. The depth of the realisation brought a tear of achievement to her eye.

Jim seemed suddenly buoyant again. Niobe rolled her eyes. He never stayed down for long.

"Then we'd better make it count," he said.

The flight to Rome was a short one. Even though she'd never flown commercially, Niobe hadn't realised she wasn't allowed to until she'd asked for the booking to be made. Her royal plane had to be chartered, as it was somehow considered less of a terrorism risk. Devin sent her some video footage of what first class was like. Niobe didn't have the heart to tell him it would've been a step down for her in comparison. He'd been particularly impressed with the size of the space he was allocated, and the quality of the champagne he'd been served. He also seemed to enjoy the extra attention of the hostesses and special entry and departure through airport security. Before the flight, he'd even recorded a small piece to camera for the show about what equipment he'd have in his first aid bag. It included the usual bandages, blocks, oxygen equipment, defibrillator and green whistles. The interviewer hadn't known what the whistles were, so Devin explained their use. Devin added that they'd be a lot cheaper when the trade agreement with Australia kicked in. Niobe smiled at the thought that at least one Tantalian had praised the deal publicly. He'd understood it was important to her, and that made her feel appreciated.

Niobe arrived at the hotel first. It was a small boutique bed and breakfast, walking distance to the Colosseum. Niobe had made sure the camera crew and her entourage stayed elsewhere. Their equipment would create attention and speculation, and she didn't want people to know where she was. Someone else had checked in for her, then passed over the room key. It'd been tough to convince the palace to let her stay by herself, but after a lot of back and forth, it was agreed Niobe being alone would be the least conspicuous way for her to be in the country. It would also reduce the risk of people targeting her overnight.

Niobe found the three-star room quite different to her usual surroundings. She liked its minimalist design, which was also how her areas of the palace were decorated, but this was odd. It was a small room, but there was ornate wood panelling on the walls and a gorgeous dark-timber bed. The star rating must've been based more on room size and services than presentation.

Devin had snuck into Niobe's room during the evening. They'd enjoyed a rich, Italian-style hot chocolate and chatted about Niobe's fears for the fight. Niobe kept thinking about the end of their conversation.

"I'm concerned he'll have counters to my preferred attacks. Gethan knows where I like to hit and how. So, if Jork knows that too, I could struggle to defeat him."

"I'm sure you'll win."

"How can you be?"

"Because I don't want this to end. I don't want us to end."

"That sounds like a line," Niobe said. Devin looked momentarily shocked. "But it worked," she continued.

Niobe smiled and leant over for a long, satisfying kiss.

Devin started to kiss her more passionately, and as the kiss went on, he started untucking his shirt.

"Not tonight. I don't need any more distractions than you're already providing."

There was a slight pause, as though he was considering saying something more, before Devin nodded, though he looked a little disappointed.

* * *

WALKING to Colosseum the next morning, Niobe couldn't help but notice how many people were in hoodies, just as she was. It was like a uniform, taken from the footage of her attacking Don Azzure and Mr Gladwell. There was a huge outdoor setup next to the Colosseum itself, where people were gathering to watch a big screen broadcast of the event.

While Niobe found the hoodies touching, the quantity of them was alarming. She had proper, actual, fans. The adoration was nice, but she didn't want to have to control their behaviour—it was too much effort. How did cult leaders like Charlie Manson do it? These were a step up from her followers in her princess days. Back then it'd been tweens who had had an overly romantic picture of what royal life was about. These fans, on the other hand, seemed interested in her philosophy. She saw several things she'd said printed on their jackets and t-shirts: 'It's the least forceful way I could defend the State', and 'It's not a privilege to be killed by me'.

It seemed even God wanted to watch the match as there wasn't a cloud in the sky on the warm summer day. Outside the Colosseum were the usual people dressed as Roman soldiers trying to trap tourists into a photograph before they demanded money. Niobe went to a side entrance away from the main gate. There was heavy security there. When she approached, a security guard said, "Move along, miss."

Niobe removed her hood. "I'm here to fight."

The security guard looked confused. "Where's your entourage?"

"They'll be here soon. Now, may I come in?" She flashed the card Jim had given her. Niobe was amused by his insistence on it, but it did produce the desired effect.

"Of course, Your Majesty." The guard stepped aside as a couple of people who'd overheard the exchange rushed towards her.

"Queen Niobe. Queen Niobe! We love you," they called out.

Niobe turned, blew them a kiss, and disappeared into the stadium.

NIOBE HADN'T BEEN to the Colosseum before but was aware of its famous history. It had been built by successive Roman kings between 70–80 AD, and was called the *Templum Pacis,* or Temple of Peace—an ironic name given the violence which had occurred there. Gladiators used to live in cells nearby and would prepare for battle underneath the ground where the fight would take place. Today, most of the warren-like tunnels were exposed, and only a segment of the oval-shaped ground was maintained to show how the surface would have looked. Similarly, the seating was in ruin, and only a small section had been restored. It overlooked the fighting arena. The camera crew had been busy and were already set up with seven cameras in a large circle over which two drones would hover. Jim was talking to a huddle of camera operators as Niobe approached. The moment he saw her he ran over.

"It's great to see you here. We've managed to sell the two hundred tickets for a hundred and ten thousand Euro each.

Advertising for the show has sold for more per ad than the Superbowl!"

Jim's excitement annoyed Niobe, and he was quick to see it on her face.

"Sorry. It's just all so incredible. There's all sorts of buzz that I'll be up for several awards during awards season."

"Jim." Niobe was firm. "How long until the fight, and is Jork here?"

Jim glanced at his watch.

"Two hours. You're nice and early. Jork is arriving at noon. The fight's at one."

"Where can I warm up?"

"There's space for you over there." Jim pointed to a large white tent on one side of the ground. "Jork's is over there." He pointed to the other side of the stadium.

Niobe felt a chill run through her at the thought that Gethan would be over there soon.

"Thanks. Do you know if Devin is here yet?"

"No, he'll be arriving just before Jork. I'll send him straight to your tent."

"Thanks," Niobe said absently.

Niobe walked to her warm-up area, slipped through the tent's doors, and began to do some yoga to stretch and clear her mind.

* * *

Forty-five minutes later, a voice called out, "Knock, knock."

"Come in, Devin," Niobe replied. When he walked through the doors, Niobe felt as though, with Devin there, everything would be all right. She almost skipped over, from happiness, and gave him a hug. To Niobe's trained senses the hug seemed a little colder than usual and it was followed by a very brief kiss. Where was the desire he'd displayed the night before?

"Can you help me run through some moves? It'll be good to try them on someone who doesn't know what I'm doing."

"Sure. Should we get a camera in here?" Devin said with enthusiasm for the idea.

"No, let's keep this between us. I don't want Jork getting wind of what I have planned."

A sudden kerfuffle outside indicated Jork and his entourage had arrived. Niobe looked Devin in the eye.

"Please, let's do this. I need to keep occupied and not think about Gethan being in the wrong tent."

"Okay."

"Thanks. So, can you go into a left foot forward stance, like this?"

Niobe demonstrated a *hidari kamae,* fighting stance. Devin copied it.

"Now I want you to step forward with your right leg and throw a front punch with your right hand. Like this. Aim for my head."

Niobe showed him how she wanted it done, then stood in front of him. "Go," she commanded.

Devin stepped forward and threw a weak punch. After training with so many people who knew you were only cheating your training partner if you staged a weak attack, it was refreshing to have someone make the mistake.

"Go back. I need you to really try and punch me as hard as you can. Like Jork is going to. Do you understand?"

Devin nodded. They spent the next fifty minutes running through various attacks. Niobe was always careful to control her punches, so she barely made contact with Devin.

When they were quieting down in the last fifteen minutes before the fight, there was as sudden parting of the entrance to the tent. Niobe gasped as Dahlia entered. Dahlia reacted to

Devin's presence with a glare. He took the hint and made to leave.

"Thanks, Dev. See you after, I hope," Niobe said.

Devin left the tent.

* * *

"I DON'T WANT to see you," Niobe told Dahlia. Dahlia's black dress annoyed Niobe. Was she going to a funeral?

"Oh, please. I'm sure you're upset about the Gethan stunt, but we thought it would work out differently. We thought you'd be sensible enough to call off the fight immediately."

"Well, I didn't, so why are you here?"

"I have another surprise for you. Ebony has a security guard follow her everywhere."

Niobe nodded. She'd seen him on set.

"He wears a camera. He recorded this." Dahlia handed Niobe her phone which had a video ready to be played on it.

"Notice the date?"

Niobe glanced at the date stamp. It was the day before she'd killed Mr Gladwell. With a rising sense of dread, Niobe pressed play and watched Jim talking to Devin. How was that possible?

"Didn't you wonder how the paramedics and police got there so quickly? The cameraperson had told Jim where you were setting up."

"They swore they wouldn't."

"My poor, naïve niece. Can't you tell when someone is lying to you?" Niobe winced. "D'you really think Jim ever wanted to do this only once? He needed a way to get you to commit to a second series, and he wanted a love interest to help the narrative. Now you have something worth fighting for. Devin. At least he's a real paramedic, but he's also a plant. After Ebony told me about him, and I met him the other week, I had this nagging feeling I'd seen him before. I ran through her security tapes and found that footage yesterday. I confronted Jim on my way over to you. He said he'd seen Devin in a promotional video to attract people to study as paramedics and guessed he might be interested in being on TV. Such a shame your relationship is all a sham."

Dahlia's tone was sarcastic and irritated Niobe. She struggled with a rising sickening feeling as she realised Devin had been the one to convince her she should go ahead with the attempt on Jork. No wonder he'd seemed so ideal. He'd been coached on what to say. Was that why he took so long to reply to messages? With a crushing realisation, Niobe twigged he'd never outright told her to go ahead with the fight with Jork. He'd guided her to that conclusion, which she'd reached herself, just like Gethan would have done. He'd played the mentor role so perfectly, and she was so used to that kind of relationship, she hadn't even noticed. He hadn't even seemed concerned when he said she'd been fighting a legitimate killer, probably because he was actually selling it as part of the challenge. She should have trusted Patterson's judgement about Devin.

"I could see that right from the outset. It's why I counselled you against it. You, my queen, can spot someone lying when they're inexperienced at it, but not when it's second nature to the person. I don't know why you couldn't see through Jim's bullshit, but you couldn't, and now you're literally about to fight for your life because of it."

"Yet you choose to show me this now? Knowing it could distract me."

"Gethan said it's what you needed. Besides, at least you'll go into the fight knowing who your true enemy is."

"So, you're really just trying to help me?" Niobe asked sarcastically.

"Of course."

"I don't buy it; I think you want me to be killed."

"It would stop the menace."

"So, you admit you and Gethan are conspiring against me."

"Not at this moment. We haven't had contact for the last couple of days. I hoped his presence would get you to call it off. So did he. You do need to stop. What you are doing is murder, not self-defence. Even if you bring peace, that's too high a price to pay. Gethan said King John had asked him to make sure you were stopped from killing. He thought disappearing would achieve that. It didn't, so he tried reappearing. That failed too. He just wants you to stop. I do too. He does love you, but he feels he must honour your father."

"He coached Jork anyway. How would my father feel about that?"

"It was probably to see how you'd rise to the challenge. He did mention something about wanting to see if you were ready for the next step in your training, should you win, I mean."

"I finished my training. At least with him."

Dahlia rolled her eyes.

"Oh, to be as young as you and to think I knew it all too. If you win, I'm sure he'll let you know what the step is."

A huge roar erupted from the crowd. A moment later they announced Jork was entering the combat arena.

"Time to go. Best wishes, Niobe."

Niobe was momentarily confused. Dahlia sounded sincere, and hadn't used Niobe's title, when addressing her, which was her usual sign of disdain. Her mind raced. She didn't know who to trust.

When her name was called, Niobe emerged from her tent. The sound of the crowd was deafening. She was sure the cheers were louder for her than for Jork. But she had to find a way to keep grounded. After all, favourites didn't always win.

Jork was already waiting in the makeshift ring for the fight. Gethan was a few metres behind him, standing awkwardly with the rest of Jork's entourage. Gethan nodded to Niobe as she emerged, and mouthed, "I'm sorry." Niobe glared at him. She wanted to mouth back, "You're next," but the cameras prevented her.

The ring was a crude taping of a line, which the cameras were outside of. Under the rules agreed to by both parties, there were to be no weapons, nor protective clothing. Niobe was dressed in black leggings and white t-shirt. Her sneakers were white leather with a lightweight sole. Her hair was tied back in a platted ponytail. Hopefully, it would make it harder for Jork to grab if he tried. Jork wouldn't face such a possibility from Niobe as he had a military buzz cut. Jork was about half a foot taller than Niobe and at least twenty kilos heavier. He was shirtless, which revealed he was muscular, but not overly toned. His skin was tanned, like Niobe's, but his eyes were much darker. Niobe assessed him and thought that from the way he stood he looked like he knew how to handle himself.

As Niobe stepped into the ring, she couldn't help herself, and she bowed to her opponent as she would for any sparring practice. Jork sneered in response.

"Little girl," he said. "I'm about to end you."

"We'll see."

An announcer's voice thundered through the speakers. "Two gladiators have come to fight to the finish. There are no rules for combat other than no weapons, nor protective equipment. There will be no rounds or time limits. The match will continue until neither can continue, or one opponent has been killed. Gladiators, do you agree to these terms?"

Both Niobe and Jork raised their hands and nodded. The crowd cheered. A fraction of a second later a similar sound echoed from the tens of thousands gathered outside the stadium.

"Begin!" the announcer commanded.

* * *

NIOBE AND JORK circled one another, sizing each other up and gauging the distance for an attack. Niobe knew she needed to be patient. After ten seconds of posturing, she moved back a step and performed a backflip kick, which made the crowd cheer. She was far enough away that she had time to complete it before Jork could seize the opportunity to rush in and throw her to the ground. It was a strategy an

Onna-bugeisha had used in battle. At the very least, it would make Jork question what he expected from the fight. Jork did move towards her, but Niobe was back on her feet before he got close enough to strike. Jork now had something she desired: momentum. She kicked out with a *mawashigeri*, roundhouse kick to his inner right thigh. The contact didn't feel quite right, but Jork's leg buckled enough for him to stumble briefly. To prevent further attack he swung round with his left arm and caught the right side of Niobe's face with his outstretched fingers.

Niobe felt blood trickle down her face. She looked at Jork's hand. His fingernails were sharpened into points. Niobe wondered if they were poisoned too, like Laertes sword in *Hamlet*. Jork wasn't above cheating, so why not? Then again, there'd be too much risk of self-injury for him to do it. The small audience cheered, and there was a scattering of applause, which became louder once Niobe resumed her fighting stance.

Jork grinned at the sight of her blood. "There'll be more of that soon."

"Unlikely."

Jork changed his stance to that of a boxer and held his hands up. Niobe moved just close enough to encourage Jork to strike. She'd need to find a way inside his range in order to hit him. Jork swung a few punches at Niobe in quick succession. She was able to block most of them, but one caught her in the left cheek, and she fell to the ground. In an instant he was on top of her reaching for her throat with both hands. Niobe went to perform a cowpinch. With a shock, she realised why her kick had felt wrong; his inner thighs were padded. Her signature move wouldn't work. Niobe knew she'd have only seconds before she started losing consciousness; she was already feeling lightheaded from her sudden exertion and the adrenaline rush of the fight. She told herself not to thrash her head around. That would only hasten her demise by stimulating her vagus nerve, as Mr Gladwell had discovered firsthand. Niobe felt herself begin to panic. Jork was too heavy for her to easily throw him off by bucking her hips. His armpits were also out of reach for an attack of his axilla.

Instead, she reached for his forearms and pressed her thumbs on the points located roughly three fingers down from the elbow crease, trying to burrow through the flexor muscles to the radial or median nerve, or both. As she attacked the nerves, Niobe felt Jork's fingers release some of their tension. She swung her arms in opposite circles and swept Jork's arms from behind them. As Jork fell on top of her, Niobe was able to use his momentum to twist so she was now on top of Jork. He used his arms to sweep her off him and they both rolled away from each other. His arms had caught her t-shirt, and as she was flung off him it was ripped off her. The world could now see her tattoo of the kanji for *wa*, the Japanese word for harmony. They could also see the scar on her side. Niobe wondered what story she'd tell if asked about it afterwards.

They each leapt to their feet. Niobe used the well-known back handspring technique for speed, whereas Jork pulled his knee up to his chest and turned until he could use his hands and feet to spring up.

Niobe felt a breeze on her stomach. Jork couldn't suppress a smile at Niobe's exposure. Niobe saw the grin and realised she now had the advantage. Jork would be distracted by her breasts, which her sports bra was struggling to keep in place after the grappling had pulled it askew.

Niobe lunged at Jork while he still seemed occupied by the sight of her flesh. He caught her movement just in time and was able to deflect her strike and counter with a punch of his own. They traded a few more blows. Jork was rapidly losing his breath, but Niobe felt her aerobic capacity was waning too. She knew from her own experience of knocking someone down when utterly exhausted that a tired opponent was still a dangerous opponent.

Jork came at her with a flurry of punches. Niobe was forced backwards. After two steps she darted sideways, hoping to launch an angled strike. Jork seemed ready for the move and caught her with a low *yokogeri* side-kick to her right shin, which was bearing most of her weight. Niobe felt her ankle dislocate, as it had done in a training mishap a few years before, but couldn't tell if anything was broken. She cried out in pain and fell to the ground, and Jork leapt on top of her again.

As he moved in for the kill, Niobe felt she was about to lose the fight. She'd never been hurt this badly in a fight before, but then those fights hadn't been to the death.

It was a cliché, but time really did seem to slow down as Jork flew towards her. It was as though events seemed to last a fraction longer than they should. Jork's fist was still coming at her at an alarming rate though. Niobe tried to react to the whole rather than the fist. Decades of training led to the reaction of accepting the punch to focus on jabbing a finger into Jork's eye. The 'fleshy-tough-squishy' feeling told her she'd hit her target. It was enough to allow her to crab crawl back and get to her feet, which made the crowd roar.

She stood in her fighting stance. Despite her high pain tolerance, Niobe was still wobbly on her right foot. Most fighters liked to have the strong foot back in their stance, but Niobe wasn't like other fighters. Her left foot was now her best weapon, so she placed it forward.

What do you do when you have nothing left to give? Niobe asked herself. She probably only had one more attack left before the pain from her foot would become unbearable. Gethan's voice appeared in her head, "Take what you need from your opponent." Jork's upper defence was good. Gethan must have known she'd go for Jork's head and had prepared him accordingly. Niobe wasn't going to be able to knock him out easily. She would have to improvise.

Niobe went to attack again. As she expected, Jork went to block her strikes. Niobe faked a kick with her right leg. As Jork dropped his hands to block it, she pivoted and grabbed his right arm with both of hers. She barely let her foot touch the ground to strengthen her balance, but it still sent a shockwave of pain up her shin. Niobe drove her knee into Jork's forearm with all her weight. Niobe could feel Jork's ulna as it snapped from the impact. The bone broke through the skin, and Jork cried out in pain. Niobe repeated the knee strike to make the bone stick out further. She placed her left hand on Jork's elbow and moved her right hand to his wrist. With a loud *kiai*, she bent Jork's arm so his own protruding piece of bone stabbed him in his abdomen near his liver. She pulled his arm free so the wound would bleed out, then repeated the stabbing action. Niobe swept his foot with her injured leg and Jork fell backwards to the ground. She stood triumphantly over him, as both screamed in pain. The audience screamed with delight. A moment later the sound of the crowd outside added to the cacophony.

Jork tried to roll away, but Niobe dropped her knee onto the abdominal wound. Jork screamed in pain.

Niobe turned to her tent and called for Devin to bring the green whistle. She didn't hide her expression of disgust when he handed the whistle to her.

"Now go away," Niobe said with such forcefulness that Devin obeyed without hesitation. She wondered if he thought the device was for her. It wasn't.

"Here, Jork, suck on this. It will take the pain away. Death should be peaceful for the dying. Hell may be here, but it hath no fury for you anymore."

Jork nodded and began taking deep breaths. In a few moments his face relaxed its contortions.

Niobe lent forward and whispered into his ear, "Besides, I want you conscious." Jork's face grew fearful. She knew what she was about to do would be debated, especially since she could have let him pass out first, but despite what Jork probably believed, his wounds weren't yet fatal. And she wanted that thrill one last time. Niobe held her thumb up into the air, then slowly twisted it so it was pointing to the ground. The crowd cheered. Niobe thrust her hand downward, guiding her thumb into the hole created by the bone piercing Jork's abdomen. He looked at her in confusion. Niobe felt her thumb go through the protective membrane, the peritoneum, and into the cavity. She gripped the flesh and pulled, ripping his skin and rupturing multiple blood vessels. Blood spattered as she flung her arm up, some hitting the sky camera. Blood began rapidly bubbling out of Jork. Niobe thrust a *nukite*, spear hand, into the hole she'd created. She felt his intestines mush, and she repeated the action a second time. The crowd fell silent as they realised his wounds were now fatal. Jork's eyes glazed over as he lost consciousness. Niobe placed her bloody hand on his carotid sinus to check for a pulse. A few moments later, she nodded. It was over. She picked up her ripped t-shirt and wiped her hand on it. The audience burst into applause.

Niobe tried to control herself, so her adrenaline rush wouldn't show so much. She needed people to know she wasn't doing it for the thrill, even though it was such a rush to finally achieve her dream of thrusting her hand into someone's abdomen.

"Is that what you wanted?" Niobe asked the nearest camera. "Can you really accept such a violent act? This is the last time."

* * *

Niobe hobbled slowly back to her tent. Devin looked up anxiously as she walked in. He could see she appeared to be okay. Niobe wondered what he'd say.

"Hey, I see you've managed to get your shirt off," Devin said with a grin. Niobe was sure she'd heard that line before.

"You may check me over. I think all I have are a dislocated ankle and this cut on my cheek. Oh wait, also some bruised ribs and a few other contusions. Oh, and a bruised neck from when he tried to strangle me."

When Devin came over to check on Niobe she rejected his attempt to kiss her. "Just check me over."

Devin started investigating each of her wounds. "What's wrong?"

"You tell me."

"Huh?"

"What do you think I found out about you just before the fight?"

Let's see if the guilty one betrays himself. Devin's face contorted into a look of shame.

"Oh. I admit it was a setup to begin with. Jim paid me to take you out. But I messed it up. I … I fell for you."

Niobe scrunched her face. For the first time she felt like she was seeing Devin with perfect clarity. Was he paraphrasing a line from a movie? What he was saying was exactly what she wanted to hear. That was it. That was how she could tell someone practiced was lying to her. Was that how Gethan had been able to tell when she'd lied to him? It seemed to make sense.

"Did you know Jim said something to me when he pitched the show to me? He said something along the lines of always being able to tell when someone desires fame. He recruits such people, helps them develop, then gets them to help him when he needs it. That's what he did with you isn't it? You're so full of shit."

"How do you remember that? Why do women always remember what was said?" Devin said accusingly. Niobe's heart dropped as she realised he wasn't concerned about defending himself. Devin began bandaging her wounds. Despite the situation, he was still in paramedic mode.

"During heightened situations, women's brains fire differently to men's. There's a region called the amygdala. In women the left one fires more, versus the right one for men. The left side of the brain also contains the speech centres, so we remember words more than men. Be thankful you haven't harmed the country, or you might make my list."

"Sorry."

"How'd you get me to fall for you?"

"I mirrored what you were saying. A lot of it was me, but yeah, I'd been coached a bit by Jim."

"Leave now."

Devin took the cue. As he started packing his bag, he turned and said, "Make sure you get your wounds checked again by a doctor, okay? You seem all right, but you'll need crutches and some of the bandages changed, and you may need stitches on your cheek. And perhaps I am full of shit and hungry for fame, but I still don't want to see you suffer, and I do think you're pretty awesome, even if I don't love you that way."

"Why did you try to sleep with me then?"

"To see if I could force the feeling. Plus, your physique is stunning."

Devin finished packing and turned to leave.

"Devin."

"Huh?"

"Thanks for finally being honest. Now leave before I start getting angry with you again. Even if I'm no longer able to kill without prosecution, I do know how to kill without detection."

Niobe realised this was why Gethan was trying to stop her, it wasn't this particular fight *per se*. Perhaps he wasn't trying to get her killed, but, in his own way, show her by overcoming the strongest possible opponent any further fights were pointless. The hunger seemed to have left her.

Devin hastily exited the tent and literally bumped into Jim as he left. Neither said a word as they passed.

"That was brilliant, Niobe! I particularly like the thumbs down sign. It was so *apropos*."

Jim's energy made Niobe aware of just how much her body was crashing now her adrenaline spike had dissipated. She was too tired to tease out of Jim what he'd done.

"Jim Jyons. I just killed a man with the bone from his own forearm."

"It was incredible."

"I wasn't as angry with him as I am you. So, tell me, what do you think I'll do to the man who's manipulated me into killing for ratings? Who turned my family against me, for ratings. Who turned my *mentor* against me, for ratings. Who created a *fake boyfriend* for me, for ratings. Who put me in danger." She dropped her voice and didn't bother trying to keep an icy tone out of it. "If I'm a danger to myself just think what I can do to you."

Jim turned white and seemed suddenly rooted to the spot. He'd gone to his dark place. Of flight, fight or freeze he was doing the latter. He needed the former.

"Jim, the time is 1.23 pm. I'll give you an hour's head start. Then I'm coming for you."

Jim still couldn't move. He looked like he was about to lose bladder control.

"I suggest you run. Go," Niobe said as icily as she could.

Jim, at last, found his feet and scarpered out of the tent.

Niobe told herself to have Patterson send him an email to say the queen wouldn't actively pursue Jim, unless he returned to Tantalia, and that he should make sure they were never in a room together. It occurred to her that since the Azzure's had made the same threat to her, she was in the clear from them.

CHAPTER 29

When Gethan entered Niobe's tent a few minutes later, she swore. "Oh, come on, can't I just have some peace? Why do men always think they have to check on the poor woman?"

"Yes. I imagine you must want some peace to provide some balance," Gethan said.

"I've joked about killing you. Now, I want to."

"You're one of the very few who could. Despite that risk, I want to talk to you."

"Go away. I'm angry with you," Niobe said, but the anger in her voice didn't sound convincing to her.

"And I deserve your anger. Congratulations on your victory."

"No thanks to you. Did you know he cheated? His nails were sharpened, and he had padding in his thighs. I'm pretty sure he had weights in his shoes too. His kicks didn't feel right."

"He wanted to win."

"Duh."

"That's important. He was a trained killer, trying his hardest to kill you, yet you overcame him. Well done."

"It's wrong that even with your betrayal, the girl inside this woman is excited by your praise."

Gethan allowed some warmth into his voice. "That's nothing to do with being a girl or a woman. Just human."

"So, has anything changed?"

"You fought as expected or better. The larger question is whether replacing or killing a single person really made a difference? That, only time will tell. Is it just a regime change, or wholesale cultural change? Tantalia will be all right though. Your people love you more than you know. When I wasn't training Jork, I've spent much of the last fortnight back in Tantalia, amongst the people. They're proud to have you as their head of state. I guess in the end all they really want is to know it's someone else's blood which is being spilled, and they're safe. You give them that assurance. When I look at your actions from their perspective—all your public comments and behaviour is spot-on to what it should be. They don't suspect the darkness within. In that regard, you are behaving like a proper queen. Like someone I'd be proud to be associated with. Unlike Jork, who even I began to want to kill after spending time with him. He was a horrible human and, as you might say, objectively an arsehole. The world is a better place without him."

"What are you saying?"

"Perhaps your father was wrong to try and stop you."

"My *father*?"

"I'll say it. Listen up, this doesn't happen often." Gethan cleared his throat. "I was wrong. I was wrong to doubt you, and even more wrong to try and stop you. I'm sorry. I should've paid more attention to the fact your mother never changed her mind. I served her too."

"I would've pointed that out to you, if you'd ever answered my calls."

"Sorry. That was also a mistake. I wasn't following any strategy I've taught you. But then, I was very angry, and stupidly I let my emotions cloud my judgement. I'm human. It was wrong of me. When it comes to you, I don't always act in my best interests."

"Like dobbing on me when I was a teenager?"

"Like that. Although, I was thinking more that I should've just resigned when the plan for Alban was hatched, but I didn't want to lose my connection to you."

"Thank you. Before, when I asked if anything had changed, I meant had anything changed with *us*. Because you *left* me," Niobe said accusingly.

"Every student needs a period of time away from their master. How else could they determine what their technique means for them? I was always intending for us to meet again," Gethan replied.

"But like this?" Niobe gestured to the stadium. "Or like a fortnight ago?"

"I admit I could've done our reunion better. But I had hoped you would call it off. It was fascinating watching the fight. I think you've improved even further since I left."

"Why'd you help Jork?"

"Listen carefully. He was never going to win. All I did was help you earn it a little more. You were fighting to defend your territory; he was attacking you to extend his. There is so much research which says defensive animals are vastly more successful than ones which rely on attack. Why do you think we spend so much time on defence; it's more effective than offence. It's why there's no first strike in martial arts and why I knew you'd find a way. You always find a way. Although, I must say I never saw this way coming. That was some pretty out of the box thinking. That expression when he realised it was his own bone mortally wounding him was priceless."

They shared a nervous laugh and warily sat facing each other. For a few seconds it was like old times.

Niobe sighed and let her hostility towards Gethan, release. "You lied to me that my solution to the riddle was the right one."

"I realise that now. But it wasn't a lie then. I told you what you needed to hear, but like the best *zen koans* the truth of the solution changes over time."

Niobe nodded. "I figured out how you could usually spot me lying."

Gethan leaned forward. "How?"

"You assumed when I was saying exactly what you wanted to hear that it was a lie."

Gethan nodded. "Well done."

"So, do you still have more to teach me like Dahlia said? Or have I figured out the last thing?"

"I do have one more thing. But … I'll still be around, if you'll let me?" Gethan raised his eyebrows with the question and continued. "I admit defeat. Your father was wrong to try to stop you. You're unstoppable, as I've now realised. Plus, look at the people. They clearly don't want you to stop."

"But now I have to."

"Yes. You'll cope though."

"I will." Niobe sighed, then added, "Yes." Inside she was buzzing. While she had thought she was above such concerns, she realised that now her people had truly seen what she was capable of and accepted it. The sensation the thought produced was of being an even better version of herself. It was intoxicating.

"Yes, to what?" Gethan asked.

"Yes, to you can hang around. I'd like that."

"Thank you. I know that can't be an easy decision right

now. Just so you know, it shows a maturity in you your parents would be so very proud of."

"Thank you."

"So … truce?" Gethan offered.

"Truce," Niobe confirmed.

"You've earnt the final lesson. You've trained for twenty hours a week for over twenty years. You may not have realised it, but you became a master of technique a decade ago."

"Ten thousand hours, right?"

"Such an arbitrary figure, but that's what the research says it takes to master something. All you've done for the last decade is expand what you're a master of. I can't teach you any more technique, but I can give you the secret to obtain a deeper appreciation of what you know. It's something I've benefited immensely from and am very, very grateful for."

Gethan paused. Had something caught in his throat?

"If you want to improve yourself further, you need to become the teacher. You need a student. Someone to pass the torch to."

Niobe headed straight for the airport. She hadn't brought more than a backpack with her, so there was nothing she needed to retrieve from the hotel. The producers of *Sovereign Assassin* had pre-paid the bill. When she arrived back in Tantalia, there was a small crowd, mostly women, gathered outside what was meant to be the VIP-only exit at the airport. They were carrying signs of support for her. Niobe was surprised, because she'd never really considered who her specific audience might be. The show was about her, not them. Her flight details hadn't been announced, nor was she expected in the country until the next day. Were these further machinations engineered by Jim?

Niobe's crutches made her easy to spot, and a cheer rose from the crowd. Several people called to her, so Niobe used her crutches to manoeuvre over. She stopped to talk to one of the people, a twenty-ish young woman.

"Out of curiosity, why are you here?" Niobe asked.

"To see you. We thought you'd want to return home ASAP, so we took a punt and came here early."

"Who put you up to it?"

The woman seemed confused. "No one, Your Majesty. We just think you're awesome. The way you kick male arse and stand up for our country."

"What's your name?"

"Barb Wenx."

"Well, Barb. Just so you know, I'd kick female arse too, if it was hurting Tantalia. I don't discriminate on gender."

"Yeah, but they've all been men, so far."

"So far? It's over. The law is about to change, so I can't do this anymore, but yeah, men seem to have been the problem—"

"You're going through with that?"

"Yep. I keep my word. And, I intend to make sure they keep theirs. *Quid pro quo.* I can't see a way around it."

Barb's expression changed to one of shock, but then a steely resolve took its place. "Leave it with me."

Niobe laughed. The woman's confidence she'd be able to change things was admirable.

* * *

Once she was safely back at the palace, Patterson informed Niobe there was to be a parade the next morning to celebrate her victory.

"A parade?"

"Yes."

"What the—?"

"Agreed. It is a little over-the-top. However, it is a fitting conclusion."

"Who authorised this?"

"Authorised, Your Majesty? No one. The people demanded it."

Niobe shook her head in disbelief.

"Perhaps parade is a little misleading, since it'll just be you in a bulletproof pope-mobile, driving along Ancora Parade to the steps of parliament, where you'll give a brief speech."

"I have to talk?"

"Yes, Your Majesty."

"Ughh. Fine. I'll think of something. See if you can get Dahlia and Ebony to meet here with me afterwards. I think they're back tomorrow. Dahlia was going to show Ebony St. Peter's Basilica before they returned."

"You're talking to her?"

"Yes. We'll be awkward for a while, but our relationship is on the mend. Same with Gethan."

Patterson raised an eyebrow.

"Very good, Your Majesty. Anything else I can do?"

"Send a doctor to check on me. These bruises are really sore, and I think the swelling in my ankle has increased. Maybe I shouldn't have flown so soon, even if it was short flight."

"Done."

A few minutes later, the palace doctor arrived. Niobe was pleased when she confirmed the cut on her face was barely more than a scratch and would heal without leaving a scar. The doctor was more concerned about her bruises and, after some prodding, declared it likely Niobe had a hairline fracture on the two floating ribs on her left side. They'd heal in six to eight weeks, and in the interim she'd have to avoid strenuous exercise. Her ankle was another matter. It had been dislocated and she'd need to stay off it as much as possible for the next week, and use crutches for a while. The swelling would go down in the next day or so, and she'd have to do some rehab to build the strength back into the joint. Niobe thanked the doctor and decided to do a *kappo* meditation for half an hour. It had always seemed to speed up healing for her in the past. She went to her bedroom, set a timer, closed her eyes and started dismissing thoughts as they appeared.

* * *

THE NEXT MORNING, it was another warm, sunny springtime day. The ride along Ancora Parade filled Niobe with a weird sense of hope. People were cheering for their monarch and their country. They had pride. Niobe recalled the story her parents had told her that even when you disagreed with the war they were fighting, you had to have respect for the soldiers who put their lives on the line for their country. Wars could be unjust, but you had to admire those who went beyond words and fought for a cause. This seemed to be the zeitgeist Niobe had tapped into.

When Niobe reached parliament, half a dozen security personnel held up large umbrellas to shield her until she was behind the bulletproof panel separating her from the crowd.

Niobe rested on her crutches and stood at a lectern to give her speech. She had a cue card with a few notes scrawled on it. Screens at speeches annoyed her.

"My fellow Tantalians. It's a pleasure being your queen."

The large crowd cheered.

"I've reflected a lot recently on the meaning of immunity and whether it's right I have such a privilege. The sovereign, your sovereign … me … I … should be the link between God and Earth, not Earth and the Devil. So, it is perhaps fitting I am now forced into retirement."

The mood of the crowd suddenly shifted. There were audible boos.

"I have a record of four kills and no defeats, which may sound impressive for a young woman, but that ignores history. Nakano, an *Onna-bugeisha*, female warrior had a kill count of a hundred and seventy-two samurai."

The crowd cheered, not as strongly as earlier, but enough to make Niobe think she still had them on her side.

"My retirement means I am not seeking another target and *Sovereign Assassin* has ended. I might consider coming out of retirement for the right target, even if it meant I was jailed."

The crowd erupted into applause and calls of support.

"As Musashi said, 'Do not regret what you have done'. I do not regret my actions, although this level of devotion is something I still find odd. Musashi also said, 'Get beyond love and grief; exist for the good of man'. I hope I'm living up to that adage; it's been at the heart of my actions for the country."

More calls of support flowed from the audience.

"It is also incumbent upon someone in my position to mend the bridges when an offence has occurred. It's why I've reached out to the families of all my victims. I may not always have succeeded as well as I'd hoped, but unless a hand is extended, the gulf will never close. To this end, I will be speaking to the incoming President of Autarchos about plans to build a new bridge between our countries across the Paine River, funded in part through the palace. Although I know I have limited political power, I have offered to use my influence to help Autarchos transition to a more democratic government. So yeah, a literal and figurative bridge. I've also directed the Prime Minister to bring forward to this afternoon the vote on the bill to change the laws of the land so I can be charged with murder if I kill again. Thank you for your support."

Niobe said her last sentence in an as upbeat as possible voice, and the crowd cheered briefly. Then they seemed to process her statement and fell silent. Niobe walked as quickly as her ankle and crutches would let her to a waiting car to return to the palace.

* * *

THAT EVENING, Niobe was standing by the window of the meeting room, looking down at the fountain she loved, when her guests arrived. Dahlia was wearing a light-coloured summer dress which fell to her calves. Ebony was just as brightly attired.

"Dahlia, Ebony, thank you for coming. I want you both to know I've spoken to Gethan and cleared the air between us. Similarly, Aunty, after our talk, I can see how you haven't been quite the adversary I thought you were. I apologise for thinking that."

Dahlia smiled. "You weren't wrong, but thank you."

"I have a proposal to put to you."

"Last time you said that it started *Sovereign Assassin.* Should I be worried?"

Niobe laughed. "No. Gethan has helped me understand that in order to progress I need to teach. I was hoping Lady Ebony could be my student."

Ebony squealed and clapped her hands.

The corner of Dahlia's mouth turned upwards. "It might help avoid some teenage angst, I suppose. What sort of commitment are you talking about?"

Niobe thought to the twenty thousand plus hours she'd been trained for over the last two decades. "Two hours a day, five days a week, before school, not after."

Ebony's face fell. "You mean getting up at six?"

Dahlia laughed at her daughter's consternation.

"You're forgetting travel time. It'd be more like half-past five. You could shower and have breakfast here afterwards. Chef makes the best breakfasts."

"What do you think, Ebs?" Dahlia asked.

Ebony hesitated. Niobe went over and whispered in her ear, deliberately making it loud enough for Dahlia to hear.

"There's a kata called *Wanshu*. I'll show it to you. It teaches you how to seize and tear off a man's testicles."

Ebony's eyes lit up. She was in.

Dahlia mockingly rolled her eyes. "Fine. I'll have to confirm it with Jacques though. He usually agrees with me on such things, so let's say yes."

Niobe smiled. She had found her student. Her smile relaxed when she heard Patterson's shuffling gait approach the door.

"Come in, Patterson," Niobe called just before he knocked.

Patterson bowed to each person in the room and then said the television should be turned on.

Niobe nodded, and Patterson switched it on. He changed the channel to a news station. It was showing live footage from outside the Tantalian Parliament.

A massive group of protestors were marching on parliament to get them to not pass the new law. Niobe noticed Barb was front and centre of the rally, megaphone in hand.

Niobe had to laugh. It was absurd. People were rallying, running a picket line to parliament, in order to enable someone to continue serial killing. What had the world come to?

The newsreader indicated the numbers present at the protest were still growing. Official estimates said over twenty-thousand people were there already. Even though that represented half-a-percent of the population, the amount was ridiculously high. That many people cared enough about the issue to stop their daily lives to attend.

"We'd better go. It looks like you'll be occupied tonight. We'll be in touch about the training," Dahlia said. She seemed unusually pensive.

Niobe nodded mutely. Dahlia and Ebony left quickly. Niobe remained in the room transfixed by the events on the TV. Despite her commitment to changing the law, she admitted a small part of her wanted the option of continuing her activities to still be there. At least she had tapes of three out of four of her kills. The last and most glorious was in multi-angle and high-resolution. She could relive it whenever she wanted. That would have to be enough.

* * *

THE NEXT MORNING Niobe was awoken by a knock at the door. She was surprised to find herself under a blanket, but still in the meeting room. Patterson must've covered her up and turned off the TV. Patterson poked his head into the room and asked if she'd be prepared to meet the PM who'd arrived to discuss the changes to the law, passed in a marathon session overnight.

"But I don't know what happened. I just woke up."

Patterson offered her a rare grin. "Then I think you should let him tell you."

"Okay." Niobe couldn't think what else to say. She straightened herself up and hid the blanket under the couch, just in time before the Prime Minister was shown into the room. He had a strange expression that Niobe couldn't interpret. Was it happiness, amusement, or a brave face for sorrow?

"Your Majesty, Patterson said you don't know what happened overnight?"

"That's true. What did happen?"

"As instructed the government brought forward a vote on

the bill to change our constitution to allow the monarch to be charged with murder. We asked for all parliamentarian's support, although, ultimately it would have to be a free vote as per the constitution regarding laws which affect you. There was some debate on the bill. While that was occurring, the amount of people protesting the change grew exponentially. We had to put parliament into lockdown, such was the risk from the crowd."

Niobe nodded. It was a drastic step.

"But we knew you wanted to keep to your commitment, so we persisted. It seemed parliamentary members thought it might be a vote killer for their re-elections if they voted for the bill, despite the instruction to do so by yourself. I then received a text from Duke Ancora on behalf of his wife, the duchess, and daughter, Lady Ebony. They suggested an amendment to the bill which would satisfy your agreement with Autarchos for legislative change to your immunity, but also stop Tantalians rioting on the street."

"What?"

"Before I get that, let me say it passed with only two nays and one abstention. Enough for the 90% threshold required to amend the constitution."

Niobe smiled. "Zack. Don't play games. Tell me or I'll hurt you."

"I'm sure you could, too. The amendment was simple. You can now, officially, be charged with murder as per your agreement. But, and it's a big one, this can only happen for murders beyond one in a calendar year."

"Are you saying I can choose a target a year?"

"Up to. Yes."

Niobe grinned so broadly she felt the scab on her cheek crack. A single drop of blood rolled down to her chin.

* * *

A few minutes later, Niobe called Duchess Dahlia to say thank you.

"But of course, Niobe. I've never hidden my belief you need to have limits, and I still adhere to that. But I think, given your unique skill set and rules governing who you target, having zero opportunity to do what you do would also be unfair. So, I applied Aristotle's maxim that virtue is a mean between extremes, and I reached the compromise."

"If you were here, I'd hug you."

"Will you make Jim your first target?"

"Is that a request?"

"No, he's just who I thought you might pick."

"He may have hurt me, but I am not Tantalia, even though I may have quipped once that the state is me. As much as I hate to admit it, *Sovereign Assassin* has done wonders for our country. So, let him live in fear that I might target him one day, even though I never will."

* * *

Gethan called Dahlia.

"Thank you for your support," Gethan said.

"You don't have to thank me. I agree it's the best way she can be monitored and controlled. Certainly it's better than giving her free rein, or making her go back to concealing the act," Dahlia replied.

"Plus, Ebony will occupy her time. It will be good for both of them."

"Hmm. I hope so."

EPILOGUE

Niobe and Ebony were sitting cross-legged facing each other after a vigorous workout. Niobe was still getting used to being in Gethan's spot, but she was enjoying the challenge of aiming higher than his standard. That was always the rule for the instructor: set the standard higher than your own, so continual progress in the art could be made. Niobe described the life cycle of stars and how they lived and died, and in their death exploded and sent their mass into space. Sometimes the dust would combine and form planets such as Earth. In turn, life formed on Earth. That meant life was made from stardust, and at some point, such as when our sun went supernova, it would return to it. Human life, all life on Earth, Niobe explained, was irrelevant over the time scale of the universe.

"If life is truly meaningless, then what is its purpose?" Ebony asked.

"The meaning of life itself is not important. What's important is the meaning attached to *your* life," Niobe replied, smiling at the thought she sounded like Gethan.

"But if we're specks of dust?"

"If your life is trivial and meaningless, you might as well enjoy it. So, embrace the absurdity of our existence. Realise it's all insignificant until *you* give it significance. Don't stress over little things, and do what gives your life meaning, what makes you happy … subject to the laws of the land, of course."

"Of course," Ebony replied. They both laughed.

"What do you think about them calling New Year's Eve Judgement Night?"

"I haven't heard that one."

"Since you said you'd keep your kill until New Year's Eve, lest anyone think they could get away with stuff, that's become its new nickname. Everyone at school keeps asking me who's next."

"What do you tell them?"

"That I don't know. Sometimes I add that if they don't stop asking, I might have to put them on a list in case I ever become queen."

"Keep that attitude. Remember the globe doesn't know if it's in darkness or light, but it shines anyway. So, be a fucking beacon. You got that, Ebs?"

Ebony nodded, appearing suddenly coy.

"Oh right, I swore. You haven't heard me do that yet. Yeah, I'm not a princess anymore."

"You're the queen!"

"And the bogeywoman," Niobe said. They shared another laugh.

A thought occurred to Niobe. Should she tell Ebony what she'd been thinking about the Riddle of the Eye? She'd told her about the puzzle already, deciding that it would hasten her development in other areas of her social life. And if she did indeed become queen, it might help her.

"You know what, Ebony?"

"What?"

"I realised something recently, about the Riddle of the Eye and my solution to it."

"What?"

"I was wrong, and so was Gethan. I'm not a prisoner in that scenario, at least not anymore. I'm something different."

"What?" Ebony leant in. Niobe loved that she looked to her as her mentor. Gethan was right; it did give her a different appreciation of what she'd learnt, and not just her martial art techniques, but for the philosophy too.

"I thought I was subject to the gaze because of my royal blood and parents' concern over my behaviour, and by freeing myself from the burden of it, I could be truly free and happy. I was wrong. I was wrong because I should never have seen myself as being subject to the gaze, so I never needed to free myself from it. My new way of being makes that clear. I thought I knew what the gaze was, that it came from other people, but that was wrong too."

"What did you realise?" Ebony asked with bated breath.

Niobe smiled in response. "Woe be to anyone who fails under its burden, because *I am the gaze.*"

THE END

ACKNOWLEDGMENTS

This book was written rather quickly due to my having the luxury of being a fulltime writer for three months while on long service leave in 2019. In a way, it was my satirical response to a certain politician claiming they could publicly shoot someone and not lose any votes. Niobe is just a more intelligent and capable version of this. Since then, there have been events which mean it's such a crazy world at the moment that someone like Niobe isn't as far-fetched possibility as I thought at the time of writing the first draft, even though she should be. I believe leaders need empathy and Niobe is lacking in it.

In a book which contains a lot of martial art philosophy and technique, it's appropriate for me to thank my instructors past and present who've taught me so much. Thanks too to those I've trained alongside. You have made training more fun than learning self-defence should be. I owe a lot to my roughly twenty-year study of martial arts, as not only has it improved my confidence and introduced me to many close friends, it's also how I met my wife.

I'd like to thank my usual suspects yet again: the Monash

Writers Group for their encouragement and support, and my family for being interested in what I write. My editor Kathryn Moore is amazing at what she does and I am indebted to her for helping me move out of my comfort zone and tell a bolder story to my earlier draft of this novel. Kim Smith did a final proofread and I thank her for finding some very stubborn typos which had been missed. I'd also like to thank the incredible Cath at Shooting Star Press for believing in the story and her support with my writing journey through publishing this book.

Thanks too, to all those people who've encouraged me with my writing over the years, be it in small ways or large. It's meant more than I sometimes let on.

Any reference to research or studies in the text refer to real research. Some other references need particular explanation:

The story of LiLi is from a Bagua manual as indicated in the text. There are many versions of this story in the public domain, but the manual is where I first encountered it.

The story of the hapless teacher discussing fixed action patterns (FAPs) is based on my own experience teaching them to a class. A group in the front of the room wouldn't stop laughing. At the end they told me to look it up on urban dictionary. As I mentally replayed all the phrases I'd said during the class, I could see why they thought it was funny. I could never teach the topic with a straight face afterwards.

The dialogue between Niobe and Mr Gladwell as he dies is adapted from *Thus Spoke Zarathustra* by Friedrich Nietzsche. The idea of *ubermensch*, which was proposed by that book, is explored in *Sovereign Assassin*, and it seemed like a good Easter egg for those who know Nietzsche's work.

Similarly, the story of Heinz is a dilemma used by Lawrence Kohlberg to ascertain someone's level of moral reasoning according to his stage theory of moral development. I've included it because it showed the difference between Dahlia and Niobe's morality, and set up their adversarial actions. I also hope the reader will consider what their own response to the dilemma would be as it may reveal something meaningful about yourself.

I hope you've enjoyed reading this book. If you have, please leave a review on Amazon, Goodreads, blog, social media or other online site.

When he was in high school, a dare escalated a little too quickly and Robert made the state final in an interpretive dance competition. Thankfully, his teacher was okay with him chickening out of the main event, thus preserving his affection for education. Whilst not a direct consequence, Robert has since spent too much of his life studying and has just embarked upon his seventh university degree, a PhD in Education. Robert has degrees in psychology, sociology, biology and education, all of which inspire his writing.

Robert studied Wado-Ryu karate for twenty years and ran his own dojo in Perth for several years. However, he is not currently training.

Robert is kosmemophobic, meaning he has a fear of jewellery. He has no idea why, it just freaks him out.